Harley Quinn™

RAVENOUS

– DC ICONS –

Wonder Woman: Warbringer
by Leigh Bardugo

Batman: Nightwalker
by Marie Lu

Catwoman: Soulstealer
by Sarah J. Maas

Superman: Dawnbreaker
by Matt de la Peña

Black Canary: Breaking Silence
by Alexandra Monir

Harley Quinn: Reckoning
Harley Quinn: Ravenous
by Rachael Allen

RAVENOUS

—DC ICONS—

RACHAEL ALLEN

Random House New York

Harley Quinn created by Paul Dini and Bruce Timm

Jacket art by Kevin Wada

 Published in the United States by Random House Children's Books, a division of Penguin Random House LLC, New York.

Random House and the colophon are registered trademarks of Penguin Random House LLC.

Visit us on the Web! GetUnderlined.com

Educators and librarians, for a variety of teaching tools, visit us at RHTeachersLibrarians.com

Library of Congress Cataloging-in-Publication Data
Name: Allen, Rachael, author.
Title: Harley Quinn: ravenous / Rachael Allen.
Description: First edition. | New York: Random House, 2023. | Series: DC icons |
Summary: Harleen Quinzel starts attending Gotham University and becomes an Arkham Asylum intern, paired with the most high-profile female inmate, the notorious Talia al Ghūl, but as they spend more time together, the lines between good and bad begin to blur.
Identifiers: LCCN 2022031154 (print) | LCCN 2022031155 (ebook) |
ISBN 978-0-593-42990-7 (hardcover) | ISBN 978-0-593-42992-1 (ebook)
Subjects: CYAC: Supervillains—Fiction. | LCGFT: Novels.
Classification: LCC PZ7.A4362 Hap 2023 (print) | LCC PZ7.A4362 (ebook) |
DDC [Fic]—dc23

Printed in the United States of America
10 9 8 7 6 5 4 3 2 1
First Edition

For Kate, Dana, Alina, and Sasha:
I couldn't have done this without you.

PROLOGUE

Gotham Memorial Hospital

BRIGHT LIGHTS. PAIN LIKE I'VE BEEN LIT ON FIRE. I CAN'T move my arms or my head or my legs. *Why can't I move?* There's a sharp pain in my arm, just a jab. And then . . . relief. Everywhere else.

From somewhere above me, I hear a man's voice, brisk: . . . *heart rate 120 and climbing. And she's so pale . . .*

And then a woman's: . . . *chemical waste . . . whatever it is, she seems to have aspirated it too . . . we're gonna need to intubate.*

We're moving now. The lights flicker, and so do the people.

Woman: *Her blood pressure is dropping. If she pulls through—*

Man: *It'll be a damn miracle. I know.*

Darkness creeps in around the edges of my vision. My brain feels thick, my thoughts sticky.

I try to hang on to a single idea.

I did it.

I think it worked.

Man: *Is she . . . smiling?*

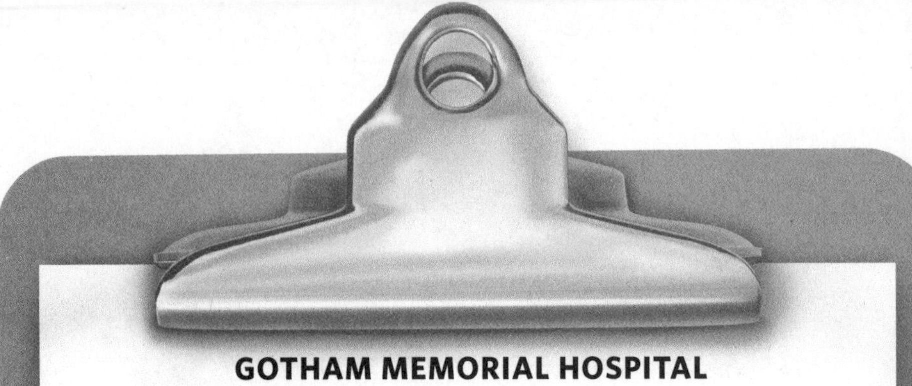

GOTHAM MEMORIAL HOSPITAL

EMERGENCY DEPARTMENT FLOW SHEET

PATIENT IDENTIFICATION

Patient: Quinzel, Harleen F

Age: 19 Sex: F

GMH#: 09111992 Date: 1/28

Mode of Arrival: Walk | W/C | (Gurney) | Carried | Police | Medic Unit

Triage Category: I___ II___ III___ IV___ V✓

RAPID ASSESSMENT

CHIEF COMPLAINT: Chemical burn and suspected aspiration, acute respiratory distress, found down in field

Does the patient have an infection or suspicion of infection?

Yes___ No✓

Is the patient on antibiotics (not prophylaxis)? Yes___ No✓

CIRCULATION

Palpable Pulse✓

Strong✓ Weak___ Regular___ Irregular✓

AIRWAY

Patent___ Impaired✓

BREATHING

Unlabored___ Labored✓ Shallow✓ Deep___

NEURO

Alert___ Oriented___ Confused___ Unresponsive✓

Clear___ Slurred___ Garbled___

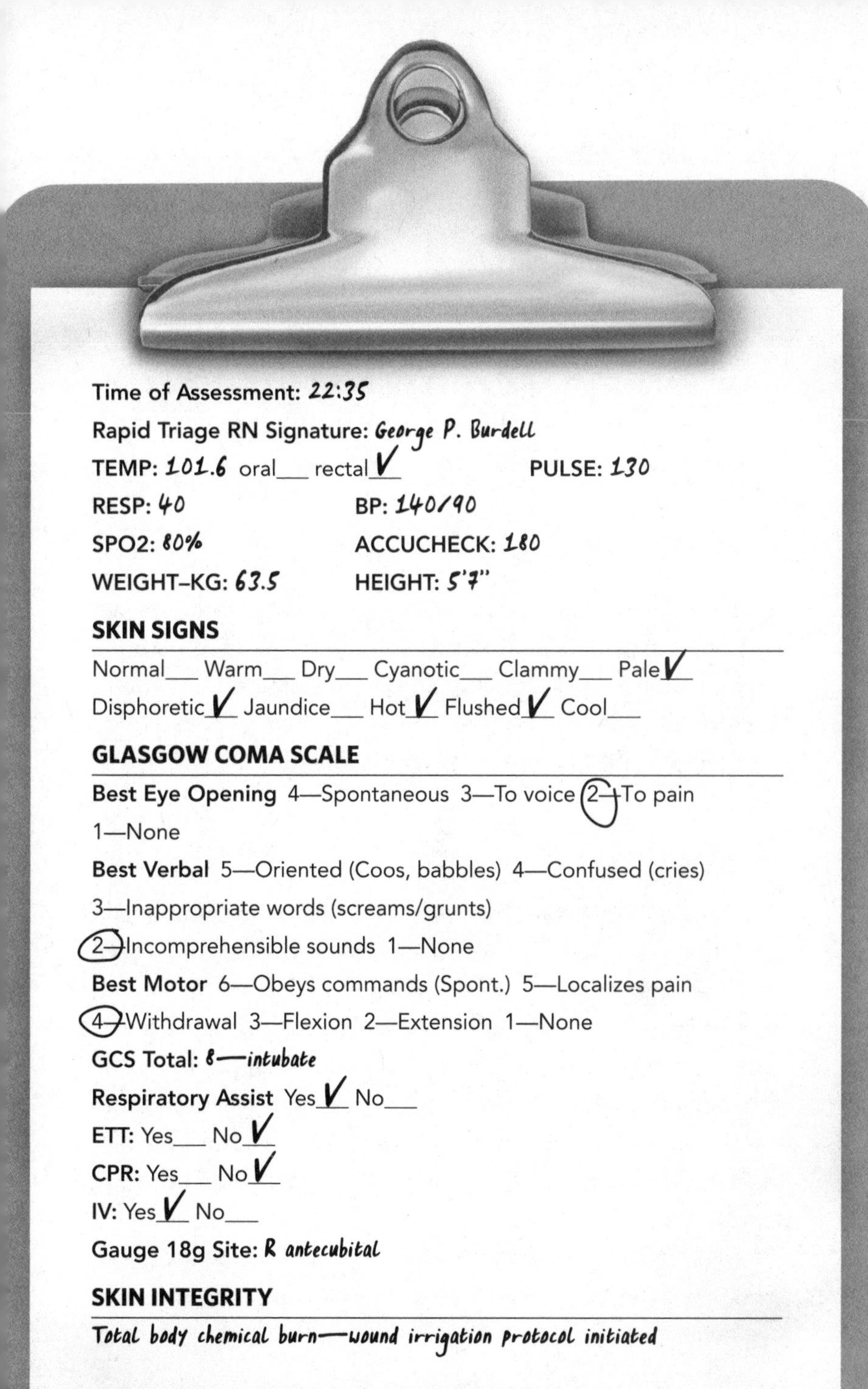

Time of Assessment: 22:35

Rapid Triage RN Signature: George P. Burdell

TEMP: 101.6 oral___ rectal ✓ PULSE: 130

RESP: 40 BP: 140/90

SPO2: 80% ACCUCHECK: 180

WEIGHT–KG: 63.5 HEIGHT: 5'7"

SKIN SIGNS

Normal___ Warm___ Dry___ Cyanotic___ Clammy___ Pale ✓

Disphoretic ✓ Jaundice___ Hot ✓ Flushed ✓ Cool___

GLASGOW COMA SCALE

Best Eye Opening 4—Spontaneous 3—To voice (2)—To pain 1—None

Best Verbal 5—Oriented (Coos, babbles) 4—Confused (cries) 3—Inappropriate words (screams/grunts) (2)—Incomprehensible sounds 1—None

Best Motor 6—Obeys commands (Spont.) 5—Localizes pain (4)—Withdrawal 3—Flexion 2—Extension 1—None

GCS Total: 8—intubate

Respiratory Assist Yes ✓ No___

ETT: Yes___ No ✓

CPR: Yes___ No ✓

IV: Yes ✓ No___

Gauge 18g Site: R antecubital

SKIN INTEGRITY

Total body chemical burn—wound irrigation protocol initiated

The memories come in flashes, piecemeal.

The sound of metal bars sliding open.

A knife against my throat.

And falling.

Falling.

F

A

L

L

I

N

G

Through the air into something that smells like bleach and burnt hair and batteries. It feels like fire. Like taking a napalm shower, swan-diving into a swimming pool made of knives.

I feel it until I can't feel anything anymore.

Sometimes I'm awake and sometimes I'm dreaming and sometimes the pain makes me wish I was dreaming, even if it's all nightmares. I see fragments of that night painted on the inside of my eyelids. Hands clasped through a fence. Running (being chased?) down a hallway. It all blinks by too fast. A face in a burlap mask tries to pry apart my sanity, and I wake up screaming, or maybe I'm still asleep, but I have to get away because the things he does are terrible and more terrible still.

My mind hides from him, and there is peace, thank goodness. I float in the place between awake and dreaming, and a conversation wraps itself around me. Two people talking urgently, but I can't tell whose voice is whose. Only that the conversation is made of heat and secrets and things we promise people in the dark.

I love you.

Do you?

You don't strike me as someone who wants to hear some "to the moon and back" BS.

No. Actions are better.

I'd do anything to show you.

Anything?

I try to hang on to the memory. I think one of the people is me, but which one? And who is the other? Unconsciousness threatens to catch me, but I grit my teeth. This feels important. Like it's maybe the beginning of everything. Or the end.

The next thing I know, I'm opening my eyes.

Fluorescent lights.

Hospital bed.

Beep. Beep. Beep. Beep.

It's too much work to stay awake.

The third time I regain consciousness, I have to fight off a snake that wants to lay eggs in my throat. I cough-cough-cough, hacking away at it, determined to expel this sinister creature from my body.

The fourth time, I wonder if it was really a snake or an intubation tube. I ask the nurse if she's seen any snakes in my hospital room. I *think* I ask the nurse that. I think the nurse is real. I think I recall declaring that snakes are nothing after you've fought the patriarchy. The nurse looks at me so funny that I wonder if maybe I was talking gibberish. I tell the nurse she's only here allegedly, so she should really stop staring at me like that.

The fifth time, I wake up for real. My eyes open and stay open, long enough for me to make out the jungle of tulips and daisies and teddy bears that surround me. Huh, people must really like me.

A navy-blue blanket forms a nest on the uncomfortable-looking couch next to me. It's empty, though. The entire room is.

I feel like I've been hit by a truck. That was carrying fireworks. And an active volcano.

"You're awake. How are you feeling?"

I startle. A nurse wearing spaceship scrubs and an inquisitive smile has appeared at my elbow. (Not the shifty nurse from before.)

"Umm . . ." It's only a small sound, one syllable, but the pain makes my hand go to my throat automatically.

Another smile, this one sympathetic. "You were intubated," she says. "Your throat might be sore for a few days."

Well, that explains why I feel like I've gargled sandpaper. It also explains that whacked-out dream I had about snakes.

She checks some of the beeping machines surrounding me, her tan arms working quickly, and I realize I'm hooked up to an IV and a lot of other things. Also that my face itches. Tremendously. There's something white covering it on one side. I go to reach for it, but the nurse stops me.

"Nope. You don't want to do that."

"What happened to me?" Again with the words scraping their way out of my throat.

A glimmer of a memory sparks in my head. Something bad. Something really bad happened. No. Was going to happen. I had to stop it. I have to—

I try to sit up, and the nurse rushes over and holds me back, gently but definitively, the way my mom used to hold my hand when we crossed the street. Which is probably for the best. The ceiling tiles are already spinning.

"You can't do that yet. With the amount of toxins in your system, you shouldn't even be alive. You have to be careful."

Toxins? I wish I could remember something, *anything*, but the pieces are tiny and hazy and oh-so-slippery. I can't hang on to any of them for longer than a fraction of a second.

There's something ominous pressing in on me. That's all I know.

"Why can't I remember?"

"Hey." The nurse puts a hand on my shoulder. Her name tag says VALENTINA, which is interesting because Saint Valentine chased all the snakes out of Ireland. Or maybe it was Saint Patrick. My head is so jumbled. "It's going to be okay. Sometimes this happens. I'm going to let the doctor know you're awake." She digs in the pocket of her shirt and hands me a little book and a pen. "But for now, take these. It might help to write down what you do know."

A journal. I know that the book she handed me is called a journal. I don't know a whole lot of anything else. I wish she'd say what's wrong with me. Is it amnesia? Brain damage? Something worse than amnesia or brain damage?

"And here. This might help too. It was with your stuff."

She pulls a black phone in a pink glittery case out of a plastic bag on the table next to us. My phone, I'm assuming, based on the hyenas on the case. (Hey! I know I like hyenas!) I turn over the phone as she exits the room. Press a button. *Attempt* to press a button. My hands are bandaged in these dainty gauze gloves, so it takes a couple of tries.

Whoa.

My lock screen is a picture of me kissing a dark-haired

boy on the cheek. His eyes are friendly, laughing, like you've just shared a secret with him, but don't worry, he'd never, ever tell anyone.

I've never seen him before in my life.

What I Know

My name is Harleen Quinzel.
I'm 19 years old.
I go to Gotham University.
I woke up in a hospital today.
I have no idea how I got here.

PART I

CHAPTER 1

Arkham Asylum

HERE'S WHAT I REMEMBERED MUCH LATER. THE GATES loomed large before the shuttle. Dark. Chilling. The letters spelling out *Arkham Asylum* twisted with a kind of brooding malevolence. Trees crouched over the building with clawlike branches.

But no, that's not reality. Or only partly. Reality shifting through the lens of a kaleidoscope made of everything I've ever daydreamed about Arkham. Also? In my imagination, it's always storming there. Vindictive clouds blotting out the sun so it's pitch-black outside, even in daytime. And I'm supposed to be walking in. Not taking a shuttle.

Ah, well. In my mind, I become Past Me, bouncing in my seat and chattering to the girl next to me. "Did you picture it with storm clouds? I always pictured it with storm clouds. Fog, at the very least."

I peer out the bus window at a sky that is full of fat, happy clouds and blue enough to make a robin's egg jealous.

The girl chuckles politely. (Great! She hates me!) But then she sizes up the vast Gothic building like she's trying to think of something to say. "At least the stone is dark?"

"YES." I seize the opportunity. "Deliciously dark. And those turrets, just—" I chef's kiss in their direction because words can't begin to convey their perfection. "It's like Cinderella's castle pledged allegiance to the dark side." I sigh, and the girl laughs, a real cackle this time, not just a polite chuckle.

"I'm Harleen," I say, holding out my hand because I've decided we're friends now.

"Aria," she replies with a smile and a solid handshake.

I try not to heave a huge sigh of relief like a cartoon character. Next to me, Aria's chest relaxes almost imperceptibly. This is the secret. Every other new intern on this bus is just as scared as we are. Every first-year in my dorm too. They're all petrified that they won't make a connection with anyone. Or that it'll happen too slowly, be too tenuous. And then that's it. *Everyone* will know, and it's like getting picked last for kickball, only instead of kickball, it's ALL OF COLLEGE. It's basically terrifying, but I find that taking as many flying leaps as possible helps.

"Are you a first-year too?" I ask. (The subsequent leaps are always easier after you've taken the first one.)

"Yep. I'm in Kane Hall. You?"

"Elliot." I still can't believe I live there. I, Harleen Frances Quinzel, go to school at Gotham University. For real this time, not just as part of a gap-year program. We're already two weeks into the semester, and I can't help but wonder how long the reality will take to sink in.

The bus spits us out in front of the main building. I hop down onto the curb and look up and up and up. I'm going to do big things here. I can feel it. Think up new ways to help patients: a more definitive test for diagnosis here, a treatment with a better success rate there. I picture my ideas rippling into hospitals and private practices across the country.

Have you tried the Quinzel Method?

Of course I have! It's genius.

Aria steps down next to me, tufts of her black pixie cut fluttering in the wind. "Did you hear they brought The Joker in last week?" she says in a hushed voice as we walk inside.

My eyes light up. "I've only read everything about it I can get my hands on."

"Same!"

We both go a little quiet because there's a metal detector ahead and guards, and I don't know, but the whole thing just feels tense. We start taking everything out of our pockets, and Aria is just setting a teal handbag (or was it navy?) on the conveyor belt when a girl behind us pipes up: "Are you talking about The Joker?"

She's less quiet, so now *everyone* is talking about The Joker as we fill plastic bins with our keys, cell phones, wallets, and, in my case, eyelash glue. (What? It's really good for a variety of emergency situations.)

A self-satisfied voice cuts through the others. "He hasn't spoken a word since he arrived."

"Really?" Fascinating. I turn around to see who might be able to tell me more about one of the most interesting minds in Gotham Ci— Oh. It's Graham. He was in the Gotham University Bridge Scholars gap-year program with me last year. (It's where overachiever kids from the roughest high schools in Gotham City do mentored research in labs at Gotham U.) But don't be fooled by the fact that his name is one-third of the ingredients necessary for a s'more. Graham is the human equivalent of biting into a chocolate chip cookie only to find out that the chips are actually raisins.

(Side note: more people should make oatmeal cookies with chocolate chips in them. Why is this not a thing?)

"Did you read that somewhere?" asks Aria, eyeing him somewhat suspiciously. "Because I've read everything out there, and I haven't seen that." (Did I mention she's my friend now?)

"Well, actually"—Graham crosses his arms and gives her the smuggest smile in the history of humanity—"one of my gap-year professors is on the board here. Dr. Crane mentioned it at brunch." He waves a hand like there are just oh-so-many brunches with important people, and he can't be expected to keep track.

I mime vomiting into my handbag, and Aria snorts, but Graham narrows his eyes at me. Oops. I thought I was out of his line of sight.

Anyway, we're through the metal detector now, and the checkpoint with the guards in riot gear, and, no, I do not currently have any weapons on me, thank you very much. (I left my pocketknife at home, and I feel positively naked without it.) Then this total Boy Scout of a boy steps in front of us in his white lab coat that I can't help but notice is straining at the biceps, and he's all,

"Hi there. I'm Winfield Callaway. I'm a third-year at Gotham U, and I have piercing blue eyes the color of the ocean, and I come from the kind of family that uses *summer* as a verb. I'm the lead intern this year at Arkham Asylum, which means I'm in charge of new-intern orientation. I'll be giving you your tour today, and I'll also walk you through the mountain of paperwork you'll be filling out."

Note: He did not actually say that part about the eyes or the summering. Also, ugh, *paperwork*? Way to suck all the fun out of putting together minds like so many puzzle pieces. I feel like he must be able to see what I'm thinking, because he throws me a sympathetic smile. With dimples. Of course he freaking has dimples. NOT THAT I'M LOOKING.

I decide to walk alongside Winfield the Lead Intern with Dimples and ask him a few of my most pressing questions. Namely:

Have you gotten to meet The Joker?

Is it true that he isn't speaking?

Do you think Killer Croc is immortal? Because I heard that alligators are genetically capable of being immortal; it's just that they get killed off first.

And: *Where are the vending machines with the best chocolate?*

His answers: *No. Yes. That's an interesting idea.* And: *Near the second-floor break room.* (In case you were wondering.)

Winfield stops in front of a panel of windows that look in on a cafeteria. Inmates I recognize from the news sit hunched over their lunch trays. King Shark, Two-Face, Mr. Freeze. You can tell who the major players are: Mr. Freeze is in some kind of maximum-security, climate-controlled pod, and Two-Face is flanked by no fewer than three surly guards AND his hands and feet are cuffed to the table where he sits alone.

It's weird, though, because even with all the extra security, they don't look exactly like you'd expect them to. More like a dulled version of the pictures you see on TV. Take Two-Face. I know it's him because of the way one side of his face is burnt and the other side looks like it belongs to some suave investment banker who uses moisturizer that costs more than a semester's worth of textbooks. But there's something almost sad about seeing him in a prison uniform—identical orange on the left and the right—instead of a flashy stitched-together suit. I watch Mr. Freeze lean forward in his pod so he can take a spoonful of soup (cold, I'm assuming). I wonder who I'll work with. What secrets they're hiding. How much longer I have to wait before I can start working through their issues like so many crossword puzzles. I'm so enamored, it takes me a second to realize what feels off about this situation: none of them are looking at us.

"This is the inmate cafeteria. The glass is a two-way mirror. Bulletproof," says Winfield, confirming my suspicions.

Now that I know, I can't help but move closer. I drift down the hall until I'm standing opposite King Shark. He's positively majestic; there's no other way to describe him. His massive head and torso look like every picture in the great white shark books I used to pore over in the elementary school library. Power walking through the hallways as fast as I could, because we weren't allowed to run, but if you didn't book it, all the sharks in all their photographic glory would get snapped right up. His shark-y upper half is so distracting, you almost forget to notice that his torso feeds into an oversized pair of Arkham standard-issue orange pants. Also that he's got arms. I stare in awe as he moves one of said arms—sharkskin-covered, leathery gray, with webbed fingers. He picks up a spoon that seems impossibly small. He takes a bite of his peas, then a bite of his mashed potatoes, then half a fish stick, then a sip of his first juice box, then a sip of his second one. He repeats the actions in this same order, so peaceful. I am transfixed.

I watch as he goes through the cycle a third time (a fourth?). He's so contentedly busy that he doesn't notice Maxie Zeus strolling up behind him. I notice. Zeus's uniform is artfully torn to resemble a toga, and he's wearing a laurel wreath fashioned out of napkins. Honestly? He looks like the kind of guy who lifts weights on the beach and trips skateboarding children. He nudges the inmate next to him. "Check this out."

He balances his tray in one hand, and with the other, he swipes one of King Shark's juice boxes (the apple one, which frankly seems a lot more treasonous). King Shark turns, lightning-quick, much faster than you'd guess his size would allow. He stands up up up, towering over Maxie Zeus. Holy crap, he's enormous. He's at least seven feet tall, and also HE'S A MOTHER-FREAKING SHARK. Maxie seems to make this realization at exactly the same moment I do, perhaps because King Shark is so large that he has cast Zeus and his friend in shadow.

The other interns, sensing an impending bloodbath, rush next to me at the window. The guards are wise now too. They materialize from every corner of the cafeteria, ready to neutralize the situation. But despite their Tasers and billy clubs, they look around like they're hoping someone else will make the first move. King Shark opens his mouth to reveal row after row of razor-sharp teeth. I'm fairly certain he could swallow a man whole. I think I remember reading that in my shark books. King Shark takes the apple juice back from Zeus gently, so that none of the juice shoots out of the straw in the exchange. Maxie Zeus gulps the way you do when your entire life is going by in flashes and you wish you could get a do-over.

And then it all happens so fast. Those great white jaws snapping shut. The bone-crunching sound of teeth chomping through something solid. I lean forward, my nose nearly touching the glass, expecting to see pieces of wannabe Greek god all over the place.

His lunch tray, I realize with relief. King Shark just bit the guy's lunch tray in half. It's almost comical, the perfect shape of a shark bite carved into the plastic, an apple wobbling in one corner of the tray. Maxie Zeus looks like he's about to pee himself, and honestly, he deserves it.

Aria whispers, "Ho-lee crap."

"Seriously," I whisper back.

Another intern lets out a low whistle.

King Shark sets his apple juice down on the table, right back where it was, right next to his grape juice. He sits, causing the entire table to groan under his weight. And then he returns to his gentle routine like nothing happened.

I am intrigued.

And, let's be real, a bit smitten. Tenderhearted monsters do that to me.

"Okay," says Winfield, clapping his hands to pull us away from the great white distraction in the window. "So, mealtimes aren't usually that dramatic, but it's a good reminder that this isn't your usual mental health facility. This is Arkham. We help rehabilitate people who are criminally insane, but a lot of the people we help are . . . unusual. Very dangerous. Very high-profile. Often those with special powers or abilities. You can never forget to be careful when you're here."

He leads us through the rec room, the staff room, the kitchens, the laundry room, the outdoor area. After a lunchtime shark attack, everything else we see feels tame in comparison. That is, until we pass a hallway that seems like all the others except for the fact that Winfield jerks his head meaningfully in that direction. "The Joker's down that way," he says. Quietly so that the other interns don't hear. "End of the hall."

"Reallllly." I notice there are two guards stationed outside a door, and I stretch all five feet seven inches of me, trying to get a glimpse of him.

Winfield glances around before he continues. "Crane has a propensity for sending in beautiful women interns to see if he'll talk. So. Be prepared."

A grin forms on my face. I can't even help it. I ask him slyly, "So, you're saying you think I'm pretty?"

And . . . he trips over his own foot. Literally. The dude practically face-plants on the sad gray floor. "What? *No.* I mean, you're not *not* pretty. I just meant—"

My grin grows bigger. "Beautiful. I think your exact wording was *beautiful.*" He is turning red, so I bat my eyelashes for good measure. It's fun to watch him squirm. "Anyway, do you think it'll work?"

He shrugs. "I don't know. He's still not talking. But one time, he seemed tempted?"

"Fascinating!" I say. But what does it mean?! I'll definitely be discussing it with Aria later.

"I'm not worried, though," he adds. "Dr. Crane is a genius. He can take the most hardened criminal and they'll be sobbing and vulnerable when he leaves the room." He stares off into space for a second like he's imagining Dr. Crane in all his psychiatric glory. Or like he's posing for a men's cologne ad. It's hard to say.

"By the way," he says, pulling himself out of his reverent stupor, "you can call me Win. If you want to."

"Sounds good, Win-if-you-want-to." I laugh at my awful joke, but I can't help noticing how his cheeks turn red, just a little bit.

We pass through another checkpoint and a huge sliding-bolt door.

"We're in the women's ward now," Win explains to the

group. And then just to me, "You know who's really fascinating?"

"Who?" I ask, eyes bright, partly because if there's someone exciting here, I want to know about it, and partly because I like the way it feels to be getting a tour within a tour. A behind the scenes, VIP, go-backstage-and-vibe-with-the-band tour that is just for me.

His eyes mirror mine. He likes it too. "Talia al Ghūl. I think she's more interesting than a lot of the male inmates here, but she doesn't get as much hype. You know she took down the mayor's entire security detail? *By herself?*"

"Really?"

Now this is a broad I want to get to know. I mean, help. I want to help her and understand her and turn her from her life of crime onto the straight and narrow, yep. I heard about her assassination attempt on the mayor, how she got so close before failing, but I had no idea she did it all by herself. That part wasn't in the news.

I glance at the cells as we pass, wondering which one belongs to Talia. And I realize she's not just the most high-profile female Super-Villain here; she's the *only* female Super-Villain. Because women don't get as much credit, even for things like mayhem? Because they're less likely to get caught? I've heard rumors about this master thief called Cat Lady or something, but she might as well be made of smoke what with the number of times someone's actually seen her. As we keep walking, my thoughts turn elsewhere. Being in the women's ward feels different, like having a bucket of ice water dumped onto my soul. My zeal for revolutionizing the treatment of the mentally ill and making a name for myself dampens a bit. I don't realize why until I see a girl with strawberry-blond hair and birdlike shoulders. And then it whacks me in the chest.

"You okay?" asks Win.

"Mmm-hmm," I lie.

The girl isn't Bernice (she's got the wrong nose, wrong eyebrows, wrong freckle placement). But she looks enough like my ex-girlfriend to tie my stomach in knots.

Bernice ended up in prison (regular prison, not Arkham). After our vigilante girl gang uncovered a campus predator. After the police busted in to find that Bernice had nearly killed him. After she took the blame for everything we had ever done. She's gearing up with a public defender to start an appeals process, but still. There's a part of me that feels so guilty, it hurts to breathe. I make a mental note to visit Bernice's sister, Stella, like she asked me to.

Dr. Nelson is in regular prison too (a fact that makes me feel decidedly less guilty). The faculty position at Metropolis University evaporated in the wake of such a horrifying scandal. Temporarily kidnapping a bunch of girls and leaving their minds in pieces is not exactly the kind of thing you can come back from. Not after Officer Montoya catches you red-handed. Not after a girl ends up dead.

I try to focus on the Arkham tour. Dangerous criminals! Constant vigilance! Win leads us out through a set of huge double doors that seems to be undergoing repairs.

"Fingerprint scan," explains Win. "It's been in the works for months, but they're finally putting it on all the major doors into or out of the wards."

"Ohhh, fancy." And then I remember what I've seen in the news. "Trying to cut down on all the escapes?"

He shrugs. "All good authentication systems have something you know, something you have, and something you are." He lowers his voice. "It's honestly about time we did this."

I think about what he just said. I guess the badge around

his neck that he's been using at each set of doors is the "something you have." And then the code he punched in would be "something you know." The fingerprint scan was the only kind of authentication they were missing.

We're on the outside now. The safe side. Win faces us and rubs his hands together. "Let's get those badges made."

He points to an office the size of a closet that houses a metal stool positioned in front of a plain blue backdrop. Across from it is a desk, some filing cabinets—and even though it's typical office stuff, the whole room feels like a cave. But then maybe that's because the man behind it is popping sunflower seeds and scowling like a disgruntled troll (the kind that lives under a bridge, not the internet kind). I'm the first of the interns to walk inside and sit down, since I was standing next to Win. I blink up at the cave troll, who's leaning on his stool, and wait for something to happen. He has sunflower shells stuck in his beard.

"You have to take off your glasses," he says, like I'm an idiot for not guessing that.

I politely remove them and place them in my lap, though I have to say, I'm not pleased. I need them. Not because of how I see but because of how they make other people see me.

"One, two, three." He hits a button on his computer.

Click! goes the camera in front of me.

He frowns at the picture that pops up on his screen.

"You're not supposed to smile," he says, rolling his eyes. Again, like I was somehow supposed to know that. "Let's try it again. Ready? One, two, three."

Click!

"You smiled again."

"Well, duh. I'm getting my picture taken. It's impossible not to smile."

Also? It is a stupid rule. I tell him as much and ask him for an explanation and whether there are any loopholes (let me tell you exactly how happy this makes him), but just as he starts to answer, I notice Graham saying something to Aria in the hallway. I can't hear what he says, but I get this prickly feeling. Maybe from the way his head is inclined toward her ear, or the way her eyes flick to me and away just as quickly. They are gossiping about me.

I hear the cave troll/prison photographer counting down again, and I shift my eyes back to the camera, quick.

Click!

"Finally." He enters some personal information (name, title, areas to be accessed), and a few seconds later, the machine next to him spits out a card with my name on it.

The girl in the picture is not smiling.

I'm probably being too sensitive. That's what I tell myself, at least.

When Aria finishes taking her badge picture, I fall into step with her and make a joke about the "smiling is verboten" photographer. Is it just me, or is there an edge to her laugh that wasn't there before?

I glance over my shoulder at Graham. Did he tell her about the stuff that happened with Dr. Nelson last year? Because people know. When a person does something that terrible, people can't stop themselves from talking about it. Especially at a place like a college campus. The juicier the rumor, the worse the offense, the more it gets dissected. The more warped and twisted and fantastical the story becomes. I never hear people talk about the toxin he sprayed the girls with, though. A fear spray plus sedative combo. Only the insiders know that part. Even fewer people know that the toxin was sent to Dr. Nelson anonymously in exchange for blood samples. Or that the supplier is working at Arkham.

I keep expecting Nelson to crack and reveal who the supplier is. Try to get a plea deal. He doesn't strike me as the kind of person who'd do well in prison. But so far, he's been as silent as the grave. Which means the supplier must be scarier than I ever could have imagined.

There's a part of me that wants to shake every tree and kick open every door until I find the person who made the toxin that killed Kylie. Because the girl who died wasn't just anybody—she was one of my best friends. We were a family—me and Kylie and the other girls in the Reckoning. But now Kylie's gone, and Bernice is in jail, and I don't really see Jasmin and Bianca a whole lot anymore. We had to choose. Our girl gang or our futures.

I look down the hallway, back toward where they keep Gotham City's most captivating and chaotic criminal minds. I feel like I'm destined to be here. To advance my career. Prove I'm more than just the rumors. I'm here to help people the world thinks are beyond repair change the course of their lives. That's why I've got my blond hair bound up in a bun. No dip-dyed pigtails this year—just brainy glasses and an expression that screams intellectual curiosity.

I'm not going to let anything drag me off the straight and narrow path to my legion of lofty goals.

We make a stop at the first-floor bathrooms before heading to the staff cafeteria for lunch. I note that the ceiling panels are those typical industrial white squares speckled with black. I also note that it'd be pretty easy to push one aside and hop up there from the back of the toilet. Not that I'm thinking of doing that.

When I go to wash my hands, Aria is already gone. Bummer. I was hoping she'd wait for me. I hurry to the cafeteria and get a plate of chicken tenders and green beans that doesn't look half-bad. Aria is getting something to drink. Oh, good. The seats are already filling up at one of the tables, but Graham is sitting there, looking like he's trying to be King of the Interns, so I start a new table, alone. It's a risk, but it's one worth taking. Besides, I'll have Aria on my side.

Just as I think her name, I see her walking toward me. I lift my hand. Wave. She scans the cafeteria tables like there's a sea of people and options instead of just two. And I know what's going to happen, even as she veers toward Graham's table instead of mine. I know, but I lie to myself—*just wave a little harder and she'll see you.* It only makes it hurt more when she sits down next to him.

I guess my fresh start isn't as fresh as I would have hoped.

Eventually, my table fills up with other interns. They can't *all* sit at Graham's table. Eventually, there are people eating and laughing, and I try exceptionally hard not to look in Aria's direction. Eventually, another girl—one with long, wavy surfer hair and a Beatles T-shirt (Ansley?)—looks at us conspiratorially.

"Wanna know something?"

"YES." Like, obviously. Emphatically. Immediately. And not just because it'll make me forget about what happened with Aria, who I plan on ignoring for the rest of time.

(Everyone else concurs.)

"I heard this place is haunted."

"What?!" I bust out laughing. So does half of the table.

But her eyes only grow more sincere. "Yeah, yeah, I'm serious." She tucks a strand of hair behind her ear. "My friend is a second-year intern. And apparently, it's true."

Honestly, this is so delicious, I don't even care that it's also ludicrous.

"What kind of haunted?" I ask, unable to help myself.

She glances around, and our shadows lengthen, and it suddenly feels less like a joke.

"A terror in a burlap mask," she breathes. "My friend calls him the Scarebeast. They say he stalks the halls at night. They say he knows everything you're afraid of, even if you don't know it yourself yet. They say people go crazy just from looking at him, because his eyes are made of fear itself. He can make you die of a heart attack without even touching you."

She crosses her arms, pleased with herself, and I try to pretend that my heart isn't skittering around my rib cage like a frightened mouse. I remember the conversation I had with Kylie's friends shortly after she died.

She had a heart attack.

There was some kind of weird toxin in her system.

Whoever killed her literally scared her to death.

He's here.

The person responsible is here, and I said I wasn't going to makes waves this year, and I said I was going to leave that vigilante costume at the bottom of my drawer. But the promises I've made myself just got a whole lot harder to keep.

CHAPTER 2

Marstellar Library

THE MARSTELLAR LIBRARY IS ONE OF MY FAVORITE BUILDINGS on campus. It's small and grand and trimmed with pink marble all around. It used to be the main library back, like, a million years ago when the school was founded, but now the main library holds ten times more books, and Marstellar is used mainly for multimedia storage. Most people don't even realize it's here, but I maintain that the only thing better than a library is an ancient library. *In pink.* I'm just saying, the founders knew what they were doing.

You know who didn't know what they were doing? Whoever put me in this French class. Madame Dumas lectures from the front of the charming wood-paneled room, and I catch maybe every tenth word she says, because I am in charming wood-paneled hell. Turns out the French program at my East End high school wasn't exactly stellar (quell surprise!). But since I've technically had four years of the subject, they put me in this advanced French course, along with thirteen Gotham U students who have clearly spent the last four years at French boarding school or wherever the eff, because they all hang on Madame Dumas's every word, and they all seem to know things like saying oui so it sounds like "way" instead of "wee" is more Parisian.

Anyway, I'm pretty sure Madame Dumas hates me. Possibly because in our first class, she asked who had been to France, and I replied (in English) that I had been to Coney Island, did that count? She starts saying something about our examens and writing on the chalkboard (I love that this library still has those old green chalkboards!), and I'm no master of the French language, but even I can understand where this is going.

Notes d'examen

A—5

B—6

C—2

D—1

My heart squeezes when she writes the number 1 next to the D. It's me. Of course it is. It's for damn sure not one of these perfect Gotham U kids with their Chanel backpacks and their shoes that never have any scuffs. Madame Dumas passes back our exams, and even though I knew it was going to be there, my eyes well up when I see the giant letter *D* written in red wax pencil. (Sidenote: Why does it have to be so red?)

I've never actually gotten a D before. On anything. All A's all through high school, though I guess that's probably true of everyone in this room, only they didn't go to high school in the East End, so their grades matter more. Beside me, my roommate, Samantha, gets a B. I had been super excited about taking this class together and becoming best friends for the rest of eternity, but now I fold my exam in half so she can't see it.

"If you made below a C, please stay after and talk to me," announces Madame Dumas (in English, for us simpletons) because this moment can't get any worse.

"I'll see you back at the dorm." Samantha smiles at me, and I don't want to begrudge her the B she got or the fact that she's smiling about it, but I do. I can't help it.

The other students trickle out, and I drift toward Madame Dumas like a criminal to an executioner. Is this the part where she tells me I'm kicked out of her class? Grills me about why I didn't study for her test?

"I studied so hard! I really, really did!" I tell her, answering a question she hasn't even asked. Begging her to believe me. "Honestly, I had a harder time with this than my chemistry exam."

Her eyes bulge. "I purposely set a light first exam to ease you all into the semester. This is French. It's not meant to be a weed-out class."

"I'm not—" How do I even begin to say something so humiliating? "I'm not like the other students here." It's the best I can do. I hope she gets the subtext. The question that I want to ask but can't. The thought that bashes itself against my brain whenever I'm at my most vulnerable.

What if I'm not smart enough to be here?

She gives me a sympathetic smile that is, frankly, unexpected. "I think you can do this. Sometimes I have students who don't score well on the first test, and they don't really course correct and they end up failing my class."

I suck in a breath, but she continues.

"But. Sometimes I have students who struggle on the first test, but they put in the work and get tutoring and study really hard for the rest of the semester and end up with a B."

B. I could be happy with a B.

"Please come to me after class anytime you don't understand something. And I would definitely reach out to the tutoring center."

What I want to do is fall on my knees and tell her I that I shall always think of her as a great benefactress, but that might be overkill, so instead I nod rapid-fire and choke out a "thank you."

On the way back to my dorm, though, the thoughts buzz around my brain like so many bees.

Like you really belong in a place with marble buildings and wood-paneled walls.

If you made below a C, please stay after.

You may be going off to that fancy school every day, but that doesn't make you one of them.

What if I'm not smart enough to be here?

I try to shake it off as I enter my dorm room—I don't want to cry in front of Samantha.

She smiles brightly when she sees me. "Want to go over our test answers together?"

I thought she caught a glimpse of my test, but maybe I folded it fast enough; she wouldn't be asking in that kind of tone otherwise, right? But then, didn't she say she'd meet me back at the dorm? I don't know, but either way, I decide the best plan is to shake my head and say, "Maybe later."

I start to lay the test on my desk but find myself tucking it into my bottom drawer instead. My fingers touch something slippery—a black-and-red costume. Glittering. Dangerous. Before, at the asylum, I was tempted. But now? Now I know that I am hanging on by the most fragile of threads. I've lost both my parents. I'm from the East End. I don't get to fail up, and I don't get a million chances. So, as much as I want to stalk through the night with a mask and a list of names, I can't. If I ever want to make it, ever want to be one of them, this is the price. And I'm willing to pay it.

CHAPTER 3

Alpha Kappa Nu Sorority House

WELCOME HOME. THE HOUSE LOOMS IN THE DISTANCE, sprawling and impressive, three stories tall, with cheery yellow paint and huge wraparound porches with lazily rotating fans. It's not a place where I would have guessed I'd fit, despite coming here with Kylie a bunch of times last year. The WELCOME HOME banner hangs from the bottom-floor porch, scrolling navy script painted on a lavender background. They left it up since Bid Day, a few weeks ago. I don't know if it's because of stuff with the Reckoning or losing my parents, but those words really get to me. I teared up when I passed underneath the banner on Bid Day, my Alpha Nu bid card clenched in my hand like a golden ticket, "Girls Just Want to Have Fun" blaring through a speaker as a hundred girls swarmed me with hugs. Walking into Alpha Nu really did feel like coming home.

"Um . . ." I can't help but gasp as I get closer to the house. It looks like it's being eaten by an enormous rainbow spiderweb.

I walk closer, jaw still hanging open, joining the other

new members on the front lawn. Thirty-six shades of yarn stream across the yard, over balconies, around corners, and out of doors and windows. I only skimmed the email about the Big-Little Reveal. I must have missed the part about the yarn.

I wander around the yard and realize that each piece of yarn ends with a note card. The one at my feet reads *Mayra*. I search for one that says *Harleen* and finally find it attached to a scarlet piece of yarn on top of a hydrangea bush.

"Don't start yet, Harleen," calls the new-member coordinator, Kelsie, who always has this tone—like she's a kindergarten teacher, but one who hates you. "We're waiting until all the new members are here."

After several long minutes of waiting, during which I do cartwheels on the lawn and search my hair for split ends and speculate with Gia about who we might be matched with, the rest of the girls arrive and find their respective pieces of yarn.

"If we each get our first choice, you, me, and Cindy will be in the Superstar family together," gushes Gia.

The older girls explained to us last week that clusters of anywhere from four to twelve sisters are called a family, complete with a name like the Princess family, the Booty family, the Angel family, or the Clueless family. Every sister could trace her line back through her Big Sis until eventually it led to one of the first Alpha Nus on campus. I look at my note card and swallow. I *really* want Sophie. She's Kylie's Little Sis, and after what happened, it felt like she was the only person who wanted to talk about Kylie as much and as badly as I did. I even went with her to visit Kylie's family a couple of times. Kylie's little sister (her biological one, not Sophie) is a senior in high school this year, and even though she's a brunette and a competitive volleyball player, she and Kylie have exactly the same laugh.

"All right, ladies," says Kelsie with a pointed look at Gia. "You've probably figured out that each of you has a piece of yarn with your name on it. Follow your yarn, and along the way, you'll find pieces of a costume. At the end of the yarn, your Big Sis will be wearing a matching costume." Her eyes sweep over us, making sure we're ready. "Everybody, go!"

Have you ever watched thirty-six girls try to untangle a spiderweb of yarn as big as a three-story house? (Chaos. Absolute chaos.) I work as quickly as I can, jumping over some strings, crawling under others, all the time winding my scarlet string around my arm. Kelsie didn't say it was a race, but let's be real, anything can be a contest with the right attitude.

I hurry up the first-floor stairs, where my yarn winds through the eye hole of a creepy-looking white cat mask.

"Umm. . . ."

I don't really know what to make of it, but I pull it on over my head anyway, even though the mask is kind of hot and makes it hard to see. Then I follow my string out a window, hanging my body halfway out and stretching my toes to connect with the railing of the back porch.

Gia laughs. "Harleen, you know you can just throw your yarn down and walk around to get it, right?" She is currently tying a pale pink bikini top over her tank top.

"I know, but this way is much more fun!"

I follow my string around the deck, almost tripping over my next article of clothing, a pair of thigh-high red boots. I examine them, my expression dubious. These plus the cat mask—*what the crap am I supposed to be? A furry?* But I swap my flip-flops out for the boots and keep going. In the kitchen, I find a fake blinged-out necklace. But in the chapter room is where it all comes together. I follow my yarn under a table, where it feeds through the arm of a black hoodie dress with a tiger and roses and the words BLIND FOR LOVE spangled on the front. I laugh as it finally clicks. Well played, Big Sis.

I slip the hoodie over my head and become Taylor Swift from that part in the "Look What You Made Me Do" video where she and her cat squad rob a bank, except the bank is called Stream Co. It's, like, metaphorical, you know? I keep following my string, running through the chapter room, which is this big, giant space where we have all our secret meetings. But you know, in that scene, Taylor also had a—

GOLDEN BASEBALL BAT!!

I pick it up and swing it around a few times like the badass I am.

"Hell yeah."

All around me, girls are starting to find their Big Sisters at the end of their strings. I pass two pirates hugging and two bunnies posing for pictures. I must be getting close. I follow my string up a flight of stairs and into one of the bedrooms.

Please. Please. Please. Please. Please.

Sophie is at the end of it. She's wearing nerdy black glasses and flannel pants and a JUNIOR JEWELS T-shirt, and she's holding a paper sign that says WILL YOU BE MY LITTLE?

I feel a sob well up in my throat, so I try to diffuse it by making a joke. "Aww. All along there was some invisible string tying you to me."

Sophie grins at me. "It's actually kind of blood-red, but close enough."

Could she *be* any more perfect? We start screeching and jumping up and down and hugging and screeching some more.

"We've got our first new Superstar!" yells one of the older girls behind me, and they rush to hug me too.

Gia appears next, wearing a pink swimsuit, fuchsia fur coat, and bedazzled sunglasses and following a lavender strand of yarn to Madison, who is dressed as full-on country music Taylor, curly blond wig and all. Cindy is close behind us, making a grand entrance as the NOT A LOT GOING ON AT THE MOMENT Taylor with her heart sunglasses and a fedora. She finishes her hot-pink string by running open-armed in slow motion over to Kate aka Zombie Taylor, who mimics Cindy's slo-mo run and wraps her in a movie-style embrace.

"Yay! Now we have the whole Superstar family!" yells Madison just as Sophie is squealing, "Harleen, come look at your presents!"

"PRESENTS!"

I start digging through my crate of goodies. Alpha Nu pencils and stationery, a water bottle, lots of candy, and a beautiful framed drawing of the Superstar family tree. I touch my finger to Kylie's name, which connects to Sophie's, which connects to mine. She's my Grand-Big.

"Aw, this is perfect. Now we can finally figure out how we're all interrelated." I look at the tree and then at Gia. "I'm way higher up on the tree than you are. Who pulls rank now, Gia?"

She makes a pretend-mad face and throws a narwhal stuffie at me, and then everyone is flinging narwhals (they are our mascot), and we dissolve into this contagious silliness that I never want to end.

"Hey," says Sophie in a quieter voice, moving away from the rest of the girls. It's the voice she gets when she wants to talk about Kylie. "I'm really glad you're my Little."

I feel the warmth down to my toes. "Me too."

"And I have to confess something." My eyes go big, but Sophie keeps going. "I've always been a little jealous of you."

"Me?!" You could knock me over with a feather right now. I don't even know. Sophie is a Gotham U cheerleader. She has wavy dark brown hair that shines like patent leather, and she's one of the most beautiful girls I've ever seen.

She shrugs. "It seemed like she had a special kind of friendship with you. And the other girls y'all hung out with too, but especially you. It was like you and Kylie had secrets that we would never have."

Her perfectly plucked eyebrows arch ever so slightly, like she's hoping I'll reveal those secrets now. I stay silent. Mostly because I'm shocked. (Also because it's my only defense.)

"Anyway, I just wanted to say that if whatever was going on last year is still going on, if you're ever in any kind of trouble and you need someone, I'm here for you." She blushes. "I hope that makes some kind of sense and I don't sound like a weirdo."

I want so badly to tell her about the Reckoning, but I can't because I know where that would lead, so instead I give her the biggest hug ever and whisper, "You're amazing."

It was fun pretending today. All the warm feelings leach out of me as I walk down the stairs from Sophie's room. I know this can't last. I saw the financial breakdown last week at our new-member meeting. Dues. Semiformal. T-shirts. An Alpha Kappa Nu badge. And that's just fall semester. There's no way I can afford this.

I am literally an orphan, and let me tell you, every book I've read is a liar, because so far no one has sent me on any magical quests. In real life, it means I have to think about every penny. Because even though I have a presidential scholarship to cover my tuition and room and board and books, and that's a huge relief, I still have to worry about clothes/shampoo/dorm room stuff/every cup of coffee I drink outside the dining hall.

"Harleen," calls a voice from across the great room. As though I've conjured my fears, there stands Alpha Nu's VP Finance, holding an envelope and looking at me like she knows exactly how many dollars are not in my bank account.

I walk over to her as confidently as I can, holding my spine in a way that I hope doesn't scream, *I'm a penniless orphan*.

"Hey, I'm sorry I haven't turned in my dues yet. I—" Do I tell her? That I can't be an Alpha Nu? That I don't have it this week, but I'm not going to have it next week either? That I have to walk away from the closest thing I've found to a home on this campus?

"It's okay," she says.

Wait, what?

"Your dues have been paid." She smiles, and all the freckles on her face shift.

"Umm . . ."

She lowers her voice to a whisper. "Kylie's mom took care of it. Don't worry. I'm the only person who knows." She passes me the envelope. "Here. She told me to give you this."

"Are you serious?" I try not to cry for the billionth time since I walked into this house. Is this what sororities do to people? Turn them into nonstop tear factories?

She nods, giving me a quick hug and then opening the back door because she can tell that (A) I'm about to cry waterfalls, and (B) I might not want to do it in front of everyone. (Have I mentioned how much I love these girls?)

I manage to keep it together until I get outside, but when I open the envelope from Kylie's mom, it's all over.

Harleen,

I'm so glad that we've gotten to know you better this year. Kylie used to talk about you all the time, and I know you were one of her very best friends. She also mentioned that she was really hoping to convince you to join Alpha Kappa Nu in the fall. She wanted to be your Big Sis. But she was worried the financial aspect might be hard for you. And she didn't want that to stop you from being an Alpha Nu.

I'm paying your dues this year and every year after. It's what Kylie would want. I know you would have done anything for my daughter. Please let me do this for you.

Much love,
Heather

What is going on right now? Is this real life? I hold the letter to my chest. This is huge. I can't believe she's done this for me. I may not have any magical quests, but I've got a fairy godmother.

She had a heart attack. There was some kind of weird toxin in her system.

A terror in a burlap mask. They say people go crazy just from looking at him.

I know you would have done anything for my daughter.

I'm just not sure I deserve her.

CHAPTER 4

Arkham Asylum

DURING MY FIRST MONTH AT ARKHAM, I KEEP TRACK OF ALL the rumors I overhear the other Team Graham interns telling about me. I think I write them down in a notebook somewhere.

> I heard she was on a Proceedings of the Gotham Academy of Sciences paper about The Joker. IN HIGH SCHOOL.
>
> Yeah, well. I heard she was only on that paper because she was sleeping with her professor.
>
> I heard she only got her scholarship because of him.
>
> I heard she killed him.
>
> I heard her girlfriend went to jail.
>
> I heard it was a suicide pact, and she didn't keep up her half.

Sometimes I amuse myself by sneaking up behind them. "I heard she kills people just for talking about her."

Apparently, you're not supposed to joke about killing people while in a facility for the criminally insane. So I work harder to swallow the comments down, planning my schedule to the minute. Completely packed. Not a second to spend thinking about the terrible things people are saying about me or the fact that a killer is walking the halls of Arkham, roaming free.

Chug another energy drink. Sleep is for the weak. Mistakes are for the weak. Anything less than perfection makes you freaking weak. If I work hard enough, I can paint over the past, blot out all the mistakes.

Luckily, our second month at Arkham brings something even more exciting than my sordid past: Assignments Day. The day each of the interns is assigned to an inmate for the rest of the school year. (Well, assigned to an Arkham psychiatrist, anyway, but everyone knows which psychiatrist to pick if you want to spend a lot of time with The Joker or Mr. Freeze or Talia al Ghūl.) It's all we can talk about as we wait for our coffees at the little stand inside the staff cafeteria.

Graham is being peak Graham, as usual. "Well, I already met with Dr. Crane, and I told him I'm only interested in staying on as an intern if I get to work with him."

The Joker. He means The Joker. Interning with Crane is the inside track for getting to work with the Clown Prince of Crime. Who, by the way, *still hasn't spoken*. Riveting.

I look Graham up and down, nose wrinkling at the scrubs he's taken to wearing, partly because Dr. Crane usually wears scrubs and a lab coat and partly because Graham likes to pretend he's a doctor and he actually thinks he has a chance of convincing some unsuspecting barista that he has a medical degree (yeah, okay, Doogie). He wouldn't even know what to do with The Joker if he found himself in a room alone with him.

And you would?

I feel my cheeks turn red at the thought. Me. In a room. With The Joker. Alone. Could I get him to tell me things he's never told anyone? Find out why he blew up Gotham Clock Tower, the crime that landed him in here a couple months ago? Last year, I managed to steal a sample of his blood from a crime scene. It was the culmination of all the research I was doing in lab—when I ran it and found off-the-charts levels of epigenetic modifications in the Super-Villain gene. That was my whole hypothesis—that people who had both the dangerous version of the gene AND greater modifications brought on by past trauma would be more likely to become Super-Villains.

I try not to think about how my blood sample showed levels twice as high as his.

I have a published paper with data from The Joker, I tell myself. Maybe I wouldn't be able to get him to talk, but I feel like I'd have a hell of a lot better chance than Graham. Which reminds me . . .

"Doesn't Crane only send *girls* in?" I'm a few people behind Graham, but he definitely heard me. I can tell by the way his shoulders scrunch up around his ears.

One of his friends shoves him. "Have fun putting on your mom's dresses."

Graham rolls his eyes and pays for his coffee. He doesn't so much as glance in my direction.

Something about it makes me snap. "I've met him, you know," I say brightly.

Every head turns in my direction, even Graham's. Ha!

He sizes me up. There's a part of him that's dying to ask, I can tell. Instead, he narrows his eyes at me.

"You're lying."

Last year I would have unleashed a thousand dark fantasies on him in my mind. This year? I keep my dark thoughts bound up so tight, I don't even let myself feel them. Only happy-sunshine-smiling. *You should smile more, sweetie.* My mind is so crammed full of pretty bright thoughts that sometimes it makes my eye twitch.

Graham stalks off toward rounds. The others follow. Not that I don't have any friends here, but the three interns I'm closest with have already staked out chairs in the seminar room where we have rounds so they can be closest to the clipboard when sign-ups start. And as much as I admire that kind of relentless extra-ness (honestly, it's probably why we're friends), some of us need caffeine to be fully functional humans, okay?

The doctor in front of me moves, and I step up to the counter.

"Can I get a macchiato and a dark chocolate Greek yogurt?"

The guy behind the counter taps in my order. I step to the side to wait for my coffee.

And anyway, I *have* met him. One time the police were chasing him through the alley behind my apartment building, and I watched from the fire escape as he got away. (Okay, so that doesn't count.) But then another time, I was really in a bad place after my dad died, even though he was kind of the worst. (Families are complicated.) So, anyway, I'm walking the sidewalks dressed in a Harlequin outfit (the one now buried in my dresser) and smashing things with my baseball bat (as you do), and out of nowhere, THERE HE IS. Not gonna lie, there was some darkly effed-up chemistry between us. He even gave me my secret name. Harley Quinn. Not that I go by it. Or wear Harlequin outfits. Or smash things. Not anymore, anyway.

Not even if you find the man in the burlap mask?

Not even for Kylie?

Don't think about that.

I peel the top off my yogurt and grab a spoon. My phone pings in my pocket, probably my friends telling me to get my butt to sign-ups already. I check, expecting to see Xander freaking out over whether someone else is going to snag Solomon Grundy out from under him. But it's someone else. My stomach does a double-twisting backflip. I haven't gotten one of these messages in weeks. I was starting to worry Jasmin and Bianca didn't like me anymore. Bianca messaged us a couple times right when school started, but it was about doing missions, trying to get the Reckoning going again.

And as much as I still wanted to light the patriarchy on fire, I had to tell her that I couldn't. I promised Montoya. We wouldn't do any more missions, and her investigation into the Reckoning would stay closed. But after I said no to Bianca the first few times, her invitations to have tea and study at her apartment stopped too.

RECKONING SECURE CHAT

Bianca: Hey! Just wondering if you all were up for doing some breaking and entering tonight? Judge Bishop is vacationing in Nantucket—time to look for proof about what the whisper network has been saying!

Jasmin: I'm free after 5. Where are we meeting?

Bianca: My place. 7:00? I could make us tostones first?

Jasmin: Omnomnom

My heart sinks. Here's the thing: I so very badly want to have dinner with them tonight. But I can't say yes to one and not the other. I type, delete. Type, delete. And then I just go for it.

> Harleen: Hey! I can't do the mission tonight, but do you want to go get ice cream on Friday? I miss y'all!!

I wait, breath held. If they say yes, our friendship is more than vengeance and danger. They like *me,* not just the girl I become when I put on the costume.

> Bianca: Oh, sorry, I actually have a thing on Friday.

> Jasmin: Yeah, I'm not free either.

I wait for them to offer another date. And I wait. Nothing. Right, so that's it, then. I bite the insides of my cheeks. I will not cry in the Arkham Asylum staff cafeteria. *I will not.*

> Harleen: Totally, yeah, maybe another time.

Jasmin dashes out a quick For sure, but I already know how that promise turns out—empty. I slip my phone back into my pocket. I thought we were family.

The barista scrawls a name on my macchiato and sets it on the counter. *Hurling.* Awesome. I take a sip and scurry off down the hallway.

Crap, I'd better hurry. The sign-ups are happening in fifteen minutes! I don't want to get stuck talking to Condiment King for the rest of the year about how mayonnaise is really an essential element in any Super-Villain's arsenal. Though if I'm being honest, I didn't pick the fastest way from the staff cafeteria to rounds.

The reason I took this route, the reason I always take this route, is because it goes past Him.

My shoes are loud against the dingy tile floor. He absolutely knows I'm coming. Well, he knows someone is coming, anyway. It's not like he knows who I am. Or waits for me. I shake my head and take a spoonful of my Greek yogurt. He's never even been at his door when I've passed, so it's not like today he's going to suddenly—

"Puddin'?"

I freeze. Nearly twist an ankle. There he is—all dove-white skin and sickly-green hair. Eyes burning holes through me from the one rectangular window in the door of his cell.

The Joker.

Just spoke.

To me.

"What?" My voice cracks, and I hope he doesn't notice, but he just continues on like this is the most natural thing in the world, and we might as well be in a park or on the subway or creaking up the hill for the very first drop of a very tall roller coaster.

"Isn't that what you're eating?"

Pud— Oh.

"It's dark chocolate Greek yogurt." I glance from side to side, but we're alone. Where are his guards?

His mouth spreads into a smile. "Scared you'll get in trouble for talking to strangers?"

"We've met before." I say it without thinking, and his smile only grows wider.

"Once upon a dream?"

He's teasing. He doesn't remember me, then, from that night in the street. Of course he doesn't. What was I expecting, that I'd confess that I saw him in the street one night and knew I wanted power like his? That I designed my girl gang vigilante costume to look like a Harlequin because of him?

I take a step closer. He's like an abyss you can't look away from. And I don't know that I mind being devoured.

I'm supposed to be putting it all behind me, being someone else this year, someone better. But cool, cool, maybe I'll just share all my darkest secrets with Gotham City's most notorious Super-Villain. That's almost the same thing, right?

He wraps a hand around one of the bars on his window, almost caresses it.

"I feel like I could really talk to you. You're not like those other girls they've been sending in here." His voice is a silk sheet—soft and rich—but you could still strangle someone with it.

I can see myself cracking his brain open like an egg, secrets spilling across the pages of scientific-journal articles that make me famous. An entire star-crossed, apocalyptic future. I wrap my fingers around the bar next to his hand, knowing it is a terrible, dangerous, astonishingly stupid idea, but too bewitched to stop myself.

"You seem like the kind of girl who's sick of being a good little robot. Who can appreciate the beauty of an explosion." His eyebrows flick upward. "The feel of a bat in her hands as she smashes it through a window."

I fight back a gasp. He does remember.

He strokes his finger down my hand. Stares at me knowingly.

"I—I—"

He leans toward the window, our noses almost touching. "I could never forget a face like yours."

I take a step closer. "Why'd you do it?"

"Blow up the Gotham Clock Tower?"

I nod breathlessly. Wait for him to turn into some dark version of Robin Hood, confess that his secret sins are a revolution against classism or health-care disparities or treatment of the mentally ill.

He grins. Crookedly. Slyly.

"I wanted to make an explosion in the shape of my face."

That's . . . it?

"Oh." I unwrap my hand from the bars.

He looks mortally offended. "OH? Chaos for chaos's sake—there's nothing more beautiful than that."

I take a step back. Tug at the collar of my white coat. I like chaos as much as the next girl (okay, let's be real, probably more), but there's always been something driving my chaos, something that makes the darkness worth unleashing. I hoped he was the same way. "Mmm-hmm. I have to get going."

"Hey! Hey, don't walk away from me. I'm giving you the chance of a lifetime here!"

"I can't be late to rounds," I say over my shoulder. And then I pause. Turn. Look fear directly in the eyes.

"And, Mr. J?"

"Yes?"

"I'm *exactly* like the other girls."

My heels click down the faded gray-green hallway like a countdown. *Tick. Tick. Tick. Tick.*

He explodes behind me, but I don't turn around again. I'm twice what he is. I knew this before, but now I KNOW it. Maybe there's another Harleen in another universe who didn't know about the genetic testing or have the girls from the Reckoning making her strong. Maybe she fell for that "other girls" BS. Followed him till he hollowed her.

When Dr. Crane says it's time for intern sign-ups, I snatch the pen from him the way only an East End girl can. And I sign my name next to Dr. Morales's, knowing exactly who her primary patient is. I'm working with Talia al Ghūl.

CHAPTER 5

Wayne Dining Hall, Gotham University

IT'S OCTOBER, AND THERE ARE SCARECROWS DECORATING the dining hall. I grab a tray and get in line at the station for omelets. A cluster of girls stand in front of me talking, their voices carrying.

"That was the girl, I'm telling you."

"I can't believe she let a professor do something like that."

"So messed up."

My heart sinks. It's intern orientation all over again. The guys in my classes. The girls in my dorm. Everyone seems to have heard from a friend's boyfriend's roommate about what happened with me and Dr. Nelson last year. I kind of wish I'd wrangled some other Alpha Kappa Nu girls instead of coming to Sunday brunch alone. They actually believe me that nothing happened—that Dr. Nelson was a sadistic creep who collected girls like pinned butterfly specimens and I just happened to get caught in the cross fire. I can't help thinking about Kylie and her newly anointed campus-wide nickname ("the Girl Who Died"). She introduced me to the other girls at Alpha Nu. She's the whole reason I joined. Or maybe it was because of Jasmin and Bianca. The fact that I so badly wanted to fill the family-shaped hole that was left when the Reckoning dissolved and my friendships with them dissolved right along with it.

The girls bust out laughing as they move on to the drinks station, and I step up to the counter glumly even though John the Omelet Guy is usually my favorite.

"What can I get ya, Harleen?" (Seriously, he knows everyone by name.)

"Veggies and goat cheese?" I glance over my shoulder at the girls to see whether they are still laughing. (They are.)

John pours whipped eggs from a jug onto the cooktop.

I stay quiet, even though I'd usually be talking with him about gymnastics or books or Gotham U's chances this football season.

"You okay, Harleen?" he asks as he sprinkles the quickly forming omelet with asparagus and red pepper.

I nod and take my plate, waiting for the girls to finish at the drinks station so I can get milk and coffee. I've heard a lot of people talk crap about the dining hall food, but honestly, it's kind of unbelievable how you can get however much food you want, and there's an amazing salad bar all the time and tea and juice and frozen yogurt on tap. I can't imagine feeling anything but grateful for three square meals a day that include fresh fruits and vegetables.

I follow the girls into the sea of tables in spite of myself, straining to hear more, waiting for them to call me a slut or worse.

"Have you seen the pictures of the accident?"

Accident?

"Oh! The ones where that factory place is still on fire? Yeah. I saw those. I heard there's ones of a campus lab that got trashed, too, but the school's keeping those pics hush-hush."

"Probably because her parents are, like, gazillionaires."

Okay, maybe this isn't about me after all, because I definitely didn't set a building on fire or trash Dr. Nelson's lab (though now I'm thinking I should have!). Also, I currently have no parents, let alone ones who are "gazillionaires."

Just then, one of the cackling gossipmongers gestures at a pretty red-haired girl sitting by herself.

"Can you imagine?" she stage-whispers, and her friends burst into giggles.

They aren't talking about me.

They're talking about this poor girl, alone, peeking through her curtain of hair, looking like the saddest person to ever eat French toast.

I watch the group of girls walking on, setting up roost at their own table like the self-satisfied harpies they are. I look back at the red-haired girl, wearing a CLIMATE CHANGE IS REAL tee and hunching her shoulders.

And maybe it's because of what happened with Aria at intern orientation, but I just can't help myself. I make the most determined face I possibly can, and I go over and set down my tray.

"Hey!"

"Hey."

(It is possible I went too hard with the determination and it's scaring her.)

I try a smile instead. "I'm Harleen."

. . .

. . .

. . .

"Can I sit here?" I ask, even though I already sat down.

The girl replies with a resigned, "Sure."

I want to get all impassioned and spout off about slut shaming and evil professors and tell her about last year and ask her a million questions, but I can tell that isn't the right way to go with this girl. Instead, I pull out my chemistry textbook and some homework that's due Monday. The girl jumps a little at the movement, and her eyebrows rise for a second. But then she pulls a copy of *The Orchid Thief* from her book bag and starts reading.

I breathe a sigh of relief as quietly as I possibly can. I thought I was going to scare her away. (I'm particularly skilled at doing that to people.)

I glance up. She really is reading (apparently she's able to focus a lot better than I can right now), and there's this little wrinkle between her eyebrows from concentrating. It's cute. *She*'s cute. HEY, WAIT, I KNOW HER! She's that red-haired girl from club sign-ups with the bumping-into and the limbs wrapping and the feeling like my legs and mouth and brain had forgotten how to work. Wow, how in the multiverse did I not realize who she was when I sat down? Well, I guess I was on a women's empowerment mission and all. Plus, her hair was covering a lot of her face. But now that I'm looking, holy hell. I wish I could remember what her name is. It's definitely her. The fact that her body language is all limbs-folded-in-on-herself-like-a-paper-airplane and she's clearly hurting doesn't hide her beauty. She has these angular cheekbones—the kind that mythical queens have, to give the bards something to write songs about. Her curtain of red hair sweeps almost to her waist, and her eyes are the color of springtime.

She turns a page in her book, and it jolts me out of my stupor. I don't want her to catch me staring.

I go back to my omelet and my book. *Try* to go back to my book.

But there are just so many things I want to say to her. I can't stop myself. "Let me tell you about Marie Curie. . . ."

Hours later, we're still sitting at the table, talking. I've explained all about how Marie Curie is an iconic badass who told the Royal Swedish Academy they could take several seats for attempting to deny her the chance to accept her Nobel Prize just because she dared find some happiness with a dude with a "thriving mustache" after her husband died. (I think it made Pamela feel a little bit better?) Oh! Also, I know now that her name is Pamela and that she's a first-year, like me (though I'm technically a year older because of my gap year), and that she lives in Elliot Hall, just like me, only two floors up. (It's kind of like we're besties now.)

Pamela's chair makes a horrible screeching noise against the dining hall floor as she stands up. She picks up a bag that looks hip and European but also like it might be made from recycled materials.

"I'd better get going," she says by way of explanation.

I don't mean to look so startled. We've been here for three hours—one of us had to leave at some point. But is it weird that I just want her to stay? We could keep talking, eat lunch and dinner here too, and fro-yo with rainbow sprinkles as an afternoon snack. I don't want this moment to end. I want to be her best friend the way other people talk about love at first sight and lightning flashes and meeting their soul mates.

I realize that Pamela is packing up her bag with excruciating slowness. Is it possible that she wants all that too?

If saying hi and introducing myself and stuff was taking a leap of faith, then what I'm about to do next is hurling myself off a cliff. Pamela zips her book bag shut. Our eyes meet. And I try so hard to sound cool and chill and friendly and non-desperate when I say it.

"Same table, tomorrow?"

CHAPTER 6

ARKHAM ASYLUM

DR. MORALES HAS THREE DEGREES. AND SHE'S AN EDITOR of a scientific journal. And the president of the Association for Advanced Neuroimaging. Oh, and also she's published over a hundred papers. I picked her initially because I wanted to work with Talia al Ghūl, to understand and rehabilitate Arkham's ~~most famous~~ only woman Super-Villain, but holy wow, this lady is amazing. And after my mentor last year turned out to be a monster who kidnaps girls and tests experimental toxins on them, I have to say, it's nice to be working with someone who's known for things like ethics and collaboration in addition to their academic accomplishments.

I hurry down the hallway because I don't want to be late for my very first time shadowing her. Why is it so hard to be on time in this place?! I swear, the hallways rearrange themselves when you're not looking. I take a shortcut through one of the inmate wings because otherwise there's no way I'm going to make it on time. A voice calls out to me from a cell.

"The Straw Man's a-coming."

I startle and search for the source. Solomon Grundy stands at the door of his cell, blue-black veins threading through gray-green skin, skin that appears to be coming off in patches. *He's like a zombie,* I remember Xander saying. *He can't die.*

I wait, just a moment. Was he talking to me?

He points directly at me with a finger dripping with swamp moss. (So, yes.)

"Straw Man's a-coming for you," he says before turning back to his cell.

I stifle a shiver. Well, that was creepy. I wonder if it has anything to do with the Scarebeast that Ansley was going on about. The face in the burlap mask. The person who gave Dr. Nelson that spray that hurt so many girls and killed Kylie. But I don't have time to think about it, because if I do, I'll be late for Dr. Morales.

Dr. Morales cuts through Arkham in a long black skirt and sensible shoes. Tall. Professional. Long legs that take long, purposeful strides. I have to walk fast to keep up with her.

"You're a first-year, yes? What are you majoring in?"

"Either psychology or neuroscience—I'm still deciding. But I'm definitely premed. And I'm thinking psychiatry would be a good fit." *I basically want to be you when I grow up. Can I just follow you around like a puppy until that happens?*

"Excellent. Glad to hear it. Well, keep your grades high, and it certainly doesn't hurt that you're interning here. Or that you already have a paper in *PGAS.*" She pushes her huge, scientist-from-the-seventies glasses up on her face. "You were doing research with Dr. Nelson last year, yes?"

She pauses to search my face, the only hitch in her step in this entire walk across Arkham.

I nod.

"Yes, well." She makes sort of a clucking sound. "I'm sorry to hear about it. I've collaborated with him, and, well, I can't say I'm surprised."

Her face goes tight, mouth pinching. She is thinking a million and one terrible things about him, but she's too professional to say them out loud to a newly minted intern on our first day working together. She shakes her head, and her black curls bounce with the motion of it, even though she has them tucked back in a loose bun.

"So," she says, a business-y tone in her voice. Whatever moment just happened has already passed.

"So!" I echo. "I'm really excited to work with you! And Talia!" Perhaps I should dial it back on the exclamation points, though, even if the inside of my head does feel like !!!!!!!!!!!! at the thought of doing my first session with the woman who nearly assassinated the mayor.

"What do you know about Ms. al Ghūl?"

I try not to startle/flinch/let my shoes squeak. It would probably not impress her if I answered, *Something something League of Assassins something something*. It occurs to me that I should have spent a little less time reading up on Dr. Morales on my phone this morning and a little more time reading up on Talia.

Oh well.

I finally settle on, "She's tenacious."

But I say it all firm, like there are multitudes in that two-word answer and I'm only just holding them back.

Dr. Morales nods, apparently satisfied with my assessment. Thank. Goodness.

"She is. She's also one of the smartest people I've ever met. When we go in there, you are to be a silent observer. You're welcome to take notes, ask me anything you'd like afterward, but while we're in that room with Talia al Ghūl, you are not to speak to her. This is for your own safety."

Dr. Morales stops walking.

There she is, I realize, trying to stifle a gasp. We're here, and beyond that two-way glass, Talia al Ghūl sits in a metal chair, legs crossed at the ankles even though they're in shackles. Her hands rest on a metal table in front of her that is likely bolted to the floor. Her fingers are laced together like she's waiting for a latte or a blind date to show or the first tee at a golf tournament. Her raven hair is tucked neatly into a high pony, and her orange Arkham uniform fits like it's been tailored. Some people just *look* like they come from money, no matter what they're wearing. Maybe I notice it extra because I know I'll never look that way.

"I've had interns who had trouble with this boundary, and they are no longer my interns. Are we clear?"

I startle, sucked back into the now. I was definitely not thinking about asking Talia how she gets her hair to look so good in prison, nope.

I attempt to make my face as earnest and trustworthy as possible. "Absolutely."

Do you know how hard it is to sit still and be quiet for an entire hour? I use every last one of my focus strategies—take detailed notes to stay attentive, fidget with the marble and mesh I keep in my pocket. But Talia is so damn interesting, and there are about eighty billion things I want to ask her.

So far, I've made it five minutes. And it's been nothing but pleasantries.

How are you doing today, Talia? (Good.)

Is everything going okay? Are you being treated okay? (Other than the fact that I'm in Arkham? Yes. I could use more books, though.)

In general, how would you describe your mood today? (Fine. Everything is peachy.)

Note: Talia did not actually say the word *peachy,* but I spaced out during that part.

Finally, Dr. Morales gets to the good stuff.

"I'd like to talk to you about your trial," she says. "Your legal team argued that you were criminally insane. They said you have early-onset dementia, if I'm remembering correctly." She flips to a page in her notes, even though I'm certain she doesn't need it.

Talia adjusts her handcuffs, nonchalant. "Yes, and Crane thinks I'm lying. He wants to have me transferred out of Arkham. I see you have a new intern." She nods at me, changing the subject. "Sad you're stuck in here instead of in the maximum-security counseling room with The Joker or Mr. Freeze? I hear they chain them to the wall."

I open my mouth to tell her that, actually, I chose her, when I catch Dr. Morales looking at me and realize that I have sworn to stay silent. I close my mouth, but the look in Talia's eyes tells me she knew exactly what she was doing. *Oh, she is good.*

Talia smiles like a lion. "This one's better than the last one."

"This is Harleen Quinzel, a student at Gotham U. My apologies for forgetting to introduce her before." She *does* seem like the kind of person who'd normally be good at that sort of thing. Maybe Talia makes her nervous too? Dr. Morales continues. "She'll be shadowing me for the rest of the semester. And incidentally, she was the first to the sign-up list."

Her voice catches on the word *list*, almost like she didn't mean to say that last part. It honestly doesn't seem like the kind of thing she'd normally reveal. Maybe I do need to be cautious around Talia.

Talia's eyebrows rise with interest. She's appraising me. I try not to squirm.

"You are young for a patient with dementia," says Dr. Morales carefully.

For a fraction of a second, Talia's lips disappear into a thin line, but she recovers just as quickly. "So you think I'm lying too?" She shrugs like it doesn't matter to her either way. "I'm not. I do have trouble remembering things."

Interesting. I'll have to ask Dr. Morales how old Talia is. She seems young—glossy hair, super fit. It's her face that feels off. She's one of those women who look like they could be any age. Thirty but with eyes that hold an old soul? Fifty but with flawless skin, like those ladies from the diamond district who stay young with some combination of Botox and chemical peels and dark magic? She could tell me any number, and I'd believe it.

"I don't think you're lying," says Dr. Morales, and Talia's head snaps up, the most emotion I've seen from her. She fixes Dr. Morales with a hard stare, like she's dissecting whether she's telling the truth. I swallow and sincerely hope Dr. M isn't lying. "In fact, I'd like to prove otherwise. Would you be willing to let us perform some neuroimaging to search for pathology that could be underlying your condition?"

"To see if I'm telling the truth, you mean," counters Talia. "It sounds like a very expensive lie detector."

"If we find something, Dr. Crane wouldn't have grounds to transfer you." There's a hint of a smile in Dr. M's eyes that makes me wonder if she feels about Dr. Crane the way I feel about Graham. I don't know why this makes me so happy.

Talia smirks. I wonder if she sees it too. "I'll allow it," she says.

Dr. Morales walks her through the paperwork, and I daydream about whether I have time to go to the dining hall and fill up my travel mug with coffee before my Intro to Capoeira class. (Side note: I'm obsessed. I can't believe it counts as a PE credit. It's a martial art that involves dance and acrobatics, and my teacher says I'm a natural. He teaches us about the historical aspects of capoeira too, about how it has roots in the African diaspora in Brazil.)

". . . to ask you about something else, something not related to you and your case."

Wait, what? These are the hazards of spacing out. Sometimes you miss something juicy.

Talia cocks her head to one side, again with that calculated aloofness, only this time it's harder for her to keep up the front.

"Some of the other patients have mentioned a creature pacing by their cells in the night. I think it might be related to the screaming fits we've been seeing. Have you noticed anything like that?"

So, it's not just a rumor! The doctors know about it too.

Talia steeples her fingers. Smiles sweetly. (It does not seem like an entirely natural expression for her.) "Yes."

"And?"

"I think you should be more worried about the people who sit on your side of the table."

My head snaps up. Who?! I am dying to ask, but I'm supposed to remain a silent observer. Is it the person who was making the fear toxin mixture for Dr. Nelson? Does Talia know who it is? Not that I'm planning on investigating that, because I'm not. I've said I'm not. I definitely don't have an entire secret notebook dedicated to it in my dorm room.

I am willing Dr. Morales to ask, and I'm waiting on pins and needles, and she opens her mouth, and my brain is all *Here we go! Here we go!* And . . . nothing. Dr. Morales brushes the comment off like it's no big deal and moves on to ask Talia about something else—I don't even know what, because I'm no longer paying attention.

Talia knows something about the person who's terrorizing Arkham. Maybe even knows who it is.

I can't stop thinking about it.

Because I want to believe it ended with Dr. Nelson—people getting taken and messed with and put back broken. I want to believe that Kylie was the last person who'd die because of him and his supplier. But I already know how these types of monsters operate. They think they'll never get caught. It doesn't matter how many close calls, doesn't matter the consequences. Testing the fear toxin on girls was probably just the beginning. Monsters like this don't stop.

Not unless you make them.

CHAPTER 7

Arkham Asylum

MY MIND CLINGS TO TALIA THE WAY IT DOES A NEW CRUSH. I talk about her to anyone who will listen. I think about her when I'm walking to class. She's so cool. I mean, fascinating. Interesting. Strictly from a learning perspective, of course.

I'm heading to grand rounds one morning (we have it each month so the interns and residents and people can learn more about stuff like cutting-edge treatments here at Arkham), and for once I'm running early. I could take the long way through the women's wing—I have time. I go so far as to walk to the entrance and stand there, full of longing. She knows something about the face in the burlap mask, the creature, the person who was sending those drugs to Dr. Nelson. I'm sure of it.

But I force myself to walk in the other direction. Dr. Morales could find out. It's not worth the risk.

I take my usual route, one that cuts through part of the men's wing. And I'm concentrating so intently that I don't notice the hand reaching through the cell window until it's already grabbing for my collar.

"Have you ever been to the Attic?"

I dodge, just missing the fingers slashing through the air near my neck.

"What?"

The Riddler stands at the door, arm reaching through the bars. He's skinny, with auburn hair and glasses, and it takes me a second to recognize him without the cane and the question marks and the flamboyant green suit. Also? The hand that is reaching out to me won't stop shaking. And there's something off about his face. He looks at something over my shoulder and screams. I startle and turn, but there's nothing there. Which makes me shiver that much more.

"Are you okay?" I ask him. "Did someone do something to you? Did you take something?"

"He takes you to the Attic," The Riddler whispers, chest rising and falling so rapidly that it looks like it's glitching.

I lean closer. "Who?"

"The Straw Man. The Scarebeast. The King of Screams. He has so many names."

I glance up and down the hall, half expecting the creature to appear.

"Where is it? Where is this attic?" I didn't even think Arkham had one. I've never seen any stairs leading up from the third floor, and the main entrance is all Gothic-industrial, with its pointed arches and vaulted ceilings. Eerie stained glass windows that twist and butcher the light so that it falls to the floor in jagged shapes—goblins and bats and wide-open jaws filled with sharp teeth. It's just not the kind of place where you can picture some crusty old attic. But maybe in the back building? Or one of the renovated wings? The Riddler hasn't answered my question. He's preoccupied with whatever is behind my shoulder. I've never really believed in ghosts, but I'd swear there's something in this hallway with us. "*Where?* How do I get there?"

"Under and never," he answers without taking his eyes off whatever he thinks he sees.

"Under what?"

"Spring to and right."

Before I can think to ask what that means, he keeps going.

"Open and closed. Wandering and lost."

He starts screaming again, this time loud and long enough to alarm every inmate on the cellblock. He sinks to the floor of his cell, shaking more now. Holding his knees and rocking back and forth.

"Under and never. Spring to and right. Open and closed. Wandering and lost. Under and never. Spring to and right. Open and closed. Wandering and lost."

I yell for help as his eyes roll back in his head.

"That must have been so scary," says Shiloh, one of my intern friends (plural!!). "And he didn't give you any indication about where this Attic might be, other than some gibberish?"

I shake my head. "Sadly, no."

But Shiloh only seems more excited. "Don't worry. I have a connection in the records office. I know there were some additions in the seventies." They tap their chin thoughtfully. "I'll see what I can come up with."

I stir the liquid cheese in front of me so that it doesn't get a skin on top. Shiloh and I are working the nachos table at Arkham Asylum's rec night. (Apparently, this is a thing they do every so often. Gather all the inmates who aren't in solitary into the rec room. Put on a movie or a football game. Hope no one dies.)

"Do you think there really is a Straw Man?"

Shiloh twists their head to look at me. "Do I think there's a giant conspiracy at a spooky mental hospital that actually has some kind of secret logical explanation? Damn right I do."

"Right. Me too." Did I mention I how much I love Shiloh? Their slouchy/casual/cool button-downs in wild patterns, and their tiny septum hoop, and the way they are 200 percent all in on anything we decide to do.

I scan the rec room and wonder if The Riddler would be here if it weren't for what happened earlier today. And then I stir the cheese some more because skin on cheese is the actual grossest.

"How edible do we think this cheese is?" I ask.

"I don't know, but he seems to have some strong opinions." They gesture at Mr. Freeze, who is currently picking jalapeños out of his dip while moaning about how hot it is.

"He seriously hasn't stopped complaining about it since we got here. Let it go, Elsa."

Shiloh snickers. "Right? Also, if Maxie Zeus makes another not-yo-cheese joke, I am going to impale myself on this spork." They push their turquoise bangs out of their eyes and heave a sigh born of the kind of suffering that can only be caused by terrible puns.

I laugh. "My friend Bianca would drive you absolutely nuts."

I spoon another scoop of lurid yellow cheese onto a plate of chips that Shiloh passes me. It lands with a plop.

"Thank you," says a voice, and I'm stunned speechless for a second at the razor-sharp smile in front of me. So many teeth. So many.

"Y-you're welcome," I stutter, and King Shark recedes with his nachos.

I wonder if he can bite through steel.

I wonder if Bianca really would annoy Shiloh.

I wonder what she's doing now.

I start to get all nostalgic about last year and the Reckoning, but I'm interrupted by shouts. I whip my head up, expecting to see fists flying and a homemade shiv, but it's just that Gotham U scored another touchdown.

"All right, all right, settle down," calls my least favorite guard, a short guy with menacing eyes and a hand that always seems to find his baton.

Two-Face scowls at the guard, flips the round piece of cardboard that serves as his coin, and swears when it comes up tails.

I wrinkle my nose. It really is too bad. I catch myself—not that I'm hoping for violence. I'm definitely not. I'm not like that anymore.

"Psst, Harleen, you can stop strangling that cheese ladle," whispers Shiloh.

"Oh." I blush and drop the ladle. But then I whisper back, "They say he's the guy to talk to if there's anywhere you're trying to go in this asylum."

"Anywhere like the Attic?"

"Maybe."

"Hmm." Shiloh stares at Two-Face and taps their fingers on the table absentmindedly.

I'm already distracted by something else.

King Shark is up to something. He lurks in a shallow pool of sunlight over by the windows, searching for something. Or hiding something. Whatever he's doing—it's suspicious. He hunches over and inspects another windowpane. And then he sweeps toward the bookshelf next to the windows.

Looking over his shoulder before darting out a webbed hand. Did he pick something up? Plant something? The windows are covered in bars—strong ones—I don't think he could thrash his way out of this rec room. But maybe with C-4?

He swipes his hand out again. Okay, that time he definitely took something. So, he's not lining the room with plastic explosives. But maybe it's some kind of contraband-smuggling operation. Drugs? Cigarettes? Weapons? I lean closer. Take a step in his direction without realizing it. The floor creaks.

And all of King Shark's seven-foot hulking frame orients itself in my direction.

Oh.

Crap.

He launches toward me, parting the sea of inmates watching football like they're not even there. Oh crap. Oh crap. Oh crap. I squeeze Shiloh's hand without meaning to, the one with the *Carpe the damn diem* tattoo.

"What are you— Oh."

Neither of us says anything else because King Shark is here. Now. In front of us. In the sharkskinned flesh. My heart beats like it's been through a particle accelerator while my brain tries to calculate whether there are any escape routes (nope), how likely he is to eat me (very), and how many seconds I have to live before the inevitable shark attack (2.4, give or take).

King Shark swells over the table. I hope everyone likes their nachos with a side of carnage.

Opens his jaws. For some reason, my about-to-be-dead brain pictures Pamela.

And he asks me for a cup.

My mouth starts talking before I can fully process the

fact that I'm still alive. "A cup. Yes! For sure. We have so many cups here! I can get you all the cups!" Just don't bite me in half like Maxie Zeus's lunch tray, okay?

"Just one," he says in a voice much softer and more tranquil than you'd expect.

"Right," I say.

I stand there stupidly and stare at his shark-y face.

Shiloh nudge-passes me a red Solo cup.

"Thank you," I tell them. I hold the cup out to King Shark like a robot.

"Thanks," he says. But he doesn't take it. He lifts his hands up, and I see that they are cupped together. "Could you hold it steady for me?"

"Um, definitely." What is even happening right now?

He opens his cupped hands. I flinch, still expecting the worst.

Ladybugs.

There are at least a dozen ladybugs crawling over his rubbery gray hands. I continue to hold out the cup and watch, stunned, as he coaxes the ladybugs inside it. Quickly but gently.

"They're happier outside," he says.

And my heart breaks into approximately two million pieces. He's not the monster; I am. I shouldn't have judged him like that. I want to make it up to him somehow. And then I see my least favorite guard leaving, and one of my most favorite guards enters the rec room.

I know just the way.

Five minutes later, King Shark, Shiloh, and I are standing outside in the exercise area with two guards and a Solo cup full of ladybugs.

"Ready?" I say with a smile.

King Shark nods and smiles back.

His grin doesn't scare me anymore. I can see the kindness in it. In him. He removes his hand from the top of the cup, and first one ladybug and then another fly out into a cloudless sky over Arkham Asylum. They soar into the air like doves at a wedding or dolphins leaping out of the ocean surf. The feeling of watching them lifts you right along with them.

"Thank you," says King Shark quietly.

Then he wades back into Arkham, leaving ladybugs in his wake.

CHAPTER 8

Burton J. Crowne Biomedical Building

I WEAVE MY WAY TO THE FRONT OF THE AUDITORIUM AND take a seat in the first row. I read an article about how the first two rows are the A-zone because the professors are more likely to get to know you and call on you. Also because it helps you pay attention, especially if you're like me and have ADHD. So, yeah, I'm never sitting anywhere else now.

I pull up the Intro to Neuroscience syllabus on my laptop so I can see who our guest lecturer is today. (It's one of those co-taught classes where different people in the department teach whichever classes they're an expert in—so cool!) Ohhh, today is Dr. Crane, and he's lecturing on the neurobiology of fear. That'll be ~~fun~~ terrifying.

"Good morning." His voice tumbles from the top of the auditorium, reaching its fingers into the far corners of the room, even though it isn't particularly deep or booming. "Who's ready to talk about fear?"

He spiders down the stairs in a beige tweed jacket and skinny jeans that accentuate how spindly his legs are. There's a stately wooden desk on a dais at the front of the room, and he sits on it and leans forward, his PowerPoint coming up on the screen behind him when he presses a button on the remote in his hand.

"My research assistant, Win, will be passing out some additional reading. The chapter on fear in your textbook is stuck in the Dark Ages. Our methods are much more rigorous today, and I hope you'll agree that the questions we're asking are a great deal more intriguing."

My eyes are drawn to the boy handing out papers a few rows back, A-zone or no. He gives a stack to each row as he passes.

"Take one and pass them," he says quietly, so as not to interrupt Dr. Crane.

He hands a few packets to the boy in the Gotham U baseball cap at the beginning of my row. Is it weird that I'm jealous of that kid? Then he crosses to the rows on the other side.

The kids in my row take one and pass, take one and pass, take one and—oh. There aren't enough. The girl next to me shrugs apologetically. A few seconds later, Win heads back across the auditorium and personally delivers a copy to me, his hand clasping the paper a second longer than necessary.

"Sorry about that," he says with a small smile that makes me wonder if he didn't count the packets and short my row on purpose.

"It's fine," I say. Except my voice is saying it's fine and my tone is saying *you're* fine, and OHMYGOSH, I did not do all this work to get into Gotham U just to fail this class on account of some pretty boy. FOCUS, HARLEEN. Fear—it's what's for dinner.

Luckily, Dr. Crane doesn't seem to have noticed that I've

been busy drooling over his research assistant instead of paying attention to his lecture.

"Fear is physiological. At the end of your hippocampus, there's a little almond-shaped mass of neurons called the amygdala, which, incidentally, is the Latin word for almond. It's responsible for emotion, but most especially for fear.

"Now, a lot of people think fear is a bad thing, but fear keeps you safe. We get scared so that we don't die. Evolutionarily speaking. A fear of snakes keeps you from being bitten." He clicks to progress his slides, and a giant image of a snake with its jaws stretched wide appears on the screen. People flinch. A few gasp.

Dr. Crane flicks an old-fashioned lighter and touches the flame to a spare handout, watching the flames lick higher, holding on as long as he can, almost enjoying it, until he drops the burning papers into a metal trash can. "A fear of fire keeps you from getting burnt."

I think about how my mom said she was never afraid of heights until after she gave birth to me, and then she couldn't ride a roller coaster without closing her eyes, couldn't even get too close to a the edge of a cliff with a picturesque view without her breath catching in her lungs and making her take a few steps back. She felt like the universe was telling her she had to be careful, had to stay alive for me. Didn't work, though. I lost her when I was seven anyway.

They're saying I've got a bad heart, baby.

I shake it off and try to focus on the lecture, ignoring the word *orphan* when it flashes in my head.

"Take the case of a patient known to us only as S.M. She has a rare disease that caused parts of her brain to waste away, completely destroying her amygdala. They call her 'the Woman Without Fear.'"

He jumps the couple of steps from the raised area where he was teaching and approaches the boy with the baseball cap. "Sounds nice, right?"

The boy nods like he's hypnotized, and I find myself wanting to shout, *It's a trap!*

"But are you sure?" Crane leans closer, his crooked nose almost touching the brim of the boy's cap. The boy looks too scared to answer. (Probably a good move.) Crane straightens and calls out to the rest of us. "How many of you would really like to live without fear?"

Okay, truthfully, I *was* just thinking about how badass it would be not to be scared of anything. I'd be like, *See ya, claustrophobia. Don't let the door hit ya, PTSD.* Even though I made a whole lotta strides with my exposure therapy last year, I still don't love being in small spaces by myself.

Dr. Crane slinks up the stairs with one of those dramatic pauses that professors like to do. He paces across the median between the tiers of seats at the front of the auditorium and the back, pouncing on an unsuspecting student, grabbing the back of her chair and speaking in a low voice. "No. I don't think you would.

"Fear," he says almost reverently, "is a gift." He pauses again to let it sink in. "One night, when S.M. was walking through a park alone, a man attacked her with a knife. For most of us, this would be horrifying. Traumatic. We'd never want to go near that park again, and if we did, we'd probably have a whole host of physiological reactions: increased heart rate, heightened senses. S.M. walked that very same route the next day."

Dr. Crane clicks his remote, and a slide with sketches of different faces appears.

"I want to note that it's only fear that S.M. had difficulty understanding. When asked to draw faces that were happy, surprised, sad, disgusted, angry, she was able to produce fairly impressive renderings of men and women showing a range of emotions. When asked to draw what 'afraid' looked like, she drew a baby."

I can't explain why the drawing of the baby creeps me out so badly, but it does. It's just a profile of a baby crawling. I guess its face *does* look a little bit off. Or maybe it's the fact that it's positioned over the word *afraid*, while the other captions have faces showing the correct emotion. You almost get the feeling that if you stare at the baby too long, it'll come crawling into your dreams at night. I try not to look at it as I type some of what Dr. Crane is saying into the "notes" portion of the PowerPoint I have pulled up on my laptop.

"But unlike those who are missing their amygdala," he continues, "in most people and animals, fear can be learned. We can pair an electric shock with a tone so that a rat learns to jump to the other side of the cage, the one without the electrified floor, whenever it hears the tone. A child who gets bitten learns to be afraid of dogs. We can even learn fear from others, through stories handed down or signs that read 'danger'—until signs or symbols or pictures begin to activate our amygdala to tell our HPA axis to tell our sympathetic nervous system, sending the body into fight or flight, eyes dilating, vessels constricting, adrenaline releasing. Mouth going dry with fear and anticipation. Heart racing like it's going to burst. It's a truly beautiful system."

I frantically type everything he's saying. I can't help but think about how it all relates to my own trauma. Isn't he describing exactly what used to happen when my dad would lock me in the bathroom when I was a kid? What happened when Dr. Nelson locked me in the wine cellar underneath his house and I thought I was never coming back up? What still sometimes happens on a bad day? I wonder if there's anything in this lecture that I could use to help myself.

Dr. Crane clicks the remote, and a slide of people happily screaming on a roller coaster comes up. "Of course, fear can be flipped to pleasure for some people. A rush of dopamine and endorphins. But what decides who's going to be thrilled by a haunted house and who's going to be terrified? Why can two people experience the same stimuli so differently? These are the kinds of things that are fascinating to me—how interconnected everything is, how complex. If you become too scared, it can interfere with your cerebral cortex so that making logical choices or even thinking clearly becomes almost impossible."

I think about when I was trapped at Dr. Nelson's. How terrified I was. How I was almost unable to pick the lock and free myself. Yep, that all tracks.

"Your hippocampus and prefrontal cortex, your memory and executive function, your logical brain, they all help you gauge whether threats are real. But what if we could override that? What if we could make the emotional brain believe that anything is real?" He closes his eyes ever so slightly, relishing whatever he's imagining. "When your logical brain can't tell your emotional brain that everything is okay, when the fear becomes too overwhelming, that's when things get really interesting."

Welp. That's not creepy at all. Note to self: Never share an elevator with Dr. Crane.

He pulls himself out of his reverie and looks at the clock. "Oops, time's up. Thank you for your attention today. And feel free to come up and ask me any questions. I have about twenty minutes before I need to get back to Arkham."

Most of the class appears too scared to approach him. (Shocker.)

Meanwhile, I'm thinking about approaching someone else. How do you make a beeline for someone without looking like you're making a beeline for someone? I'm flashing hidden glances at Win, putting my laptop into my bag as slowly as humanly possible, and then I look up, and wham. There he is. Standing right next to me.

"Um, hi," I say, promptly dropping the reading on the floor.

He just grins. "Let me get that for you."

Again with the handing of the paper. Again with the hanging on a moment too long. Again with the tingly feeling in my stomach. No, wait. That's new.

I don't know what it is about this guy. He's absolutely not my type. He's so . . . clean-cut. And, like, polite-looking. A mayonnaise sandwich for sure.

"Are you the TA?" I ask.

He shakes his head. "No, just helping out Dr. Crane today, thank goodness."

He seems genuinely and intensely relieved. Which makes me suspicious. "Why? Is the main teacher a jerk or something?"

"No, but if I was your TA, I couldn't ask you on a date." His cheeks turn red when he says it. If he hadn't blushed like that, I'm pretty sure I would've said no. And even so . . .

"Aren't you my lead intern?" I cross my arms like it's a whole thing, but really it's just fun to watch him squirm.

And he does. Inordinately. "I mean, technically, but since you didn't pick Dr. Crane, we're not really gonna be interacting much."

"Oh." I don't know why I'm so disappointed by that.

"At work," he rushes to add. "We could interact over chips and salsa this Friday?"

I narrow my eyes, skeptical. "That sounds dirty."

His cheeks turn red again, and he actually holds up the Scout's honor symbol. "I promise I didn't mean it that way. So . . . see you Friday?"

"Yes," I say slowly, coyly, and his smile gets so big, it almost breaks my heart.

Maybe that's what I like about him. The way he treats me, the way he looks at me—it feels nice. Safe. Boring? NOPE. Not even gonna go there. Gosh, it's like half of me is constantly trying to self-sabotage the other half. And, okay, even though Winfield Callaway is one of those double-last-name people that I very likely have nothing in common with, and even though I don't get that dark/hot/dangerous feeling when he talks to me, maybe that's okay? Hell, maybe it's even preferable. Win is the kind of person who gets ahead in Gotham City. (I mean, his name is even Win, for Pete's sake.) So if I want to be a winner too, he's the kind of person I should be with. The kind of person I should pattern myself after. One more way that I'm going to be different this year.

I walk my different, new-and-improved self to the student center and buy a sandwich and swipe my G-card. There's a table near the big glass doors where Sophie and some other Alpha Nus like to hold court on Wednesdays.

"Harleen!" squeals Sophie. "We're going to take our lunches back to the house so we can pomp. You in?"

"Um, *yes*."

Alpha Kappa Nu has won Best Homecoming Display three years running, and I'm nothing if not competitive. I will run a three-legged race blindfolded; I will train for an epic tug-of-war in a mud pit; I will spend tenfinity hours stuffing colorful squares of tissue paper into chicken wire until the front of the Alpha Nu house resembles a pirate ship (that's what pomping is).

We squeeze through the maze of tables to the door, the pack of us cutting a wake with our matching T-shirts and paper-white smiles. I shift to let a couple guys in Gotham U sweatshirts pass, and my shoe catches on someone's ginormous backpack.

"Sorry!" I call, blond hair flipping as I turn my head.

And then the moment freezes. Because the person staring back at me is Bianca.

"Hey," I say softly.

"Hey." There is hurt in her eyes, even though I'm the one who got ditched.

Jasmin sits across from her, eating soup in a bread bowl. I can't not stop.

I touch Sophie's shoulder. "Hey, I'll catch up with you, okay?"

She looks at us, puzzled, but nods. "See you at the house."

She and the rest of the Alpha Nus float out of the dining hall, chattering about boys and parties and intersectional feminism and the merits of liquid versus pencil eyeliner. Bianca watches them until they're gone. Hurt? Jealous? Scornful? It's hard to say.

I pull up a chair next to Jasmin. "How have you guys been doing?"

It comes out stiff, and I unwrap my sandwich and take a bite so that I have something to do with my hands.

"I'm well," says Jasmin.

"Good, I'm good." Bianca fiddles with the lid on her protein shake. "I'm glad we ran into you. We were thinking about pulling a mission. I don't know if you've heard about this, but there's been a huge increase in kidnappings all over the city. Almost entirely girls in their late teens and women in their twenties."

"No, I hadn't heard about that." Human trafficking has always been a thing in Gotham City, but I didn't realize it was on the rise. My stomach turns just thinking about it.

"Well, I thought we should actually do something about it, since clearly the GCPD isn't." She sits up straight, getting more excited now, her hands moving as she speaks. "I've got some leads on the human-trafficking gang responsible. The spots they usually hit. The cars they usually drive—I heard one of them likes to troll through the East End in a shiny black Mercedes and a nice suit. Anyway, we're gonna follow him back to wherever they're keeping the girls and then take out the entire gang. This Friday!"

"Oh," I say, and Bianca's hands freeze. "Well, I actually have plans this Friday."

Thank goodness I said yes to that date with Win. It's not even a lie.

"Right, right, you're too busy for us," Bianca says flatly, her eyes tracing the route my sorority sisters walked just minutes ago.

"Bianca . . . ," says Jasmin warningly.

"Excuse me?" I shoot back. "You're the one who doesn't want to hang out with me."

Jasmin's eyes widen. "Harleen!"

"I've asked you to go on missions three times. Four, if you count today."

"Yeah, *missions.*" Because apparently I'm not good enough to just be friends with. The thought makes the feelings I've held hostage bubble over. "I'm trying not to screw up my life this year." Or get killed trying to fight a whole-ass gang with just two people.

Bianca hunches her shoulders. "Oh, okay. Well, good. We don't need you anyway." She narrows her eyes at me. "You're so hungry to be just like them, you've forgotten all about us."

She grabs her protein shake and her backpack (the tactical pack we used to take on missions) and stalks off. Jasmin puts her head in her hands like she's very tired.

"I'm sorry," I tell her, calmer now. My anger always seems to recede once I've blown things up. "I'm just not willing to take the risk. I'm kind of surprised you are." I say it kindly. Not like a judgment. More like a question.

Jasmin twists the silver ring she always wears around on her finger. "She's been different," she finally says. "Ever since Bernice got taken away. I think Bianca still feels guilty about not stepping in and doing more."

"We told her not to." As hurt as I've been by how our friendship has dissolved, that was never a part of the reason.

"Yeah, but you know how she is about loyalty."

I nod. I do.

"She's been beating herself up because she felt like we let Bernice take the fall for us, and a couple months after Bernice got arrested, she started doing these missions again. But they're not like before. This time, it's almost like the danger is the point. And each one is more intense than the last. She originally wanted to break into Judge Bishop's house while he was home. She was going to truss him up outside City Hall, with all the evidence we found scattered around him. I only just talked her out of it."

Ohmygosh, that's intense. And so is going up against a human-trafficking gang. Way more than we ever did as the Reckoning. "Why are you helping her, then?"

Jasmin winces. "Someone has to watch out for her."

She didn't mean it as an accusation. But at the time, I took it like one. Put up invisible walls to protect myself. (Dug an invisible moat and filled it with invisible sharks while I was at it.) I let it drive us farther apart. But looking back, I can see she just wanted my help. Because maybe together we could have saved Bianca.

CHAPTER 9

Casa Julio

THE CHIPS ARE GOOD. THE SALSA IS BETTER. THE INTERACTing is best.

Win and I sit crunched into the same side of a wooden booth. (It's better for people-watching. Also snuggling.) We eat chile rellenos and carnitas fajitas and make up pretend dialogue for the people eating around us. So far, we've decided that the couple behind us are in a fake marriage because they're actually Finnish spies (why do all the spies gotta be Russian?), and the couple on our left is composed of a woman having a clandestine romance with the captain of her high school's rival cheerleading squad, with whom she recently reconnected on Instagram. (I maybe had to convince Win on that one, but look, I've written enough *Bring It On* fanfic to know what I'm talking about.)

I'm feeling like most of our guesses are well within my 95 percent confidence intervals. The two guys across the way, though, they're tricky.

"It's a breakup," I tell Win. "The guy in the blue shirt looks like he's about to puke."

Right as I'm saying it, the guy runs a hand through his dark curls, looking, if possible, even more nervous.

"Told you."

But Win just shakes his head. "Why must you be so cynical? He's about to declare his undying love."

I eye the other guy, who is looking at his phone and has absolutely no idea that the guy eating tacos across from him is freaking out internally. That he almost just spilled his water. Twice.

He gets up to go to the bathroom.

And the guy in the blue shirt reaches into his pocket.

"Ohmygosh, we're both wrong," I whisper, nudging Win in the ribs.

"What are you— Oh. Ohhhh, this is really happening."

I kind of love that he's so excited. That he can't help but absentmindedly tap his fingers on the table like a drumroll.

Blue Shirt opens the ring box and sets it on the table facing the chair of his hopefully soon-to-be fiancé. I squeeze Win's leg under the table when I see Phone Guy walking back. We both suck in our breath as he approaches the table. Phone Guy sees the ring box. Covers his mouth with his hands and immediately starts crying. Blue Shirt starts crying too. He gets down on one knee. OMG, IS THIS SERIOUSLY HAPPENING? We wait. If Phone Guy is responding, his voice is too quiet to hear it across a crowded restaurant, even if people at the other tables are noticing them too now and falling silent.

"C'mon. C'mon. C'mon," whispers Win. Like I needed another reason to fall for this guy.

And there it is. Phone Guy nods. Blue Shirt hugs him. Win and I can breathe again. Everyone in the restaurant who's paying attention erupts into cheers.

I collapse against Win's shoulder, clutching my heart. "This is the most romantic first date I've ever been on."

He grins. "Does that mean you'll give me a second?"

I don't miss the way my stomach flips when he asks it. "Yes. Ohmygosh, yes. Actually, oh! We should do something. Right now! To commemorate this romantical first date!"

His eyes flick from side to side, almost like he's scared. "What do you have in mind?"

"Hmm . . ." I tap my fingers against my chin. "Oh! I got it!"

I whip out my pocketknife.

"Uhhh . . ." Win definitely looks scared now.

"Don't worry. I'm not about to ask you to take any blood oaths. That's, like, third-date stuff." I run my fingers over the wooden back of the booth. "I think we should carve our initials."

"Oh, I don't know." Win checks over his shoulder like he's expecting a police officer to be standing RIGHT THERE.

But I've already dug my knife into the wood. "Yep. It's happening. Cover me."

I quickly carve + *W,* leaving an obvious space in front.

I pass Win the knife.

"I've never vandalized anything before." His face is pretty pale.

"You've got this. Our server just went to the kitchen."

He takes a deep breath. Looks all around like a damn owl. And then he just goes for it. Carves an *H* as fast as he can and flicks the knife shut, facing forward like, *No, I didn't touch anything. Especially not the back of the booth. With a knife.*

"You rocked that," I say, admiring his handiwork.

"Whew. Wow." He shakes his head like he can't believe it. "My heart's beating so fast."

I want to put my hand over his shirt so I can feel it. I want to kiss him until I can't remember my own name.

He asks our server for the check. I think he wants to kiss me too.

On our way out, we end up behind Blue Shirt and Phone Guy, and I can't help but tell them, "Congratulations-ohmygosh-y'all-are-so-cute-I-can't-stand-it."

"Aw, thank you," replies Blue Shirt with a smile so big it would break your heart. "I'm so glad I get to spend the rest of my life with my Schmoopie."

They stroll off down the street, hand in hand, and I turn to Win.

"Schmoopie," I hiss.

He smirks at me. "What, you don't like Schmoopie?"

"He legit almost ruined the whole thing with Schmoopie."

"Hey, don't judge Schmoopie. Schmoopie is clearly working out for them."

I narrow my eyes. "Are you trying to see how many times you can say the word *Schmoopie*?"

I like the sly look in his eyes. I like the way his shirt hugs his chest.

"I might be."

He manages to say *Schmoopie* eleven times on the way from the restaurant to my dorm, and he doesn't look a bit sorry. Not until we get to the front door.

"I don't want this night to end," I say. I don't care if it makes me bold/reckless/thirsty.

"Me neither." He looks well and truly bummed out. "But . . ."

"But?"

"I actually have to get back to Arkham tonight. Dr. Crane texted me."

"At ten o'clock at night?"

Win shrugs apologetically. "We've been working on a special project, and we're at a really critical stage."

"Ohhh, secret project." I waggle my eyebrows.

He blushes. "It's not really a secret."

"Can you tell me about it?"

"Well . . ."

"Then it's a secret." I grin triumphantly, and Win laughs.

And then he gets quiet, scuffing his shoes against the sidewalk.

I step closer.

So does he.

"This is the part where we kiss," I stage-whisper, and he laughs again, but he can't hide the way he looks at my lips.

"Can I tell you something?" he asks quietly.

I lean forward. You're falling in love with me? Can't stop thinking about me? Have a secret notebook where you've doodled Mr. Winfield Quinzel?

"You scare me."

Close enough!

I move so close that our lips are only inches apart. I think I like scaring him. Something about it makes me feel hot all over.

"Can I tell you something else?" He says the words practically into my mouth.

And then we're kissing, and I don't know if I started it, or maybe he did, but our lips crush together, gently at first, and then hungrier. More urgent. Win pulls away first, dazed but determined to finish his thought.

"I like it."

CHAPTER 10

Arkham Acres

PAMELA STEPS OFF THE SHUTTLE AFTER ME WHEN IT PULLS to a stop in front of Arkham Acres.

"Thank you so much for coming with me," I tell her.

"Sure thing." Her eyes are drawn to the flower beds out front and the gardens that wrap around the side of the building. "It's beautiful here."

I smirk at her. "But?"

"But they really shouldn't plant primroses in full sun."

"Knew it!"

She rolls her eyes, but in a good-natured way.

We've been doing this a lot—this hanging-out thing—since that time we had brunch and I bombarded her with facts about Marie Curie. Meeting up at this indie coffee shop that serves lattes in chipped teacups or studying in the green space outside the chemistry building because that's where Pamela's second-favorite tree is. Dining-hall pancakes on Sunday mornings, my (often failed) attempts to drag her to sorority events, and her bringing me along to meetings of the ecology club that she started in the wake of Greener Earth

Society's implosion. Some people have been reluctant to join because of the scandal surrounding Greener Earth Society and Dr. Woodrue and the accident, but then Pamela talks to them one-on-one, and there's just something about being up close and personal with her. She's so charismatic when it comes to the environment. Anyone within three feet of her wants to do whatever she's asking.

I glance sideways at Pamela. There are so many questions I still want to ask her about the accident and Woodrue, but now isn't the time. She follows me into the lobby of Arkham Acres. It's the noncriminal sister facility to Arkham Asylum, so there's significantly less security.

"We're here to see Stella Watkins," I tell the receptionist. He knows me from the last few times and knows I have permission from the Watkins family, so he lets us go on back to the rec room.

"So, who is this we're visiting?" asks Pamela.

"Stella? She's, um, a friend of a friend. Well, a sister of a friend." The sister of my ex-girlfriend, who is currently in jail for attempting to revenge-murder our professor last year, but there is no way I'm telling Pamela that. Yet. Maybe someday. I do feel like she's the kind of person I could tell things to—big things, dark things—and she wouldn't run scared or even make that pinched, judgy face people get. Even so, it's scary trusting someone that way.

"Hey, Stella!" I call out.

A girl who looks so much like my ex-girlfriend that it makes my heart ache looks up, and her face spreads into a huge smile. "Harleen!"

She glances at Pamela with question mark eyes.

"This is Pamela," I say. "The friend of mine from Gotham U that I was telling you about. You said I should bring her?"

Stella nods like she's trying to put a puzzle together. "Oh, right. I'm glad you did."

"How have you been?"

Pamela and I take seats across the table from her.

"Good, yeah," replies Stella, only this time her smile is less convincing.

"Do you want to play Labyrinth?"

She nods and goes to get the game, her favorite, from the bookshelf nearby. I don't comment on how shaky her hands seem as we set up the pieces, but I do wonder if maybe she's changed meds recently or if it's something else. After the first couple of times I visited, she really opened up, asking me about school and gymnastics and if I'd heard any word on Bernice. It was kind of hard to explain what had happened—with Bernice and Dr. N, and both of them going to jail—without stressing Stella out, but I did my best.

Stella's unusually quiet today. Because Pamela's here? For some other reason? Honestly, it might be Pamela. She's amazing, but it's really hard to get her to open up to people. That coupled with how beautiful she is and how rich she is and that serious, almost severe, face she's almost always making . . . well, I've heard more than one person in our dorm call her an ice queen, which is stupid because (A) that is just her thinking face—I asked, and (B) hardly any plants grow in ice. But I guess "forest queen" doesn't have quite the same ring to it.

"So, what are you majoring in?" Stella asks Pamela, all shy and polite.

"Biochemistry. But my focus is botany." Pamela's arms cross like she's waiting for Stella to make fun of her or something, even though Stella is seriously the most unassuming person ever.

"Oh," says Stella. "I was an aerospace major when I was at Gotham U, but there was this botany class I always daydreamed about taking. Ecology of the Tropics? It's the one where—"

Pamela's eyes light up. "Where you do the first half of the semester in the classroom and you spend the second half on a boat in the Amazon, taking samples and learning about how to reduce human impact on the tropics? I'm on the waiting list."

TEN MILLION POINTS TO STELLA. Pamela is now hers for life.

They talk easily about ethnobotany and Brazilian culture and the best waterproof hiking boots and giant snakes for the next half hour. Pamela tells us all about how she wants to run a nonprofit someday, or maybe be a lobbyist or an environmental engineer, or maybe all three.

"Whatever I can do to have the biggest impact on our earth." Her eyes shine as she says it. "There are so many ways we could do better. Little changes that each of us could make, but honestly? Big business and government policies are killing us. Seventy-one percent of global greenhouse gas emissions come from the same one hundred companies. If we could pass legislation and make changes on a global scale, we could really transform things."

She's sitting so straight and tall and talking with her hands, and the excitement just pours out of her. Like, her face is making its own light. She's always one of those girls who look like they could be in makeup ads, but this takes it to a whole new level. She's so beautiful, it almost feels like a weapon. Like she could slice your heart with a glance and make entire legions of men leap off a cliff to their deaths with a mere flutter of her eyelashes.

And then she's suddenly hesitant again, shoulders hunching, shy at what she's revealed.

"Um. So, what about you, Harleen?"

"Oh!" I think about this a lot. (Probably too much, if I'm being honest. If you could climb to the peak of your goals using sheer angst, I'd have summited Everest by now.) "I want to be a doctor. A psychiatrist, I think. I really want to find out what makes people tick. And, like, help them. I think that would be the best."

"Maybe you could help me someday," says Stella brightly.

She just throws out the comment kindly, meant as encouragement. But a burst of sadness smacks me in the chest. What about Stella's hopes and dreams? She was—is—brilliant at science and math. And now she's here because of Dr. Nelson and that experimental toxin. And the person who made it? They're still gainfully employed at Arkham (at least according to Talia al Ghūl). I feel guiltier than ever about not trying to unmask who it is and bring down a world of hurt on them.

"I'd love to help you," I tell Stella. Because it's true? Because I'm trying to assuage my guilt? I look around the rec room at the women doing puzzles and playing video games and reading magazines and books. "I'd love to help all the girls here. Someday."

And even as I say it, I know that part is true. My devotion to women's rights hasn't stopped because I stopped being in the Reckoning, I tell myself. It just changed its course. I'm so busy convincing myself, I almost don't notice the screams down the hallway. Stella does. She drops her water bottle with a loud *thwack*.

"Sorry," she says, rushing to pick it up. Her hands are shaking again as she sets it on the table.

"You okay?"

"Yeah." Her eyes dart to the door to the ward. "We just haven't had the best day here."

She says the last part so quietly, it's practically a whisper.

I match her voice. "What happened?"

Stella shrugs. Eyes dart around again. In the direction of the screams or to see if someone's listening?

"That's the third screaming episode today," she finally says. "We're all a little on edge."

Screaming episode. "You mean like the kind you have?"

Stella's eyes flick to Pamela. Oh. Maybe I shouldn't have said that in front of her.

But then Stella answers: "Yeah. Selective catatonia, that's what they're calling it. At least six girls here have it."

I scan the room wondering which ones. What about them? What about their hopes and dreams? How do we help them? I try to remember if I've learned about selective catatonia in any of my classes. I think we covered catatonia when we talked about schizophrenia last year, but I'm almost certain this specific subtype wasn't in my Abnormal Pysch book, which means it must be kind of obscure. And now that I'm thinking about it . . .

"Why do so many girls at the same facility have this particular kind of catatonia?" I wonder aloud.

Pamela makes that piercing thinking face. Stella nods emphatically, like, *right?*

"The doctors from Arkham are worried about it too," she says. "They've been collecting blood samples from us, trying to figure out what we have in common."

I wonder if that's a good thing or a bad thing. I narrow my eyes at the nurse across the room, watch him sort pills into tiny paper cups.

Six girls. Six. All with similar and unusual symptoms. I think about how quickly the Reckoning would have jumped at the chance to solve this last year. I wish there was something more I could do to help.

As we take the shuttle back to the subway and the subway back to campus, Pamela grows quiet. Not her usual quiet. Thinking quiet. I managed to convince her to come with me to a Nighthawks game this week. (*Pamela. You cannot go through your first year of college without attending a football game. It's like a rule.*) But now I'm worried she's seconds away from bailing. She comes with me to my room to get ready, though, and even agrees to let me put GU temporary tattoos on her face. Just as I'm about to apply the first tattoo, though . . .

"What happened to those girls?"

She fixes those piercing green eyes on me, and I would tell her my darkest fears and most embarrassing secrets and the nuclear launch codes if she asked. I wonder if she knows she's capable of having that sort of power over people.

I realize my hands are frozen in midair and put them in my lap.

"I don't know about the other girls, but Stella was sprayed with this toxin that's part fear activator and part sedative. We're not sure what happened after that. We just know that the man who took her dumped her on a bathroom floor hours later, and she can't talk about what happened without screaming so hard that she passes out."

"Holy geez." Pamela's eyes widen.

"I know. It's so awful." I pause. Hold up the GU tattoo. "You ready?"

Pamela nods, and I gently touch the colorful side of the tattoo to her check, smoothing over the paper side with my thumb. Then I take the washcloth that I wet with warm water from the sink and press it against the tattoo.

Touching her cheek. Being so close to her. The moment feels charged. Also—I hope my breath doesn't smell. I glance at the timer on my phone. Ninety-eight more seconds. My mind is drawn to memories of last year and everything that happened. When the timer on my phone buzzes, I startle.

So does Pamela. I realize she was staring at the floor in a sad/angry/wild sort of way.

I've been wondering about the accident and the lab and her professor, like an undercurrent or a heartbeat that keeps persistently thrumming in my mind whenever we're together. I've been working up the courage to ask her. So as I apply the tattoo to her other cheek, I take a deep breath and risk it. "What happened with Woodrue? If you don't mind me asking."

"Oh." She pulls back automatically, then remembers the tattoo and the washcloth and tries to hold still.

"Sorry. You don't have to answer."

"No, it's okay. I . . . think it would feel good to talk about it." But then her eyes flit all around the room like she'd rather do anything but. "Dr. Woodrue . . ." She takes a deep breath. "He was like a cult leader for the Greener Earth Society kids. And for good reason. I mean, we weren't just sitting around talking about recycling. We were protesting pollution by big businesses in Gotham City. Sometimes more than protesting. It felt powerful."

I nod. I know what that's like.

"I was desperate to be an undergraduate research assistant in his botany lab." She bites her lip, embarrassed. "I was so taken by his ideas that I let him test experimental plant compounds on me. I didn't realize that many of the compounds were actually poisons till later."

"Whoa," I breathe, accidentally letting the washcloth fall from her face. The timer buzzes at the same time, though, so we're good. I can't believe a professor would do that.

Can't you?

I also can't believe she's okay. *Is she okay?* I want to ask, but I don't. Instead, I carefully peel the paper from her cheek to reveal the green-and-blue GU there. Her skin is like porcelain with the tiniest freckle near her temple. It doesn't *seem* like the toxins did anything to her. I lean a little closer—because I need to check the tattoo? Because I'm pretending I need to check the tattoo, but actually because she smells like fall leaves and cinnamon and walking through an apple orchard, trees hung thick for the picking? Gosh, she's beautiful. She could ask me anything right now and I would say yes.

"I feel like such an idiot," says Pamela, snapping me from my stupor. "But I'm not crazy."

So, she's heard what the other students say about her. About her going berserk on his lab.

"I don't think I was the only one he experimented on. My girlfriend—" She sucks in her breath like a hiss. "The girl who used to be my girlfriend. She died the night of the incident." Pamela's eyes flick to mine. "I'm guessing you heard about it?"

I try to say yes in a way that doesn't look judgmental or suggest that I Googled her.

"Yeah, so, everything about that night was off. It was supposed to be a controlled thing. Sneak into one of the worst polluters in Gotham City. Detonate explosives to take out a few key pieces of equipment. But something went wrong, in a way that seems awfully convenient. I barely pulled Nina out in time. And even then—" She pauses, unable to speak. Eyes filled with emotion. "There was something strange about it. So I went to confront him. And now everyone's saying all this shit. But really, I was just sad. And then angry. And then I destroyed all his samples so he couldn't hurt anyone else." She juts out her chin, defiant, like she'd do it all over again given half the chance.

"Oh, I'm not judging. I totally got you," I say, pulling out a Nighthawk tattoo and bringing it toward my own face.

"Do you want me to do that for you?" Pamela asks.

I freeze. "Sure."

"So that your tattoo doesn't get messed up."

"Yes. Definitely. I don't want that." I feel like my mouth is suddenly producing a lot of saliva and I have to gulp and I hope she doesn't notice.

She starts touching my skin, that fall leaves/apple orchard smell drifting toward me again. I start talking about what happened last year with Dr. Nelson, partly because I want to make her feel like she's not alone and partly to take my mind off the fact that she's touching me.

"What happened with Stella," I say, "it was my gap-year professor last year who did it."

Pamela's hand flinches.

"I didn't know that at the time," I rush to add. "But I was in this group called the Reckoning."

She waits to see if I'm going to elaborate on what exactly the Reckoning is. I'm not sure if I should—we were supposed to keep it a secret. Always. But telling Pamela also feels like the right thing to do. I turn it over in my head while I spray blue hair paint onto one pigtail and green on the other. (Pamela declines. Apparently, we have reached the bounds of her school spirit, and they do not include multicolored hair.) I catch a glimpse of myself in the mirror—face tattoos, mismatched pigtails. I can't help feeling more like myself than I've felt in a long time.

I shake it off because we really need to leave for the game already. Also—I tell Pamela about the Reckoning. Well, not who was in it or anything incriminating, but the good stuff. How we made sure Dr. Nelson went to jail. How we became a family. She asks me lots of questions as we leave our dorm and pass by tailgates and people grilling and canopy tents lining the road in blue and green and white sprinkled with the occasional Metropolis University red.

Everyone is dressed head to toe in Gotham U colors. Little kids wearing the jerseys of their favorite players. Little girls dressed in cheerleading uniforms. The campus looks like a circus. We stroll past stands with cotton candy and hot chocolate, vendors selling Gotham U hats and sweatshirts, inflatable games, and a couple of radio station vans.

The fraternities blare music through giant speakers on their front lawns. I wave to Sophie as we pass the Alpha Nu house, all of the girls decked out in sweater dresses and Gotham U scarves and boots with blue or green socks showing at the top. At first I thought the whole point of sorority girls coming to football games was to look pretty and flirt with boys. Then I realized that Sophie and the rest of them spend the games shouting themselves hoarse and yelling obscenities that would make a trucker blush whenever the refs make a bad call.

"So, are you still in it?" Pamela asks as we pass through a massive arch of blue and green balloons that marks the entrance to Nighthawk Alley, a stretch of road lined with fans to cheer the players as they walk into the stadium. We're running a little late, though, so the players are already inside.

"Oh. Well. There was a lot of stuff that went down. It's a long story." I feel guiltier than ever about turning down Bianca and Jasmin when they asked me to do more missions with them. Bianca's mission to find that trafficking gang was last night. I hope it went well. I hope she and Jasmin are okay. Why does doing the right thing feel so wrong?

Pamela nods, but in a way that makes me feel like she's disappointed somehow.

"But I think the person who was supplying Dr. Nelson with the fear toxin is working at Arkham." I rush to redeem myself. "You can't tell anyone, but they were giving him spray cans of the stuff in exchange for blood samples from his victims."

Pamela makes a face like WTF, but I keep going.

"Anyway, now that I'm an intern there, I can figure out who it is. Take them down or make them pay or whatever." Did I really just say that? Wasn't that exactly what I've been promising myself I *wouldn't* do? But being around Pamela has a way of making me forget about things like rules. Or maybe not forget. Maybe question why they're there, and whether they should really be followed, and who they ultimately benefit.

"I want to make Woodrue pay too," says Pamela, eyes gleaming. She pauses as we get to the lady who tears the tickets. "Thank you," she says politely. And then to me, in a lower voice, "Also, I feel like I have to tell you because if you haven't seen the pictures yet, you're going to. The night of the incident? We accidentally blew up a whole building."

"Wait, seriously?!" I am intrigued. And impressed. And

a little giddy, though maybe that's the sixty-five thousand cheering fans.

Pamela blew up a building. And not just because she wanted to see an explosion in the shape of her face. I tamp my excitement down quick, though, because her eyes look so indescribably sad.

"My girlfriend was thinking of blowing the whistle on Woodrue after she learned he was experimenting on me. And she ended up dead. But none of it makes any sense. I thought I pulled her out in time. I can't help but wonder if I'm not the only one he used those experimental toxins on. I want to find out the truth about what happened to her."

"We should make a pact," I say. "To help each other."

It'll make Pamela feel better, I just know it. Plus, I love pacts. They feel like tying your dream to an arrow and shooting it into the sky. Like metaphorically pricking your fingers in a blood oath that twines you together for life.

"Okay," says Pamela, and something about the look on her face makes my stomach do a backflip.

Gotham U's all-star cornerback intercepts a pass, and thousands of people stand and whoop. Hold their breath as he passes the forty-yard line. The thirty.

The two of us sit. Our own little world on the metal bleachers. As he returns the interception for a touchdown, we hook our pinkies together. And as everyone around us screams, we make a vow.

We will help each other uncover the truth.

We kiss our thumbs, never breaking eye contact, a current sizzling between us made of justice and loyalty and fire and the righting of wrongs.

"Wow," I say.

"Yeah," breathes Pamela.

I'm kind of relieved she felt it too.

And then she gets this shifty look on her face. "Does this pact start . . . now?"

"Of course it does! Why?" I am jumping at the chance to prove myself, but Pamela looks sheepish.

"I need to sneak into the morgue."

CHAPTER 11

Gotham Morgue

I AM LITERALLY JUMPING UP AND DOWN NEXT TO THE BRICK wall at the back of the morgue.

"How many dead bodies do you think are in there?"

"Do you think there are any zombies?"

"What if one of them bites us and kicks off a zombie apocalypse and we're patients zero?"

Jump. Jump. Jump.

"Harleen!" says Pamela.

"Sorry. I just had to act like a grown-up for *three whole hours* in chem lab!"

Pamela shakes her head, but I think she's more amused than annoyed. I try to remind myself why we're here—to sneak a peek at her former girlfriend and hopefully uncover the cause of death—so that I can keep my excitement to a minimum. I know this is a big deal for Pamela, and I feel buckets of empathy for her, I really do, but also it has been months (MONTHS!!!) since I did a mission like this. And there's definitely a part of me that feels a little guilty that I'm here doing this mission with Pamela but I didn't do

Bianca's mission with her, but mostly I feel like my legs are spring-loaded and my brain is made of Pop Rocks.

"So, I cased the place earlier this week . . ."

Ha-ha, she said *cased*.

"And they keep that back window open, I think because the smell of formaldehyde or whatever is so strong, so I was thinking we could get in that way." She tilts her head up at the window and grimaces. "But it's fifteen feet off the ground."

I study the window. And the tree next to the window. The tree with a beautiful, smooth branch jutting out horizontally at almost the exact height of the high bar in uneven bars.

"Got it," I say confidently.

Pamela is confused. "Got what?"

But my gymnastics game face is already on. I do a quick run and then a leap, hands grasping the branch, legs jackknifing around, torso spinning. And just like that, my top half is above the branch, arms down straight to grip it, hips resting against the bark. Just. Like. Bars.

"Ta-da!" I squeal.

"Where in the actual eff did you learn how to do that?"

"Gymnastics," I say. Like, obviously. Like, this is just a life skill people pick up.

I pull myself up into a standing position on the branch, then climb two branches higher and slip gracefully through the second-story window. (Luckily, the room is empty. I was so excited about showing off, I forgot to check while I was still on the branch. I make a mental note for the future.)

"I'm in!" I call down to Pamela.

"Um. I can't do that," I hear her call back. "Neither can most people who weren't secretly injected with squirrel DNA. Or leopard. Or whatever it is you are.

"Harleen?"

But I don't answer her, because I'm already sneaking down the stairs to the back door. I ease it open to find her still talking to the window.

"Harleen, I seriously hope you're not expecting me to follow you."

"C'mon!" I say, my voice all bouncy. I giggle when she nearly jumps out of her skin.

"You are ridiculous."

"I know," I reply happily as she follows me up the stairs.

But when we get to the top, the mood suddenly changes. Like the air has been sucked out of the room, or maybe like there are dark clouds pressing in. Something ominous is coming. The lightning has flashed, and the thunder is about to roar, and there's nothing you can do but weather the storm.

The metal drawers lining the wall seem so innocuous until you remember they have people inside them. Pamela consults the log on the desk so we can figure out which drawer is Nina's. I imagined there would be a name and a photo or something, but she's just a number on a cold metal box. Drawer twenty-six.

"This is her," Pamela says quietly, eyes filled to the brim with dread.

"It's going to be okay. I'm here," I tell her. Then I think about how long ago it was that I heard those girls talking about Pamela in the dining hall. "I'm surprised she's still here. How long has it been?"

Pamela doesn't take her eyes off the drawer. "Almost five weeks. But sometimes they keep them that long. If they think it could be murder. It's the toxicology tests that take a while. Her parents told me the results just came in a couple days ago."

She goes on in a delicate, wobbly voice. "There were plant toxins in her body. Similar to the ones he used to dose me with."

That sadistic waste of air. "If that's what we find"—I grit my teeth—"I will help you make it right."

"Thanks, Harleen," she says in a ghost of a whisper.

And then she opens the drawer.

This is where it gets hazy. Because unlike all my other memories, where I am in my body, reliving the events of my past, in this memory I am watching myself. I'm outside of myself. The drawer slides out on creaky rails, and I watch myself shrink away from it. I remember wondering if the morgue was haunted and if Nina was about to rise from the grave. Or, well, the drawer. I remember Pamela pulling back the sheet.

And then her voice, hard and shattered at the same time. "The explosion didn't kill her." A painful pause. "She was poisoned."

I watch Harleen—I watch *me*—looking horrified at whatever it is she's seeing. But I can't see it myself. My consciousness hovers in the corner of the room like a ghost. One without the power of motion, so I can't get closer no matter how much I want to see what's happening or how hard I try.

"What are all those black lines?" I watch myself ask.

"I used to get those," replies Pamela. "Whenever he would inject me, there'd be these veiny black lines radiating from the poison site. Except it didn't kill me." She doubles over, sobbing. "I'm a monster. He turned me into a monster."

I watch myself comfort her, but I can't hear what she's saying, can't remember what I said or thought.

I hear the next part, though.

"We could get revenge?" the me in my memory suggests. "I'm, like, *really* good at that."

But Pamela says it's too late. Woodrue already fled.

CHAPTER 12

Arkham Asylum

WIN KISSES BETTER THAN A BOY SCOUT HAS ANY RIGHT TO. We're in the back hallway, the one that leads to the only stairwell to the basement that hasn't been permanently sealed shut, and he tastes like he's been aggressively chewing wintergreen gum on the off chance that he'd run into me and I'd lead him to a dark corner of Arkham. (Side note: Can I still call it an off chance if I try to ensure it happens at least once a day? PROBABLY NOT.)

He kisses my mouth, my throat, my collarbone. At one point, I think I maybe hear noises from the basement—clanging or moaning or something—but the sounds disappear just as quickly. Ah, well. I chalk it up to part of Arkham's charm. Eventually, Win pulls his lips away from mine.

"I have a meeting with Dr. Crane in ten minutes," he says, panting. "I should probably try to be on time."

I smirk at him. "Are you sure? Because if you wanna stay, I don't mind being a bad influence."

I look him up and down in a way that is all kinds of suggestive.

He turns the color of fire engines and beets and fresh sunburns. Success!

"C'mon." I link my arm through his and pull him in the direction of Crane's office. "I'll make sure you're not late for your meeting with your hero."

He kisses me on the nose. "Thanks, Schmoopie."

I can't believe I let him call me that, but it kind of just stuck. I check my phone to see what time it is—I have a meeting with Dr. Morales too, and I want to be early because I was hoping to talk to her about something important.

I'm still holding on to Win's arm as we round the corner to the hallway where the offices are. Graham is leaning against the wall, scrolling through something on his phone, and Win and I separate abruptly. As much as I enjoy our stolen kisses, I try to maintain a layer of professionalism in front of everyone else. It's hard enough after last year, black-rimmed glasses or no.

Win peels off toward Dr. Crane's office, and I knock on the door next to Graham, the one with the brass nameplate that reads LILY MORALES, MD. She doesn't answer.

"Yeah, she's not there," says Graham without looking up from his phone.

"Are you waiting for her too?" Gosh, I hope not. I don't want to have to—

"She said I could watch her perform a PET scan today."

Greaaaat.

He pockets his phone. Fixes me with those beady little eyes. "You had a girlfriend last year. That Bernice girl, right?"

"Yes." I'm not sure I want to know where this is going. A lot of people have tried to get information from me about the Nelson scandal. I don't think I'll be able to stomach it if Graham does the whole "feigned concern" thing.

But his eyes flick down the hallway. "And now you're with Winfield."

"Yeah . . ."

"So you're straight now?"

FFS, I cannot with this kid. I try exceedingly hard not to shoot laser beams through him with my eyes, but I'm not a saint, so it's impossible to keep the edge out of my voice. "No. I'm bi. I was bi last year when I was dating Bernice, and I'm bi now while I'm dating Win, and I'll be bi next year no matter who I'm dating or in ten years if I get married. Ya got any other stupid questions?"

He refrains from answering. (The first good move on his part, possibly ever.)

Then Dr. Morales appears, and Graham and I both snap to attention.

"Sorry I'm late." She breezes past us and unlocks her office. "We'll go down and meet Ms. al Ghūl in about twenty minutes. Harleen, do you still need to meet with me first?"

"Yes, it'll only take a few minutes." I follow her into her office and try to rearrange my facial features apologetically as I shut the door in Graham's face.

Dr. Morales eyes the closed door. "Is everything all right?"

"Yes," I say. "Well, actually, no."

She sits at her desk, and I pull up one of the cushy teal chairs she keeps in front of it. Where to start? My fingers clench and unclench on top of my dress pants.

She looks me directly in the eyes. Kind but also serious. "It's okay, Harleen."

Right. Yes. I can do this.

"I have a friend I visit at Arkham Acres," I finally say.

Once I've started, it's easier to keep going, and I spill all about Stella and the other girls with selective catatonia and how I'm concerned for their welfare and I'd like to know more about the research being done there. After it all spews out, though, I feel hesitant. Apprehensive. Is she going to believe me, and will she think it's important, and what happens if she doesn't?

But she gets this expression on her face, like the kind Bianca used to get before she'd suggest some over-the-top/amazing/ingenious way to take down someone monstrous. Are we going to go to the police? Storm someone's office? Stage a protest?

"We're going to put in a formal inquiry with the IRB."

Oh. Yeah, I guess that works too.

Dr. M explains how the Internal Review Board oversees all the human research at Arkham and its affiliates and how they'll help us put a stop to anything untoward. Maybe even get the government involved if it's bad enough. I help Dr. Morales fill out the form, and the darkness I felt building inside me leaches away. Feels less intense, at least.

Maybe this is how it's supposed to be. You see something that needs to change. A wrong in the world that needs righting. And you go through legal channels to change it. Maybe I don't have to smash things and break into offices and rappel off buildings at midnight and create the coolest, most diabolical plans. Maybe paperwork is how people get things done without paying the price of their futures.

This could be my life. Fighting wars with paperwork to help protect girls who need saving. Learning cool things about neuroscience. I click Send on the form, and we go downstairs to scan Talia al Ghūl's brain, and I feel like the luckiest girl in the entire world.

◆

Radioactive tracers look less exciting than you'd think. I was expecting the glass vials to shine like glow sticks—pink, yellow, green. Dr. Morales draws up the clear (read: woefully boring) liquid, and I can't help but be disappointed, even though this is our third Friday in a row doing brain imaging with Talia and I should know better.

"Are you certain you aren't trying to give me superpowers?" Talia asks with the barest hint of a smile.

Dr. Morales smiles back. "Thank you for being willing to do so many of these. The pattern of pathology we're seeing in your scans is very unusual, so I wanted to run some additional tests. Today I'm using a compound I've developed that specifically binds to a pathological subtype of tau."

"I assume you've already tried Pittsburgh Compound-B?" butts in Graham.

And . . . record scratch.

Dr. Morales looks at him sharply, like, do you not remember the conversation we just had outside when I said it was fine if Dr. Crane wanted you to shadow today, but you must remain silent?

"Yes. Last week," says Dr. Morales tightly.

I grip the back of the chair in front of me. Hard. Yes, thanks, Captain Obvious, but I'm pretty sure the head of neurology at Arkham Asylum doesn't need your radiotracer recommendations. I pretend that's the only reason I'm annoyed. That I'm not at all bothered that Graham seems to already know what PiB is, even though I was so excited to learn about it last week. It binds to fibrillar amyloid-beta (the stuff that makes the plaques in the brains of people with Alzheimer's disease), and it lights up when you get a brain scan and helps predict things like brain atrophy and cognitive decline.

Graham opens his mouth again, but Dr. Morales is not playing around.

"There were increased levels in Ms. al Ghūl's brain. If you have any other questions, we can talk afterward."

Ha! Graham looks like he's swallowed a slug. I have to pretend to be very interested in a poster behind me about how PET scans work, while I wait for my smile to go away.

It makes me wonder, though. He spoke in front of Talia, and he's still here. Meanwhile, I haven't said a word for weeks. It. Is. Killing. Me. She knows something about who is haunting Arkham, maybe even knows who makes the fear toxin. All I'd have to do is—

"You'll need to sit quietly," announces Graham. "If you move around too much, the tracer may not get absorbed in the right areas."

My jaw actually drops. I can't help it. Did he seriously just mansplain PET scan protocol to Dr. Morales (who invented a mother-effing PET tracer) and/or Talia al Ghūl, who is clearly not at her first rodeo? I clench my fingers into fists. The old me—the one who lived last year without fear or remorse—would have said it out loud. She would have entertained daydreams about grabbing him by the collar and— No. I don't do that anymore. I used to let myself imagine what it would be like—smashing and taking and saying and doing whatever the worst parts of me wanted. It was like a release valve. Can't tell off this misogynist postdoc? Let your subconscious knee him in the groin!

Until the feelings started getting stronger. The pictures in my head darker. More violent. Harder to tell from reality. I came too close this one time with Dr. Nelson. Damn near killed him. Because the me in my head was so consumed, she didn't realize the knives were real. Not until she'd almost plunged one through his throat.

And these days? I don't even let the darkness have a taste. Because I don't know how strong she is. But I do know that she can't be trusted.

So I'm good now. Yeah. Not only do I not do ~~fun~~ terrible things, I don't even *think* about doing them. I'm stronger now. So strong that sometimes I accidentally break pencils and glasses of water, but that's to be expected, right?

"Graham, can I speak to you for a second?" Dr. Morales inclines her head toward the hallway.

I don't watch them leave—I won't be able to stop myself from raising my eyebrows at him.

The door shuts with a snap behind them. I take a step in their direction, straining to hear what she says to him. Talia glances at me slyly.

"Why don't you let her out?"

I startle. "What?"

I realize I just spoke to her, and I suck in my breath. But she just shakes her head.

"The other you. The more interesting one. I think we'd get along."

I start to answer. Look at the door to make sure it's still shut and Dr. Morales's voice is still trickling in from the hallway.

"How did you—?"

The door handle turns, and I stand up straight. Nothing to see here.

Talia leans back in her chair like a queen or a cat or something else that is proud and wins a lot.

How did she know that about me? Is it that obvious? Or is she just that good?

She's also one of the smartest people I've ever met.

This is for your own safety.

Dr. Morales and Graham come back, only this time, the

technician who operates the scanner is with them too. I note with more than a little satisfaction that Graham leans against the wall with his arms crossed, sullen.

After about an hour, Dr. Morales takes Talia to the other room and helps her lie down on an exam table that slides in and out of the death cave—I mean, PET scanner. The opening is only about as big around as a large pizza. I shudder. Then Dr. Morales comes back into the tech room where we are, and there's some buzzing and clicking and movement from the scanner as it begins.

The scans take a while, but when Talia's brain pops up on the computer screen, it's beautiful. Like art. Swirls of blue and green and pinpoints of yellow-orange-red. The pretty colors are bad, though. Well, potentially. More colors, especially warm ones, equals more pathological tau in Talia's brain. It's not a good thing, not at her age.

"What do you notice?" Dr. Morales asks, and I light up because she's directed the question at me and not at me + Graham + the technician. As strict as she is about intern observers being quiet when the patients are around, she's always asking questions when they're not. She takes it very seriously that this is a teaching facility.

"Definitely a lot of pathological tau," I say. "More than what we'd expect for someone as young as Talia."

Dr. Morales nods. "This amount is more like what I see in my patients who are in their eighties. Younger if they have Alzheimer's or a tauopathy, but nowhere near as young as Talia."

Just like the plaques last week!

"And the distribution and localization?" I ask.

She smiles—a proud mama-bear kind of smile, and I bask in it. I can't help it. "That's unusual too," she says. "Not like

Alzheimer's or another neurodegenerative disease. Not like a tauopathy."

"Maybe a vascular disease?" suggests Graham (this time without a heaping helping of douchebaggery).

Dr. M frowns. "Mmm. Not a bad idea, but it doesn't really fit."

I pore over the scans, wanting like anything to solve this problem in the next thirty seconds. To offer a solution that really wows Dr. Morales.

"Trauma?" I say it as soon as it pops into my head. "From repeated head injuries or . . . something else?"

"I'm not sure that would do this either." Dr. Morales pulls at her Arkham Asylum lanyard as she mulls over the scans. "But you bring up a good point. We should think about whether there are any clues in Ms. al Ghūl's history." She nods in that way of hers that feels more like a decision than a tacit agreement. "I'm going to go over these scans with the technician one more time to make sure we have clear images for every brain region. Would you mind going in and checking on Ms. al Ghūl?"

Behind her, Graham's mouth falls open, and it feels like sweet, delicious victory.

"You mean I can talk to her?" I blurt out. Smooth, Harleen.

"Only about how she's doing and only to help her up." Dr. Morales's stern voice is back. "I'll go over everything with her after I've had more of a chance to review."

I try really, really, really hard to look professional and not like I'm made of fireworks as I walk to the door to the scanner room, but then I pass by Graham. Screw it. I give him the barest whisper of a wink as I head in to talk to Talia al Ghūl. (What can I say? My eyelids are petty.)

I stand next to Talia as the table slides out of the scanner, her wrists and ankles bound in the plastic shackles that are always used in the imaging suite.

"Do you feel all right?"

"Yes," she answers as I help her sit up.

"Good." Because I'm claustrophobic, and the idea of being stuck in a narrow tube—alone—for forty-five minutes is enough to make my skin crawl. "Glad to hear it." I try to say it how Dr. M would.

I play the role of the dutiful intern, and I definitely don't even think about asking her what she meant by *the people who sit on your side of the table.* Much.

But what if she knows something that could help me? Does it have something to do with the face in the burlap mask? What if it's all somehow related to the girls at Arkham Acres? I could—

"In ninety seconds, that camera feed is going to be cut," Talia says, jerking her head in the direction of a small camera covered with a black sphere in the corner of the ceiling. I've always thought it looked like a robot eyeball. "You'll know because the idiots on the other side of the wall will start panicking."

Wait, what? First of all, Dr. Morales is definitely not an idiot, and second of all: "How could you possibly know that?"

Talia doesn't answer my question. "You should leave." She picks a piece of lint off her uniform sleeve. "The power is going to go out any second too."

What she's saying finally starts to set in. "You're escaping?"

"No," she explains, like it's simple. "The locks will still be closed. But they won't be able to get in. And we won't be able to get out."

There's something about the sharpness in her eyes when she says it. I should feel nervous. Scared. There's a part of me that does. But mostly? A dangerous excitement I haven't felt in months bubbles to the surface.

"For how long?"

Talia shrugs. "Ten minutes. Maybe fifteen."

It doesn't make sense. If she's not trying to escape, why is she doing this?

"Ten seconds. You should really get going, Harleen."

I cross to the door. Touch my fingers to the handle. And then I glance back at Talia.

"I'm not scared of you."

I take my hand down.

And the lights go out.

Talia's cool voice echoes across the room. "Too late."

I answer in the darkness.

"For who?"

CHAPTER 13

In a Locked Room, Trapped, with a Known Assassin

IT'S DARK AS INK IN THE SCANNER ROOM, THE COLOR OF moonless nights and coal-black hearts. And secrets. I can't see Talia yet—my eyes haven't adjusted to the darkness. But I can hear her breathing. I can tell she's still across the room, sitting on the scanner table. For now.

I wrap my hand around the pen in my lab coat pocket like a knife, just in case. I don't know why I stayed in here.

Don't you?

I haven't been able to stop thinking about her—about what she knows—since that first session.

I think you should be more worried about the people who sit on your side of the table.

If Dr. Morales found out, she'd remove me from her service so fast it would make my head spin.

I should keep quiet. Think about the future. I know where this path leads. To Montoya and questions about the Reckoning and visits from the police and an anger I can't control.

"The person who haunts Arkham—what do you know about them?"

And . . . there it goes. I've never been good at being one of those people who behave themselves. I can pretend, pass for a time, but my insides feel the strain of it. Some people say they've got a brain full of angry bees, but me—I've got a thousand screaming velociraptors trapped inside me. Feminist velociraptors too (sharp claws, hunt in packs), and each one is an unjust thing that's happened to me or a wrong that needs righting. And you'd better believe they're testing the boundaries of my sanity, systematically.

Talia lets the question hang there for a while before she answers it. I hear banging on the other side of the door.

"Harleen!" I can only just hear Dr. Morales calling to me.

"I'm fine," I call back, turning my head, but only for a fraction of a second. Talia's not the kind of person you want to show your back to.

"Well?" I ask.

"You work here. You probably know him better than I do."

"So, it's a him!" I blurt it out way too excitedly and cringe at my own eagerness.

"Might be," says Talia coolly.

"And you know who it is?"

"I might." She says it like a challenge. Like she's about to say "Jump," and I'd better be able to leap high enough for her liking.

"Who?"

Through the murky darkness, I can see the motion of her crossing her arms. I can't see her smile, but I know it's there, just as certain.

"First, I need you to do something for me."

"I'm not going to help you escape." Again with the blurting. (At least I'm consistent.)

"Child, does it look like I'm trying to go anywhere?"

Now that she mentions it . . .

"No. What was the point of all this, then?"

Her head tilts to the side. "Is that really what you want to know? I'm only answering one question."

"Yes. I mean, no." Why is it so hard to be clearheaded in front of her? "I want to know who the monster is. I want to know who's making the patients here scream in the night."

"Then I need you to tell me something, cricket." Her voice is soft and even, but I'm not fooled. Whatever it is, it's going to cost me. "That new security system they're putting in, with the fingerprints—when does it go live?"

I balk. "I can't tell you that."

"Well then, I guess you don't really want to know who the monster is."

"But I don't even know! They don't tell interns stuff like that."

I can feel her shrug, even if I can't see it. "If you want a name, I require a trade. We may not get another chance like this."

She's right, but—

The lights come on. Talia's eyes flick to the door. "Tick-tock, cricket."

"I'll find out. *I promise.*"

Talia narrows her eyes. "It's the same person who's conducting illegal experiments on the prisoners here."

The door bangs open.

"Are you okay?! What happened?!"

"I'm fine. Everything's fine." I can't help but hold my hands up like Dr. Morales is a police officer and I'm trying to prove my innocence.

Meanwhile, my brain is all: Illegal experiments!! What kind of illegal experiments?!

They take Talia away, and I watch her eye the clock, calculating, as she leaves. Meanwhile, I sit there trying to figure out if what just happened was a figment of my imagination. Dr. Morales is so frazzled, she doesn't see the smile Talia gives me over her shoulder.

But I do.

CHAPTER 14

Arkham Acres

I REMEMBER I COULDN'T LOOK DR. MORALES IN THE EYES for days afterward because I was scared that she'd know. Probably not the best way to hide your guilt, but luckily she assumed I was still feeling jittery from what happened.

So this one particular day I'm sitting at one of the shared computers in the intern office area, munching on Pocky with my friend Shiloh while we analyze data, and Dr. Morales taps me on the shoulder.

Oh gosh, is she going to ask me about Talia again?

"Harleen, can I talk to you in my office?"

She's not frowning or anything, but my brain is still a teleprompter with the words *Oh crap, oh crap, oh crap* in one giant loop.

I follow her down the hallway and take the seat across from her. It creaks loudly because I'm guilty.

Dr. Morales laces her fingers in front of her on her desk. "About Talia . . ."

"Nothing happened! I told you!" I blurt out.

She gives me a funny look. "So you've said." Shakes her

head. "But I actually wanted to talk to you about her scans. The longer I examine them, the more I believe that they're different from anything I've ever seen."

"Really?" I breathe. (Partly from relief and partly from the wonder of brain science.)

"I was hoping you could do some further research for me. A thorough review of the literature. Look for any other strange cases with tau or PiB or other tracers that might be similar."

I sit straight up in my chair. (It protests.) "Yeah, I'd love to!"

Her mouth spreads into a smile. "Perfect. I think we could write this up as a really interesting case study, with Ms. al Ghūl's consent. And I also wanted to ask if you would do the writing. Would you be interested in being first author?"

Would I? "Are you serious? Yeah, yes, that would be great. The press will eat this up. Talia al Ghūl. Would-be assassin of Gotham City's most polarizing mayor."

Dr. Morales clears her throat. Or maybe it's a sound of disagreement. It's hard to say. "We won't be including her name in the paper. I know what happened last year with Dr. Nelson's Joker paper—"

My Joker paper.

"But ethically, it's important that we protect the identity of the participants in our research. Historically, people have used initials instead of full names."

I think about Dr. Crane's fear lecture. "Like S.M."

Dr. Morales nods. "Exactly. We'll simply refer to Ms. al Ghūl as 'a patient.' "

I wince. "Last year—"

"I think it's fair to say that last year your mentoring was lacking in a lot of ways. I don't think you should consider the Joker paper your fault." She takes a long sip of the coffee on her desk. "But I do think it's important to think of people like Talia, and even The Joker, as not just Super-Villains but people. When you slap a label on someone, think about them as a group, it's easy to forget about their humanity."

Is that what the person performing the nighttime experiments does? Pretends that what they're doing isn't horrific because it's on Super-Villains? What *are* they doing, anyway? I'd bet any amount of money it involves the fear spray Dr. Nelson was being sent, but what's the endgame? How do all the pieces connect?

Which reminds me . . .

"Have you heard anything back from the IRB yet? About our inquiry about the Arkham Acres girls?"

"Not yet, but these things take time."

I guess she's right, but this seems so urgent. I was hoping they would move faster.

I'm still thinking about it the next morning as I head to French class with Samantha. About how walking the straight and narrow is kind of exhausting. And how it involves so much waiting. (SO. MUCH. WAITING.) It's almost a relief to have to focus every brain cell on French for the next hour. We end a bit early so Madame Dumas can hand back our most recent exams.

"This exam was a little harder than some of our previous ones. A lot of people seemed to have a tough time with it. Please see me if you need help." (At least, I think that's what she says. She's speaking entirely en français.)

She writes the exam breakdown on the chalkboard, a moment I've come to dread even though I haven't made another D after that first one.

Notes d'examen

A–4

B–4

C–5

D–1

Oh, great. Here we go again. I remember thinking it was a really hard exam when I took it. Remember cursing myself for not studying more, even though I definitely spent hours conjugating French verbs and went to Madame Dumas's office hours twice that week.

She places my exam facedown on the table.

"Trés bien," she says with a small smile.

I flip the paper over. Holy crap. Sacrebleu. I just got an A- on a French test.

"Hey!" I say to Samantha, but she's shoving her exam into a leather messenger bag and trying not to cry.

Oh. I'm pretty sure I saw a C+.

She stomps in the direction of our dorm, not really waiting for me. I rush to keep up with her.

"Hey, I'm really sorry," I say.

"I can't believe I got a C." Her face is red and splotchy, and there are tears streaming down her cheeks now. She's not sad-crying, though. Angry-crying. Set-things-on-fire-with-your-mind-crying.

I frown sympathetically because I know exactly what that feels like. "It was a really hard test."

She stops midstep and narrows her eyes at me. "*You* got an A."

Like I did it to personally wound her.

Something about the way she says *you* makes me feel hot all over.

"What's that supposed to mean?"

"Never mind."

She stomps off, and I'm left to wonder. I always felt like we were from different planets—East End versus old money, sorority girl versus future hipster—but I thought we were friends. Well, kind of. I start to come down with this restless feeling, one I used to get all the time last year. One I used to say yes to.

And when one of my intern friends shoots me a text that says, Hey, want to sneak around Arkham tonight and try to find the Attic?, I reply:

Harleen: I'm in.

CHAPTER 15

Arkham Asylum After Everyone Has Gone Home

WE WAIT IN THE SHADOWS. UNTIL EVERYONE LEAVES EXcept the night staff. Until it's nearly midnight. Me, Win, Ansley, Xander, Shiloh, lurking in an old exam room in the basement. It's deliciously creepy down here. An old metal table with leather straps. Rusted surgical tools. A drain in the floor that occasionally makes a gurgle like a dying sea monster.

Win nudges me. "So, this is your idea of a date, huh?"

I laugh. I don't mind the teasing. Frankly, I'm just glad he didn't bolt (he did kind of have this caged-animal look for the first half hour). I guess I did technically tell him to meet me at Arkham at six o'clock for dinner and a movie. And he probably thought I got off at six and was just using Arkham as the meeting location. Probably wasn't expecting burgers and sweet potato fries and watching a scary movie double feature on Xander's laptop with three other people in the basement of an asylum.

I gesture at the array of sharp objects behind us. "Hey, you've gotta love the horror-movie ambience."

When the movie credits roll, I sit up from where I'm snuggled into Win's shoulder.

"Is it time?"

"I don't know," says Xander. He's always the most cautious of all of us. Well, besides Win. But we don't usually invite Win along when we're doing mayhem and shenanigans.

"It's eleven-thirty-six. How much later does it have to get?" Ansley pushes her blond hair out of her eyes, frustrated.

"I could go check," offers Win. "I'm here a lot of late nights anyway, working on experiments for Dr. Crane. The night staff are used to seeing me." He shoots me a sly glance. "Want to come with me? We could go to the second-floor vending machines and—"

"Get the good chocolate!" I finish. "Yes, we are absolutely doing that because nothing says haunted sleepover secret mission like sixty percent dark."

Everyone else agrees, so Win and I slip from the basement to the second floor. He walks down the hallway like he owns the place, which is honestly probably the best tactic, even though doing somersaults and peering around corners dramatically is a lot more fun.

We get to the vending machines without incident, which ~~is disappointing~~ bodes well for the rest of the night. Win purchases a buttload of chocolate, which, FYI, is an actual unit of measurement. I go to retrieve it from the vending machine slot, but he grabs my hand.

"Harleen?"

"Yeah?"

He looks serious. Way too serious for sneaking around and midnight chocolate.

"I need to talk to you about something."

"Okay." My heart skips a beat. Does he know something about the illegal experiments? Is that what this is? Has he seen something during all those late nights at Arkham?

"I was thinking." He glances from side to side, fear clear on his face. Fear of what? The man in the burlap mask? "Would you like to be my girlfriend?"

"Ohhhh." And . . . it all makes sense now.

But I guess my thinking face looks too much like my I'm-going-to-say-no face because Winfield starts to panic.

"Oh gosh, you don't want to. I just thought . . . I've really enjoyed these last few weeks. And I thought you did too. And you're like no one I've ever met. And I—"

I put a finger to his lips. "Yes."

His eyes bulge. "Yes?"

I push him backward against the vending machine and kiss him. "Yes."

"Yes." He says it like a sigh of relief.

"And, uh, Harleen?" His face is panicky again. We're talking throw-up-on-your-own-shoes level of panic. But then he brushes my hair from my face so gently. "I love you."

My mouth falls open in the shape of an O. I wasn't expecting words like that from someone like him. Especially not so soon.

But I can tell by the way my heart surges in my chest that he's right.

"You don't have to say it back," he says quietly, tracing my cheek like he's afraid I'll disappear. "But I wanted you to know."

There's something so heartbreaking about him putting those feelings into the world, thinking that they're probably not reciprocated. The fact that he's not afraid to be the one who loves the most makes me sure that this is the right decision. I stare up into his ocean eyes.

"I love you too."

His hands find my back, my hair, wrapping themselves around me almost desperately. His chest rises and falls so quickly.

And then my phone buzzes in my pocket, and we both jump.

"It's just Pamela," I tell Win.

The side of his mouth tries to turn upward in a smile but doesn't really make it. "You spend a lot of time with her, huh?"

"Well, yeah, she's my best friend."

"Right." He nods.

I bump him with my hip. "Don't be like that. Boyfriend."

"Boyfriend." His cheeks turn red.

He practically floats all the way back to the basement.

Shiloh is waiting for us with their arms crossed. "Twenty minutes is a long time to get chocolate."

"Well, we had to make sure we didn't get caught. Right, Win?"

"Um, yeah." He turns the color of fire engines and stolen kisses. Smooth, Win. Real smooth.

"BUT, HEY, LOOK." I make it rain chocolate on the metal exam table, and my friends forget to interrogate us.

We chomp down on at least four different kinds of chocolatey goodness while we pore over the Arkham Asylum blueprints that Shiloh has spread on the table and held down with ancient Bunsen burners and scalpels. (A fact about Shiloh: They are extra AF about this kind of thing.)

"Okay." Shiloh presides over the blueprints like a general. "I've circled all the areas where the dimensions listed here don't seem to match up with the current layout of the Asylum. Well, all the areas in Arkham that I have access to. I figure those are our best bets for a hidden area like the Attic that The Riddler was talking about."

"Or some kind of portal to a nightmare dimension," says Ansley brightly.

"If there was such a thing, I'm certain I could find a mathematical way to explain it," says Shiloh, brown eyes sparkling at the thought. "So, I was thinking we'd split up and each investigate one or two of these areas and meet back here when we finish."

I smirk at them. "You want us to all go off alone. In an asylum. In the dark. Did you not see how well that worked out in the movies we just watched?!"

"Oh." Shiloh eyes the plans again, thoughtful.

My phone buzzes in my pocket again, but I ignore it. I'll text Pamela back later.

"I'm just messing with you. I think it's a great idea." It'll be like going to one of those creepy fun houses. "But I'm bringing a baseball bat."

Win side-eyes me. "Where are you going to get one of those?"

I pick up the poster tube leaning in the corner, the one I placed there as soon as we arrived. Poster tubes are these big long plastic tubes—imagine a can of Pringles. But, like, bigger around and five feet long and with a shoulder strap. They're the ideal size for holding a scientific poster. And also—as it turns out—a baseball bat.

I unscrew the cap with a wicked grin. "Hello, my name is Harleen Quinzel, and today I'll be presenting on the effects of smashing things with baseball bats."

I upend the tube and let the bat fall to the floor with

a clatter. It's the wooden one I brought to school from the apartment—I would've liked to bring my new gold one, but metal detectors can be such buzzkills.

I wind the bat behind my neck. Rest one hand on either end.

"Who's ready to find the Attic?"

The hallways at Arkham have more spiderwebs when you walk them alone. And the shadows change shape behind you. I ignore the chill that trails its fingers across the back of my neck and keep walking.

I've already checked out a room off the cafeteria that was on the blueprints but doesn't seem to exist in real life. (It was a bust.) Turns out someone blocked the door with a huge storage shelf, but all that was hiding behind the cans of string beans and peaches was even older string beans and peaches. Ah, well. At least searching the cafeteria gave me the chance to swipe a couple of juices for King Shark—one apple and one grape, just what he likes. I sneak to his floor and whisper *psst* at the door to his cell. He gives me the most buoyant smile when he sees what I'm holding.

I'm meant to go to a hallway on the third floor next. The shortest route would be to cut through the women's ward.

It's the same person who's conducting illegal experiments on the prisoners here.

I swipe into the ward. Just because I'm going in here doesn't mean I have to pass by her cell.

My phone buzzes, and I check to see if it's Pamela again. It is, but that's not who it was before when we were looking at blueprints. It was my dad, I realize, coming to a dead stop in the hallway.

I mean, it wasn't actually him—he's not with us anymore. Died last year when some guys beat him to a pulp over gambling debts. But it's a notification from my calendar. Today is his birthday.

I pace the hallways, my baseball bat—*his* baseball bat—swinging at my side. I want to put it through several windows until the terrible aching feeling goes away. But I can't do that here. My dad and I didn't have the best relationship (understatement of the century). He's the reason I have PTSD. The reason I went after the Gotham U Presidential Scholarship like it was survival. Because it was. But I still find myself crying in an empty hallway at Arkham.

"Are you all right, cricket?"

I startle at the sound of Talia's voice. Did my feet take me here by accident, or did my subconscious lead me to the very hallway where her cell is? I don't love the fact that she's seeing me broken like this. I try to pull myself together.

"I'm fine," I tell her, swiping at my cheeks. And then I remember something I read about using honesty to build trust. I think it was in a psychology book. Or maybe that *Silence of the Lambs* movie. "Actually"—I clear my throat—"it's my dad's birthday. He passed away last year."

"I'm sorry to hear that." Talia's face is sympathetic in the window of her cell.

"I hated him."

I choke the handle of the bat as I say it.

"Fathers are . . . complicated." Her eyes are clear of emotion—she's too smart for that—but her mouth is tight in a way that suggests she knows what she's talking about.

"I felt like everything I ever did was to get away from him. To not be like him." I shake my head angrily. "And now he's gone, and I feel like I don't even know if I'm going in the right direction anymore, so I just keep trying so hard to be so perfect. To prove I'm different from him." I shouldn't be saying all this to Talia, but I'm beyond the point of caring. "I don't even know why I'm doing half the stuff I do anymore."

I flop onto the floor of the hallway and lean against the wall. Talia watches me thoughtfully.

"Living your life to spite someone else is an exhausting business."

And now I'm watching her.

"So, you've done it too?"

She chooses her answer carefully, but I still get the feeling she's telling the truth. "I have. But in time, I realized that my goals aligned with my father's more than I thought. Even if we did have very different ideas of the best means to achieve those goals."

I can't even begin to know what she means by that. But before I have the chance to ask, she keeps talking.

"It was the injustices in the world. The corruption. I began to realize that I'm the type of person who would rather burn it all down than watch it happen."

I nod. "I know something about that."

CHAPTER 16

Arkham Acres

I'M STILL THINKING ABOUT MY MIDNIGHT TALK WITH TALIA while Win drives me to visit the girls at Arkham Acres a few days later. I hope it's not weird that I brought a boy. Or that I'm wearing a nineties-style minidress made entirely out of playing cards. (We're going straight to my sorority's Anything but Clothes party afterward. I was mildly concerned about how Win would react to the theme, but then he showed up wearing "leather" pants made out of a Twister mat, and, yes, I would put my left hand on blue, thank you very much.)

Stella looks confused when we meet her in the rec room. "Wow, you guys are really excited to play games with us, huh?"

"Oh." I laugh. "I mean, yes, *always.* But also, we're going to Fall Party after this, and the theme is Anything But Clothes."

"Good. Because I had some concerns." And then she blushes because she never says stuff like that. "So," she adds, still blushing, "want to play Unstable Unicorns?"

"YES." I have no idea what that is, but sometimes you just know when something's your destiny.

"Cool. I'm gonna get my friend who wanted to play."

Stella runs off to the other side of the rec room. I bump my hip against Win's.

"Nice pants."

"Hey, I do what I can."

I'm thinking about kissing him when Stella returns.

"This is Remy," she says, holding out one arm awkwardly, like she's so proud to be presenting her friend to us.

And I get it. Remy is . . . cool. She's wearing a white cottagecore dress, and her artfully disheveled hair is the color of faded cotton candy, and she has the most curated ears I've ever seen. Tiny studs and dangling charms and delicate diamond cuffs and a trio of the daintiest silver flowers.

"I'm Harleen," I say. "And this is Win."

"Remy," she replies, even though Stella already told us. "I love your dress. Do you mind?"

I shake my head. "Pick a card, any card! But, like, not really, because I don't wanna end up naked."

She touches one of the cards—the queen of hearts. They overlap each other like a fringe. And something clicks.

"Have we met?" I feel like I'd remember someone with hair that color.

"I don't think so," says Remy. "I've been here for a while, but I think I'd remember you."

I smile. "Same."

Weird, though. I'm getting the eeriest sense of déjà vu.

I try to shake it off because Stella's already dealing out the unicorn cards.

"So, how did you two meet?" asks Remy as we try to destroy each other using rainbow auras and sadistic rituals and alluring narwhals.

"Harleen and I are interns together." Win grins like his

entire body is made of sunshine. "And I was lucky enough to convince her to go to dinner with me."

I am suddenly very aware that we are having this conversation in front of the sister of my ex-girlfriend, who is currently incarcerated. My eyes dart to Stella. Her mouth is tight. Does it always look like that? Maybe I'm imagining it. Either way, I feel compelled to change the subject, stat.

"How 'bout you? How did you meet?" I ask, and then want to facepalm myself because of course they met at Arkham Acres.

But Remy jumps right in. "Oh! We were part of this special program for students who are good at science. We met at Gotham U."

She can't mean . . .

I keep my smile plastered on my face even though it feels brittle now. "Was it Bridge Scholars? I was in that program last year."

"Yep, that's the one." She takes out one of my baby unicorns with a glitter bomb like nothing is wrong.

Remy was at Gotham U. And now she's here.

She was in Gotham University Bridge Scholars, a program managed by a man with a penchant for picking off girls and experimenting on them and leaving them so shattered they'd end up at a place like Arkham Acres. Was Remy's one of the faces we printed out and stuck to Bianca's wall? Was she—

"Excuse me, I have to go to the bathroom."

I leap up from the table, trying not to take out one of the nurses and a game of Jenga in the process.

I know where I've seen Remy.

I run into the bathroom and make it inside a stall just in time to dry heave over the toilet.

When we were at Dr. Nelson's house—when Bernice was trying to convince me to kill him, that it was the only way to stop him from hurting more girls—there was a cabinet. And inside it were cans of fear spray and the envelopes he used to send blood samples off to Arkham Asylum, but there was something else. People who commit serial crimes like to keep trophies. And Aaron Nelson was no exception. On a shelf above the cans of mind-melting fear toxin was a rack of glass vials. Each one contained a lock of hair and had a label carefully affixed to the side. One of those vials had pink hair inside. And the name on the label was Remy.

"Are you sure you're okay?" asks Stella.

"Totally," I lie. "I think it was something I ate. The campus pizza place isn't what it used to be."

I take a sip of ginger ale for good measure. (Win dashed to the vending machines like a white knight within seconds of my return.)

I pick up my cards and pretend the hands that are holding them aren't shaking. The girls playing Jenga, reading magazines, watching a movie—I look around at them with new eyes. How many of them were preyed on by Dr. Nelson?

Across the room, a nurse draws up a syringe full of blood. How many of them are still being preyed on? Is that why they're all here? I always wondered how Stella's parents could afford this place. I thought maybe the school was trying to perform some kind of restorative justice, but of course that's not it. These girls are here because they were an experiment. I think of the screaming fits Stella mentioned last time I was here. They're *still* an experiment. And the person who helped rain down hell on them in the first place isn't finished with them yet.

When we're done playing cards, I ask Win if he'd mind pulling his car around.

"I need to go to the bathroom. Again." I swallow like I'm trying not to spew vomit all over him, and his eyes go big and he stutters out, "S-sure."

I could get in trouble for what I'm about to do. Possibly be stripped of my internship. Dr. Morales would remove me from her service for sure. Maybe that's why I don't tell Win. Because I don't want him to get in trouble too.

It's a lie, and I know it.

Dr. Crane has always given me the creeps, but Win thinks he hung the moon. It's not enough to keep me from dating him, but it's enough to make me more careful around him.

I should wait until we know the results of the IRB inquiry, I tell myself. What I'm thinking of doing might not even be necessary. But my darkness wins again, and instead of walking to the bathroom, I stop at the nurses' station.

I began to realize that I'm the type of person who would rather burn it all down than watch it happen.

"There's a girl crying in the games closet," I tell the nurse—thankfully, there's only one at the moment.

And as soon as he rushes off, I tear a page off his clipboard—a list of all the girls with selective catatonia and a schedule of their blood draws—and I shove it into my pocket.

CHAPTER 17

Arkham Asylum

AFTER I SAW THE LIST OF GIRLS, EVERYTHING CHANGED. I could no longer tell myself that maybe women weren't getting hurt anymore with Dr. Nelson safely locked away. I had proof that *something* was happening, even if I didn't know what. I made it a point to seek out Talia and talk to her every chance I got. Even if it meant breaking the rules. She was my only lead on the Straw Man's identity. I had to take it.

I'd come down from the ceiling on a sheet, Cirque du Soleil–style, while Talia was in her cell reading a book. *Do you know anything about who's taking blood samples from the girls at Arkham Acres and why?*

When I knew Talia was on laundry duty, I'd sit inside one of the giant dryers, waiting for her to open it. (An observation: Talia does not like to be startled.) *Do you think it's connected to what's happening with the Arkham inmates?*

I'd bribe Two-Face with pork rinds and bruschetta made from locally sourced vegetables, so I could talk to her during recreation time. *What's your favorite kind of breakfast sandwich?*

"I'm more of a black coffee person myself," she says, setting down a broken-spined book from the library. "But I'd rather talk about that list you took."

"Oh?" I wonder if this means she knows something. I try to contain my smile.

"How did it make you feel?" she asks in a velvety voice.

"What?" I ask stupidly. This is not where I thought we were going.

"Stealing it. Tricking that nurse. How did it make you feel?" She says it slowly and then watches me, appraising.

"Powerful, like I was doing something."

She nods.

"And dangerous."

A hint of a smile now. A speeding-up of breaths, hers and mine.

"But also scared. It could ruin everything for me if I got caught."

"I see," she says, and I feel like I've somehow disappointed her. "And last year, this is why you stopped being in that group?"

I freeze. "How do *you* know about that? Not that there's a that. I can neither confirm nor deny a that."

But Talia just waves me off. "I read some news articles, put two and two together, and made an educated guess." She looks me up and down. "Clearly, I'm not wrong."

And because I am still sitting there dumbfounded, she adds, "Don't worry. I'm not planning to tell anyone. I just want to know—why did you stop?"

Because Officer Montoya made me?

I squirm in my chair like I've done something wrong. "Because I had to. I don't have all the chances the kids I go to school with have. I have to work twice as hard and be twice as careful. I can't let myself get sidetracked doing stuff that'll get me kicked out of school and thrown in jail."

But Talia isn't buying it. "You had to stop," she says. "Because society says that what you were doing isn't okay. But why isn't it? You were fighting for women's rights, yes? That's a good thing."

"Yeah, well, I guess the law prefers these fights to happen in courtrooms instead of with cannons."

"Batman doesn't fight in courtrooms."

I suck in a breath.

"And the police don't capture him," Talia continues.

"So you're saying you don't think the police would come after me if they knew what I did?" I ask skeptically.

"Oh, they would. They absolutely would. But why is it okay for Batman to be a vigilante but not you?"

Huh. I never thought about it that way.

"Well, I guess Batman's helping people," I say eventually. Then I shake my head. "But so was I. I was helping women."

"Exactly. And maybe the police and the mayor and the good citizens of Gotham City would rather their vigilantes stick to a certain agenda. Batman is promoting the status quo. He's a glorified police officer without any of the rules. No police brutality charges for him.

"And us—what kind of vile, depraved things are we fighting for?" She nods at me. "Women's rights." A finger pointed at herself. "Or the dismantling of an economic system that only benefits the rich." Swings her arms wide. "And the rest of us? King Shark is in here because he tried to free some dolphins that were being abused in a cesspool of an amusement park."

I cock my head to one side. "Well, that doesn't sound so bad."

"He bit a few people."

"Oh."

"And Mr. Freeze just wanted to save his wife, but health care in this country is abominable, and The Joker's been calling our attention to treatment of the mentally ill—whether he means to or not. And I hear Catwoman donates a percentage of her heists to Gotham's poorest.

"Meanwhile Batman is fighting for what? Law and order? Safety for the one-percenters? In a city where Gotham's richest have created an environment in which the marginalized feel like their only way out is to become a supervillain."

She's right. She's 200 percent right. Isn't that why we started the Reckoning last year? Before I can respond, Two-Face pops both of his faces into the rec room. "Time's up."

I stand, ready to leave (reluctantly), when Talia grabs my wrist. "Remember, cricket. Heroes and villains are defined by the systems they support or dismantle."

Her words stick in my brain like peanut butter to the roof of your mouth. I can't escape them no matter how fast I walk from the rec room to the shuttle. She brings a convincing argument for why I should be helping her. Why I should be calling Bianca immediately and agreeing to any mission she's got planned.

But, no. I've been through this. That isn't the way to get what I want out of life. Dr. Morales's way. That's the way. I think about whether I really believe myself. If I'd tell a friend the same thing if they were asking—sometimes it's easier to be kinder to a friend than to yourself. More objective.

And I think of Pamela and how she feels about the environment and what I would tell her if she asked me the questions I'm asking myself. If she asked me whether she should sneak into some giant polluter company and expose them or go to any lengths to prevent toxic chemicals from leaking into our rivers.

Dr. M would tell Pamela to go through legal channels. Because that's working out so well for the environment.

But I know exactly what I'd do. I'd tell her yay for blowing up a building, and then I'd swing her around in a circle and take her to get cotton candy.

So I guess I know what I'd tell myself, if I'm being honest. I know the choice the darkest part of my heart wants to make when it comes to helping the Arkham Acres girls.

I can feel myself getting closer (to the truth or to Talia?). But I still don't have the information she needs. Until one day, I do. I wait until Talia is in the exercise yard, and then I go outside to get a breath of fresh air.

So, I'm standing on the staff side, and Talia's on the inmate side, just waiting for the guards to change shifts. And when they do, I don't hesitate.

"The fingerprint scanners go live next week. They made us all go to the badge office and have our fingerprints taken yesterday."

We face opposite directions—no one would ever guess we're talking. It means I can't see her reaction. But I feel it all the same. Even though she doesn't say anything. Even though there are ten feet and a fence between us. This throws a kink into whatever she's planning.

"Are you certain?" she asks after a few seconds.

"Yes." I've been debating whether to tell her this next part, but I decide it's necessary. "I think someone is doing experiments on some of the girls at Arkham Acres too. I think it has to do with a fear toxin that someone from Arkham was sending to a campus predator last year."

"You mean Dr. Nelson?"

I stifle a gasp, telling myself that it was all over the news, so it isn't that surprising that she knows.

"What exactly *is* going on with the Arkham inmates?" It could be the key to stopping whatever is happening to the girls at Arkham Acres.

Talia rustles on her side of the fence, and I realize she's double-checking that no one is watching. Or listening.

"There's a secret lab in Arkham Asylum that is always locked, always heavily guarded. If you really want to know what's going on, you'll have to break into the lab. I can help you there."

I do want to know. I want to help Stella and the rest of the girls. The prisoners here too. But breaking into a lab where classified experiments are being carried out is huge. I'm supposed to be different this year. Breaking and entering is not how you become a successful doctor. There has to be an easier (more legal) way.

"Why are you so afraid of the darkness growing inside you?"

"What?" I say, stupidly caught off guard.

"You don't hide it as well as you think," Talia continues in a low voice. "I see the real you. You've got it in you to kill a corrupt mayor or two."

I'm flustered, but I try not to show it, even though she can't see my face. "I don't know what you mean." And anyway, she didn't kill the mayor. She missed.

"You should embrace it." Talia is smiling now. I can hear it in her voice. "Women like us, we can change the world. But only if we're not afraid to do what needs doing. Gotham City is rotting. It needs to be purged, starting at the very top."

She's right, not that I'm ready to admit it to myself. Yet.

I try to ignore that Talia is beginning to feel more like a mentor and less like a patient. Sometimes a realization can split you in two. Bisect your life. Past and future. Before and after.

I'm scared of who I'll be on the other side.

CHAPTER 18

Secret Rooftop Garden at Gotham U Library

"WE ONLY HAVE ONE MORE FINAL LEFT IN OUR FIRST-EVER Gotham U finals week, and I got us lattes!!" I plunk down on a couch beside Pamela in the lobby of the chemistry building.

She jumps. "Are you sure you need caffeine?"

"Um, *yes.* I have been awake for twenty-seven hours, and I just accidentally went to the boys' bathroom, and then, when a boy walked into the bathroom, I gave him a dirty look and he ran back out. And then I noticed the urinals. It was awesome. So, coffee?" I slurp down a huge gulp.

"Yes, please." Pamela takes a sip of hers. "Hey, you remembered I like cardamom in mine."

"Well, yeah," I say, pleased that she noticed. "Hey, where do you want to go? We have three hours to cram for this bio exam. It's time to put the *stud* in *study.*"

"I cannot believe you just said that."

"I blame sleep deprivation. But seriously, where to? Nighthawk's? The library? The Alpha Nu house? I don't know, the Alpha Nu house is starting to get kind of loud now that half the girls have finished their finals, and the library is crawling with people."

Pamela's eyes light up. "Oh! Have you ever been to the secret rooftop garden on top of the library?"

"Wait. WHAT?" I love secrets. And rooftops. And Pamela loves gardens. "How have you never told me about this before?"

She kind of blushes and shrugs. "I don't know. So, we're going?"

"Hell yeah, we are." I'm already up and slinging my backpack over my shoulder. "There's no way I'm studying on the ground floor with the peons now that I know there's a secret magical haunted garden."

"Um, I never said it was magical. Or haunted."

"But, like, it probably is."

"Um . . ."

We go inside and scan our G-cards, and the first floor of the library is indeed packed. Every computer. Every table. Every study carrel.

"So, how do we get there?" I scan the library floor like I'm expecting a beanstalk to burst through the burgundy carpet and take us all the way up.

"The back elevators," she says. (I should have known.)

I try to contain my unmitigated glee as we traipse past all these poor, finals-laden students who know nothing about the secret garden. The back elevator is behind the ~~old~~ rare-books section and across from the boys' bathroom, and I'm sure people who aren't scared of being trapped in small spaces would find it to be positively charming. (It is tiny. And old. And really freaking tiny.)

"All the other elevators stop at six," says Pamela in the low voice people use for telling ghost stories. "But this one goes up to seven. Do you want to press the button?"

I love her for asking because *of course* I want to press the button (ANY BUTTON!), and also it takes my mind off the fact that we're enclosed in a rickety death trap. I press the button. She pulls out a key hanging from a necklace hidden under her shirt and inserts it into a lock at the same time.

My eyes widen. "OMG, could this get any better?"

"Everyone in Dr. Roesch's botany classes has access," says Pamela, even though she is no doubt part of some secret society.

"Course they do," I say, winking at her.

"You are so weird."

The doors creak open when we reach the top floor, and I can't help but gasp. It's December, so not everything is growing, but I can imagine what it would look like when it's lush and full. Thick climbing vines wrap their way around pergolas and over arches to form living tunnels, grasping with their woody brown fingers. Huge pots and planters surround seating areas, forming cozy nooks. Some of the pots are empty, but the larger ones hold entire trees. How did I never notice this place was up here? Pamela leads me along a mosaic-tiled path to a greenhouse.

"It'll be warmer in here."

"This is amazing," I tell her.

She grins. "You should see the gardens at my house."

(SHE WANTS ME TO SEE HER HOUSE. DID ANYONE ELSE CATCH THAT?!)

The greenhouse is beyond beautiful. All glass panels and sunlight streaming in and green, so much green for the cusp of winter. Plants drip down the walls, spill out of cement containers and terra-cotta pots. The air in here is different too—hot, steamy, *alive.* I feel like I've crossed through a portal and into another world.

And if we're in another world, Pamela's the queen of it. She strides past orchids and climbing vines of coral honeysuckle and passionflower, stopping here to talk to a snapdragon or there to caress a morning glory. It must be the wind or the extreme lack of sleep, but I could have sworn the plants reached out their tendrils to her when she passed.

I stop to admire a pinkish flower. "I love pitcher plants."

"They're carnivorous." Pamela lights up at the thought. "Dr. Roesch let me bring some of these from home. I have one at my house that's six feet tall. They're not actually supposed to get that big, but I've been doing some experiments. The insides of the pitcher are still smooth as glass, and the pool at the bottom has enough liquid to drown a person. Not that I'm thinking of drowning people. Sorry, is this boring? I get weird when I talk about plants."

"Are you kidding? I think it's awesome." People who like weird niche things enough that they could spend three whole hours regaling you with fascinating facts are my favorite.

We do have to study, though, so we set our book bags on a potting table and quiz each other on cell membrane composition and how enzymes work and everything else that might be on our biology final. After a while, our brains start to feel like they're oozing out of our ears, so we take a break.

"Have you thought any more about what you're going to do about that lab?" asks Pamela.

She means the secret lab at Arkham, the one Talia told me about. Let's be honest: I can't stop thinking about it. It's science. That's secret. How could I not want to know everything I possibly could, even if the science being done there is evil and nefarious?

"I'm scared," I finally say. I like that I can tell her things like that. She always listens, but she doesn't just tell you what you want to hear. She really thinks about what she says. "This is the kind of choice that changes you." And I'm trying so damn hard, ravenous for this future that feels, and has always felt, out of my grasp.

"But maybe that's exactly why you should do it," says Pamela. She tucks a sheet of red hair behind her ear. "I know you. You're passionate about justice. And, yes, it may feel wrong to do it, but I bet it feels more wrong not to." She blushes at the passion in her voice. "That's how I feel about protecting the environment, anyway."

"You're right." I say it because I want to make her feel better. But also, SHE IS. I do want justice, and I have a chance to achieve it. For Stella. For Remy. For Kylie. For Bernice. For every girl who was hurt by Dr. Nelson and whoever it is at Arkham still making that toxin and experimenting on prisoners and the Arkham Acres girls. How can I let something like that slide? Are my own career goals really worth it if I can't look myself in the mirror in the morning?

"Thank you," I tell her.

I reach across the table and squeeze her hand, so grateful to have found this friendship. Her face pinches, almost like she's in pain. It reminds me of something I've been wondering about but have been afraid to ask.

"Are you okay? Did the experiments hurt you or anything?"

I'm a monster. He turned me into a monster.

She looks terrified, and for a second I'm certain she won't answer.

And then:

"I . . . have powers." Pamela's mouth drops open like she can't believe she just said it. "I've never told anyone that," she admits, squeezing her arms tight around herself.

I try to make my best nonjudgmental face. "What kind of powers?"

Flight? Invisibility? The power to make perfect French toast?

Pamela lifts one arm in the air delicately, hand cupped toward the sky like she's making an offering. It takes me a second to realize that the vines in front of her are moving. Another to realize that she's making it happen. Plants don't grow that fast. Don't move on their own, not like that, anyway. And they certainly don't sprout leaves at the flick of a wrist.

"Holy crap," I say.

The vines in front of us have knitted themselves together to spell *Harleen*.

It's beautiful. Like living calligraphy. Also awesome. And powerful. I tell Pamela as much. And then the full implications of her abilities start to sink in.

"Wait, seriously?! This is amazing! Can you make a rosebush grow as big as a house? Oh! Can you make a Venus flytrap eat my chem TA?"

She laughs, a hopeful, fragile thing that makes me realize she was holding her breath before. That she was worried about how I'd take this revelation. She was offering everything to me in that moment, and I didn't even know it.

"Thank you," she says.

"For what? Confirming that you're clearly awesome?"

"For making me feel like I'm not a freak."

I hate that she could think that about herself, even for a second.

"Are you kidding? This is a gift. You're the coolest person I know." Her cheeks turn so red when I say it, hair falling forward to hide her face, sending a wave of this evergreen-juniper-holly smell until I can't think of anything but how I'd do anything for her. Can barely remember my own name. I manage to get out a sentence through the haze. "I'm really glad you're my friend, Pamela."

"Thanks." Those red cheeks again. Curling in on herself. And then she sits up tall. "Actually, I've been thinking about going by the name Ivy."

"Ivy," I say, turning the name over on my tongue. "It suits you."

She could not look more pleased.

We go back to studying because we do have a final in less than an hour. But when it's time to leave, Ivy passes me a pitcher plant in a resin pot.

"It's one of mine. I want you to have it. I've never had a best friend before."

When she says it, there's a place in the hardest part of my heart that opens like a flower.

CHAPTER 19

The Laboratory

I'M IN THE SECRET LABORATORY. NO MATTER WHAT HAPPENS next, it was worth it to get in here.

The minutes pass, but it feels like hours. This is the very definition of being closed in, and I try to keep my heart from racing and my breathing from quickening and everything else we learned about in Dr. Crane's fear lecture. This will be worth it, I tell myself. I'll finally know the truth.

After several eternities, I hear a voice—Dr. Crane's. Does he have something to do with this?!

"I'm going to strap you into the operating chair now. Just relax, and everything will be fine. Try not to move."

I wait, tensing my muscles. I hate that it's pitch-black and I can't see anything. Hate the crushing, boxed-in feeling. I hear the clinking of the straps, but I don't feel them. Of course I don't feel them, not from my hiding place. C'mon, c'mon, c'mon. I'm running out of air.

Dr. Crane speaks again. "Now I'm going to—"

CRASH.

A diversion down the hallway. Just like my intern friends

and I planned. They don't actually know what's going on, of course. It seemed safer that way.

"I'll be right back," Crane says, anger flashing in his voice like hot oil in a frying pan.

I close my eyes, listening. The door shuts with a snap.

And I pop out of King Shark's mouth.

He's currently strapped in the operating chair, mouth open extra wide like he was worried his teeth might get me. (Which is definitely appreciated.) I strip off the plastic poncho and plastic pants that I had on over my regular clothes. They're torn in a few places where they snagged on his teeth. I discard them in the trash can with a shudder. Glad he wasn't feeling snack-y.

I look up at King Shark, who has his mouth closed now. Without all those razor-sharp teeth showing, he almost looks kind of noble. I hate seeing him like this—strapped to a chair. Helpless. A part of me wants to let him go. Grab the nearest bludgeoning device and tear through Arkham with him like it's freaking Shark Week.

But then we'd never know the truth.

He agreed, I tell myself. He wants to do this.

I touch a hand to King Shark's leathery gray face.

"You're very brave. I promise I'm going to help you."

Kindness flickers in his eyes, and it tears my heart in half knowing what I'm about to do next.

I hop up onto the counter and push aside a ceiling tile. Climb through the opening to wait for Crane to come back. I balance on a support beam inside the ceiling, carefully, carefully. Don't want to crash through the ceiling on them, as tempting as that sounds. I pull the powdery white square of tile back into place, all except for the smallest crack.

Dr. Crane sweeps back into the room, still irritated from

the interruption. He opens a big black case—like something you'd store weapons in. Only hidden in this one are medical tools and clear bags of tiny white plastic chips (pellets?). And spray cans, I realize, lungs working overtime. Unmarked black cans just like the ones in Dr. Nelson's house. The ones he was using to terrify and torture girls. And next to those, an old, wadded-up piece of burlap.

I didn't notice it at first. I guess I thought it was just a bag. It isn't. Dr. Crane removes it from the case, almost lovingly, and he pulls it over his head. It's the mask. The one the patients were talking about. He's the specter haunting the halls at night. Torturing people within an inch of their sanity. It's just an old feed bag with eyes and a mouth cut into it. It's like something you'd see on a scarecrow on a farm, only painted to look scarier. I thought it would be worse, and I'm not just saying that to seem braver than I am.

King Shark doesn't seem scared either. Though he jerks in his chair when Crane comes closer with a surgical instrument that I think is called a trocar. I remember that Talia once told me King Shark hates needles, and, well, this is kind of like a tiny metal straw or a big effing needle.

The Scarecrow stands over King Shark and inserts the sharp end of the trocar into his arm, under the skin, like placing an IV, except on the top side and not near any veins. He slides the pellet or chip or whatever it is into the part that looks like a straw and then uses a little metal plunger to push the pellet under King Shark's rubbery gray skin.

It doesn't take effect immediately, but the waiting, the knowing, almost makes it worse. It's like watching time-lapse photography—of a plant bursting out of the ground or a sun setting. Only it's horrifying.

I have to swallow down bile when it dawns on King

Shark that he's in a living nightmare. When he jerks at his restraints, trying to get away. When The Scarecrow laughs, a thin, heartless sound with no warmth at all, as he leans closer just to see King Shark squirm.

He puts a ladybug in King Shark's webbed hand.

I wait to see if King Shark will be terrified of that too, but he isn't.

The Scarecrow brings a black recorder the size of a fountain pen to his mouth.

"Crush it," he says.

King Shark does.

CHAPTER 20

Arkham Asylum

I DON'T GET A CHANCE TO TALK TO TALIA AGAIN, DON'T even see her, until Dr. Morales and I meet with her to go over her brain scan results. Not that I'll be doing much talking. I trail behind Dr. M, feeling like I'm about to spontaneously combust.

Through the window to the holding cell, I can see one of the guards standing over Talia. He startles when Dr. Morales opens the door, and he moves away quickly. Talia sits there, smiling in that victorious way she has. And without his body obscuring hers, I see that she's holding a Diet Coke. She takes a sip.

Dr. M eyes the guard sharply. "Did you give her that? You know that's against the rules."

"Hey, I don't know how she got it." He spreads his hands wide, but a faint blush creeps in around his neck.

Dr. Morales rolls her eyes. "Mmm-hmm." She goes to take the can from Talia, but Talia slips it away, turning sideways.

"Hold on. I'm almost finished." She tilts the can as high

as her handcuffs will allow, neck curving like a swan's. I can't help thinking that even in her bright orange prison uniform, she looks like a magazine ad.

She hands the can to Dr. Morales after swallowing the last gulp. "Here you go."

She smiles that Cheshire cat smile again. Dr. Morales takes the can and hands it to the guard with a look that says, *See that it doesn't happen again.*

He makes a hasty retreat, and I sit back in a wooden chair, feeling more than ever like my insides are made of napalm, as Dr. Morales walks Talia through the results.

"I'm concerned that your scans suggest substantial neuro-degeneration for a person your age," Dr. Morales continues. "That means the cells in your brain are dying at a faster rate than they should. And that there's more pathology."

"I know what neurodegeneration means," Talia says shortly.

"Of course." Dr. Morales shuffles the files and scans in front of her. It's weird to see her nervous.

Talia eyes the scans. "So, I have Alzheimer's disease or something?"

Dr. Morales shakes her head. "That's the thing. It's like nothing we've ever encountered."

Talia's face reveals an uncharacteristic amount of emotion. It's almost like a mask falling off. Dr. Morales sees it too. She grapples for something reassuring. "The good news is there's no way Dr. Crane can transfer you now. The evidence is there."

"The bad news is I have brain damage," Talia quips.

"About that, I was wondering: Is there anything you can tell us about your past or your medical history that would help shed some light on these findings?"

Dr. Morales spreads some of the scans out on the table, ready to explain in more detail the changes in the brain that she's referring to.

Talia's nose twitches like she has an itch. She raises her handcuffed hands to her face and moves one of her knuckles under her nose. Then she folds her hands primly in front of her.

"I had a . . . *rough* upbringing," she says. "Nontraditional. Combat training. Martial arts. Weaponry. Explosives. But also exposure to rare toxins. Sleep deprivation. And more. The type of training that prepares you in the event that you are captured."

It is all I can do not to gawk at her, slack-jawed. I can tell Dr. Morales feels the same way, though she's much better at covering it. Talia has never revealed this much about her personal life or her childhood. Ever. Not when I've been present, at least. Even when we talked that time after I broke down crying on my dad's birthday—when I look back on it, I realize she was actually pretty vague on the details about her own father.

"My father taught me a dozen different ways to kill a man by the time I was seven." Talia's mouth twists, like she's agonizing over whether to reveal what she's about to say.

And then it all happens so fast. Talia spits, and her entire body arcs with the motion. Something silver flashes past my left side—toward Dr. Morales. As I turn, it strikes her in the temple.

"And how to knock a man unconscious." Talia says it with a smile.

And I realize there's a Coke tab on the floor next to Dr. Morales's chair. Just as she falls forward with a thump onto the table.

I scoot away from the table in shock. Flash back to when Dr. Morales took the can. Was it missing a tab? "You—you just—"

"Charmed that guard into buying me a drink so I could pull off the tab and disarm Dr. Morales with it? I did." Talia looks entirely too pleased with herself. And entirely too calm.

"You killed her?" I manage to choke out the words.

"I said *disarm*. Though if I'd wanted to kill her, I could have. It would have required the smallest of adjustments."

Are you kidding me? "So then you almost killed her? What if you'd adjusted wrong? What if she had died?"

"I never miss." Talia sits proudly. Confidently.

But what if she had missed? *This* time? My mind spins alternate scenarios, ones where Dr. Morales ended up more than just passed out.

"Could you calm down, please? She's only going to be out for half an hour or so, and we have a lot of things to discuss."

I stutter a nonsense response that she seems to take as permission to continue.

"Tell me what you saw in Crane's lab."

It's a command, not an ask, but this is exactly what I've been dying to talk to her about, so I comply. I tell her about Crane being The Scarecrow. About what happened to King Shark. About what was in the black case.

Talia explains that the little white pellets I saw were solid-state silicon microchips that allow slow, controlled release of The Scarecrow's fear toxin. Only these don't deliver his traditional fear toxin or the sedative–fear toxin drug cocktail from last year. These use fear to control people's minds.

"That's what happened with King Shark," I say. "He couldn't control his own actions. But how does that relate to the Arkham Acres girls? Do you think he's chipped them too? Or that he's planning to?"

"I have reason to believe he's been using blood samples of people dosed with previous iterations of the fear spray to develop these slow-release chips. And that he's testing the chips in some of the Arkham patients as part of a bigger plot."

Something bigger? "What could be worse than what he's already doing?"

"I think there are other players involved. I think they've been kidnapping girls all over the city."

"The trafficking gang," I breathe.

Talia's head snaps up. "You've heard about it."

"A friend of mine. She mentioned something." Bianca. Bianca knew about this months ago, and I had the chance to help her, and I didn't. The guilt churns in my stomach, almost unbearable.

"I want to stop him," says Talia so firmly that I have no doubt that she will. "I could destroy the chips, the lab notebooks, the data, everything. Crane is supposed to be making a delivery of the chips soon, and I think it involves the kidnapped girls. I could protect these girls—I have reason to believe they're being held somewhere."

Again, just like Bianca said. She was willing to risk everything to find them.

"But I need your help."

Now it's my turn to snap to attention. "Me?"

"I've orchestrated the jailbreak to end all jailbreaks, but there's a fatal flaw in my plan. A part I can't do alone."

"The fingerprint scans."

Talia nods. "They have created an additional hurdle. But if you could help me . . ."

A jailbreak. She is asking me to help with an Arkham

Asylum jailbreak. And who knows what else. "I have to think about it."

The disappointment shows on her face. I can't help but feel the sting of it.

"I thought seeing the lab would convince you." She shakes her head. "Well, think quickly, cricket. We don't have much time."

Dr. Morales begins to stir next to me.

"The delivery is happening in two days. The escape is set for tomorrow."

CHAPTER 21

The Call

THIS IS IT. IT ALL COMES DOWN TO THIS MOMENT. THIS choice. Should I do it? Could I potentially trade my entire future for the chance to destroy The Scarecrow's fear chips? I'd need Win's help. And Ivy's. Could I really put them at risk like that? The stakes are so high.

And then there's the IRB investigation. Shouldn't I at least give the pieces Dr. Morales and I put into motion a chance to reveal the truth? She's okay, by the way. She woke up just a couple seconds after Talia told me the escape is set for tomorrow and kind of groggily asked what happened. And then Talia said, "Oh, you dozed off for a second. It was kind of strange. Are you feeling well?" And Dr. M looked at me, and I found myself nodding and covering the metal tab with my foot.

I didn't miss the way Talia smiled at me after I did that. Like she'd already won. I'm still feeling guilty. What if someone saw on one of the cameras? What if Dr. Morales knows deep down that it was more than just nodding off? I can't do what Talia's asking. There are other ways to help that don't involve committing multiple felonies. But why are they all so damn slow?

How does anyone ever decide how they're meant to change the world? It's like you know there's this one way, and it would be guaranteed to make an impact. Eventually. Slowly. *Painstakingly.* Which kind of sucks, but, hey, at least there's a plan and people who have gone before you and succeeded, leaving a bread-crumb path for you to follow.

But then there's another way. One where nothing is certain. Maybe you'll flame out. Crash and burn. Maybe it's just a siren's call tempting you to certain doom. The risk is high, and you can't be sure it's worth taking. And the road that leads there is made of stones that crumble with each step, and maybe you'll make it to the top of the mountain, or maybe the floor is lava and always has been. And when you finally do get to that future—a fragile freaking future—you find it's made of spiderwebs and spun glass. Delicate, lovely, breathtaking things, the stuff of crowns and fairy princesses. But it might be worth it?

After pacing around campus for eleventy billion hours, I still don't know what to do. I tell myself I don't know what to do. That the best thing would be to get some unbiased advice. The first person I call is Bianca. It's how I know I'm lying to myself. Calling Bianca means I've already climbed the mountain and walked to the edge of the cliff. I just need someone to give me a push.

The phone rings and goes to voice mail. I try her again. And text. Look, I don't care how desperate I seem; this is an emergency. I want her to know that she was right about the trafficking gang. And that we may have a way to do something about it. I take my 911 call to Jasmin next. She at least picks up.

"Hello?"

Here goes nothing. "Hey, Jasmin, it's Harleen."

"Hey, what's up?"

She doesn't sound annoyed. That has to be a good sign, right? I pause for so long, she must think the call got dropped.

"Harleen?"

"Yeah, sorry." Why is this so hard? "I was hoping to get your advice. Well, and maybe your help. There's someone at Arkham doing some really nasty stuff, and I have a chance to stop him, but it's complicated. I think he may be the person who was supplying the fear spray to Dr. Nelson last year. And I also think it may have to do with the trafficking gang Bianca was after. I was hoping you and Bianca would want in."

Now it's my turn to wonder if the call got dropped. When Jasmin finally speaks, her voice is made of sharp edges.

"So, when it was Bianca's mission, it was too risky to bring back the Reckoning, but now that it's your mission, it's all cool?"

I suck in a breath. That wasn't the answer I was expecting. Guess I deserve it, though.

"You weren't there for her, Harleen. She needed you."

"I'm really sorry—"

"No, I don't think you understand. That mission you were too good to help with last semester, when Bianca wanted to follow the trafficking gang and take them out? There were too many of them. Bianca got hurt trying to escape. She took a bad fall off a building."

I press the phone closer to my ear. "Ohmygosh, is she okay?"

"She didn't die. She was lucky she wasn't too high up. But she broke her back. The pain's been so bad, they flew her back to Santa Prisca for some experimental treatment."

"I'm so sorry." I can't imagine how painful that must have been. How scary.

"I've actually been pretty furious with you for not coming to visit her in the hospital. But you really didn't know, huh?"

"I swear I didn't." I feel like I should have, though. It's almost worse.

"I know things have been different between us, but if something like that happened to you, I'd be there. I'd like to think you'd be there for me too." Jasmin's usually so even, almost stoic. Hearing the emotion creep into her voice like that cracks my heart in two.

"Of course. I'm just sorry I wasn't there for Bianca." I wish I could afford to fly to Santa Prisca and visit her. As soon as I get through this jailbreak mess, I'll send her an email. Or maybe a letter. She seems like the kind of person who would like getting a letter.

I hang up the phone feeling more confused than ever. If I was calling to look for a push, then finding out about Bianca's accident is like a hook pulling me back, keeping me safe but also scared. Stagnant.

I call Ivy next. I tell her about Talia and the prison break and Dr. Crane and the fear chips. I tell her about Bianca and how she got hurt. I tell her everything. She listens in her quiet, intense Ivy way. Then she asks me a question.

"Does helping Talia feel like the right thing to do?"

"Yes," I say, gripping my phone tight like a lifeline.

"Then, I'm helping you."

"I haven't even told you what I need you to do yet."

"Doesn't matter. We have a pact. You're not doing this on your own."

Her words unlock something in me, and I nearly dissolve

into a puddle of tears. I manage to choke out a "thank you" and explain what her role in the plan will be as I walk across campus to Win's. And then I hang up and knock on his door, wondering how in the world I'm ever going to convince him.

An hour later, and I'm still in Win's dorm room, and I still haven't told him. His room is drafty, and I'm pretty sure his ancient radiator is only one puff away from a timely death. I curl closer to him under the covers, trying to get warm.

"I love you," he whispers into my ear.

"Do you?"

He kisses my shoulder, my neck. "You don't strike me as someone who wants to hear some 'to the moon and back' BS."

"No. Actions are better."

His hand around my waist is desperate, a declaration. "I'd do anything to show you."

I think about why I came here in the first place. "Anything?"

He nods his head against my neck.

And I take a deep breath.

"Win, there's something I need to tell you."

He's wide awake now. Completely alert.

"What is it?"

"Someone at Arkham is doing really bad stuff."

"What do you mean?"

"One of the doctors is developing a technology to control people's minds and they're using the inmates as guinea pigs. I think that's where all the Scarecrow rumors are coming from."

Win gets this concerned, leap-into-action look on his Boy

Scout face. I can see it, even in the dark. "We need to tell someone. Dr. Morales. Or Dr. Cra—"

"No!" I practically shout it. "I mean, no, I don't think we should tell anyone just yet." I hold off on telling him Crane is The Scarecrow. There's a part of me that worries he won't help me if he knows. There's another thing I wonder about—a worse thing—but I keep it chained up in the back of my mind. Don't allow it to take root.

"Well, we can't just sit back and do nothing."

"Talia knows how to stop them." I wince as I say it.

"Talia?" Even in the dark, I can see his nose wrinkle skeptically.

But I'm not second-guessing myself. I've already decided. At least, I think I have.

"I'm going to help her. But I need to borrow your ID badge."

"What for?"

"I need you to swipe me into the restricted wing."

He lets out his breath through his teeth in a low hiss. "I don't know, Harleen. This sounds really dangerous."

"It's the right thing to do."

He gives a sigh, the kind born of love and desolation.

"Let me think about it."

I'm awake long after Win falls asleep. I think about what a contrast it is, telling him versus telling Ivy. She was so in agreement and on the same wavelength—like, instantly—and without any convincing. I try to ignore the way that makes me feel.

Even though I asked them both, had to work to convince

Win, there's a part of me that feels torn in half. Can I trust Talia and are we going to get caught and will I get kicked out of Gotham U and is this going to ruin my chances of ever getting into medical school? I'm not sure whether I'll really know if I can go through with it until it's tomorrow and I'm right in the moment.

And then I get the phone call.

"Harleen?"

The girl on the other end of the line is crying. Her voice is familiar, but I can't quite place it.

"It's Remy," she says, and the puzzle pieces connect inside my head.

"Are you okay?"

I step out into the hallway so I don't wake Win.

Remy can barely get out the words between sobs. "Stella had a heart attack."

The floor dissolves underneath me, and I free-fall to the basement. It's hard to even string words together, but I try. "*What?* But she's so young."

Remy sniffles on the other end of the line. "Something triggered her fear reaction, and it reached a fever pitch she couldn't come down from. She's in the hospital."

"I can get there from campus in thirty minutes. Just let me get dressed." I'm pacing now, a switch flipped, and bam! Action mode. This is all my fault. I knew something bad was happening there, and the legal channels were taking too long. I should have done something.

"They're only letting family see her. They wouldn't even let me go. But. I'm scared." She lowers her voice till it's practically a whisper. "They're supposed to be helping us here, but it seems like a lot of us are getting worse. It feels—I don't know, maybe I'm imagining it, but it feels like there's something big and bad lurking over us. That sounds ridiculous, I know. I'm probably losing it."

I grip my phone so hard I almost break it.

"You're not wrong. And you're not crazy. I'm pretty sure I know who's behind it all. I'm going to fix this. Don't you worry."

I hang up the phone and let the rage flow through me.

Tomorrow, I am going to Arkham Asylum.

Tomorrow, I am ending this.

CHAPTER 22

Arkalamity

THE DAY OF THE JAILBREAK IS HARDEST TO REMEMBER. I put together the pieces as best I can and try to link events to the particular time they happened.

8:00 a.m.

I wake up to a hand on the small of my back. Open one eye to peek at the beautiful boy on the pillow next to me.

Win is already awake, watching me. "Hey, Schmoopie. You sleep okay?"

I nod.

"Today's the day," I whisper.

"Today's the day," he repeats. "Are you sure you want to do this?"

"I'm sure."

2:00 p.m.

Win and I are at Arkham now. Our footsteps echo ominously in the hallway. It's a Saturday, and the place is emptier than usual. But once we're a few yards away from the restricted wing, I pause, just out of range of the security cameras. I can't take him to Dr. Crane's lab without telling him everything. Will he actually believe Crane is the Scarebeast? It's followed by a more harrowing thought: What if he already knows?

I shake my head. Win could never be part of something like that. I turn to him, ready to spill the truth. But then our eyes meet, and I hesitate.

"Oh, thank goodness, you're rethinking the plan too." He rakes his hands through his hair, and I suddenly realize how much he is sweating.

"Ummm . . ."

"I just—I really think there's a good chance we could get arrested or worse. There's got to be another way to stop this from happening. Are you sure I can't tell Dr. Crane?"

My eyes bulge. "Promise me you won't."

He takes a step back, confused by my intensity. "What, why—?"

I grab him by the shirt. "Swear it!"

His eyes dart to the side. Great. I've terrified him. I release my boyfriend.

"I love you," he says. "But sometimes I'm scared of you."

It doesn't hurt as much as it should, because there's a part of me that already knows. "I'm sorry. You—you don't have to do this."

He breathes this huge sigh of relief like he didn't have a choice. Do I do that to him? I think about Ivy—shouldn't he feel like my equal in every way? Am I toxic for him?

"You don't have to do any of this."

Win goes still. "What do you mean?"

"Does this relationship feel like it's tearing you to pieces?" I reach out my hands to him, and he backs away stubbornly.

"People say love is pain. And sacrifice. And compromise."

"Win." I wrap my arms around his neck, and this time he

lets me. "I'm so sorry for dragging you into this. I love you too much to watch what this relationship does to you." I inch backward as I talk, pulling him with me to ensure we stay out of range of the security cameras. "So, here's what we're going to do. You're going to go home with your future intact. And I'm going to go do jailbreak things. And we're going to always carry a special place for each other in our hearts, even if we're not together."

I wait for his reaction, expecting an explosion. Breakups can't happen without weeping and gnashing of teeth, right?

Win looks shell-shocked for a moment as what I'm saying sinks in. But then something shifts behind his eyes. "Okay," he says. It hurts that he looks so awfully relieved. And then his brows knit together. "Is there someone else?"

"No, of course not. Why would you even say that?"

He shakes his head. Can't quite meet my eyes. "She's not what you think."

She? "You mean Pamela? She's not—I mean, we're not—"

My cheeks flush as I say it, even though it's true. Win notices.

"I would have been good to you."

"I know you would." And I would have eaten you alive.

I press my body against his, squeeze him tight in one last hug. Then I watch him walk away toward sunlight and a bright future and the other side of the asylum.

I hold up one hand to wave goodbye.

The other is behind my back, holding his badge.

4:00 p.m.

I counted to two hundred after Win left, and then I went to the office suite where I work for Dr. Morales. I started drafting the introduction section for the paper about Talia. See? Just an enthusiastic intern coming in on a Saturday because of her devotion to science. I work on some computer modeling next—it's something I've been teaching myself. With Talia's unusual brain pathology, I thought it would be cool to develop a model that calculates brain age based on scans. I've fed hundreds of scans to my model, teaching it how to estimate brain ages and then testing it on scans from control brains and brains with neurodegenerative diseases like Alzheimer's to see if it works. And so far it has! The people with the neurodegenerative brains are estimated to have an older brain age than the people with typical brains. I sigh. I'm so proud of my deep-learning robot child.

And then I give it Talia's brain scans. Moment of truth . . .

One hundred and fifty years old. Crap, there must be something wrong with the model. I'm just thinking about how I might try to tweak it, when a text comes through from Sophie.

Sophie: Want to go out tonight?

Harleen: Can't. At Arkham working on a paper

Sophie: Boo.

I don't get back to work on the paper, though. My phone reads 4:00 now, and you better believe we synchronized our watches. It's time.

I close the door to the office suite and consider shoving a chair under the handle for good measure but decide it would raise suspicions. I hop up onto my desk. I'm wearing one of those small hiking backpacks that move with you like part of your body. It was sitting on my desk in my dorm room when I got home from Win's this morning. (I have zero idea how Talia pulled that off, but I'm impressed.) I unzip the bag and pull out a headlamp.

The ceiling rains down flecks of white dust like ash when I move one of the tiles. It tickles my nose, makes me sneeze. I climb up into the ceiling and put the tile back where it was, marking it with a glow stick.

I've studied the maps that were tucked in the front pocket of the bag. As long as I don't fall through a ceiling tile and die, this should be super easy. I click on my headlamp. It's just like walking a balance beam, I tell myself. If the beam was an entire story off the ground. And you had the floor of the next level pressing down on you so you had to walk like a bear. And you were surrounded by dust and spiderwebs and possibly mice.

I slither and slip through the space above the ceiling, counting my steps and left turns and right turns, trying not to let myself get spooked when there are voices underneath me. Eventually, I reach the corner I'm looking for. It's clear I've come to the end of the regular lab and office space—I've hit a cement-block wall. I carefully balance on a wooden crossbeam as, breath held, I lift up the ceiling tile and . . .

Bingo.

I'm hovering over the corner of a hallway—the bit just in front of the door to the restricted wing, if I'm being specific. There's a camera attached to the wall directly underneath me, but in the time between when Win and I were here and now, someone has blacked it out with spray paint. *Talia must have people everywhere,* I think. Something about that realization makes me shiver.

I swipe Win's card and punch in his number—his birthday, bless his heart; I saw him enter it one time—feeling mildly guilty when the little light turns green. There are no cameras on the restricted wing (Dr. Crane doesn't want anyone to see what he gets up to, I bet). Still, I can't shake the feeling I'm being watched. I clip through the hallway, arms tensed, ready for a fight. I use Win's card to swipe into Dr. Crane's lab—the regular one, not the secret one. It's empty today. Lights off. Experiments waiting. Empty labs are like cemeteries. Or old churches. The light streams through the windows in a way that feels significant.

I pick the lock to Crane's examination room, a regular lock for a regular metal key. If I hadn't escaped the secret lab that time with King Shark, I wouldn't know where to look. As it is, I can barely find it. I walk around the exam room, past the chairs and the stereotypical therapy couch, investigating the file cabinets and the whiteboard on one particular wall. Run my fingers down the side of a cabinet, feeling the smoothness of the metal. Then something changes. There's a slot in the side, a card reader you wouldn't notice unless you knew what to look for. Win's card isn't going to work on this one. One, and only one, card opens the secret lab. But there's more than one way to light a firework.

I pull a balloon out of my backpack and a tiny canister of helium. Did you know you can use balloons to set off sensors and open doors? I didn't until Talia told me. Apparently, most auto-lock doors have an ingress (enter) and egress (exit) side, so you may have to swipe your card or scan your retina to get in, but not when you leave. There's a motion sensor at the top of the door that sees you coming and trips the lock to let you go. So, you could concoct elaborate eyeball-stealing schemes or be an expert-level hacker with a genius IQ . . . or you could just bring a balloon.

The fingerprint doors they installed are swipe in *and* swipe out. Let's hope this door isn't the same.

I slide the balloon under the door (it's clear, and I've filled it with red and black glitter confetti, not that it matters). I keep the neck on my side of the door, so I can put the lip around the nozzle of the helium canister. Open the tank. Let the balloon fill. Since I can't see it filling, I have to guess when to close the tank. I think I did it right. I tie a knot in the balloon and wrap a string around it, unspooling it so that it travels up, up, up toward the sensor.

A hiss and a click. And then. The whiteboard slides toward me.

I'm in.

4:30 p.m.

I had hoped there would be more smashing involved. Planting viruses that cause destruction on a local and cloud level and deleting files and shredding schematics just isn't as much fun. I do get to light some lab notebooks on fire in a trash can (science sacrilege!!!), which gives me a nice fizzy feeling in my veins, but honestly, I'm starting to feel restless. I grab the briefcase of fear chips. Talia said to bring them to her so she could destroy them personally. Apparently, it's more complicated than simply smashing them repeatedly.

I think of the girls at Arkham Acres, my friends in the Reckoning too, Kylie-Stella-Bernice-Remy. She's lucky I don't have my baseball bat.

4:50 p.m.

Dr. Morales opens the door just as I hop down from replacing the ceiling tile.

"Harleen, hi. I thought I heard someone in here."

"Hey!" I throw on a big, bright (hopefully innocent) smile. "I was just working on the case study paper. I've been having trouble finding time during the week."

Luckily, I left the helium canister and the briefcase full of fear chips in the ceiling. Yeesh.

"Well, that's wonderful," says Dr. Morales. It feels wrong

that she's impressed with me when I'm lying to her. "How's it going?"

Now that she mentions it . . .

"The model I was working on is having some issues. It thinks Talia's brain is one hundred and fifty years old."

"Huh. Well, I'll be honest, deep learning isn't my forte, but I can reach out to some colleagues if that would be helpful." She ponders it further, tapping her chin. "Her scans do appear to come from a brain that is extremely old. And the pattern is so strange. But one hundred and fifty?" She shakes her head. "It doesn't make sense, but I'll think about it some more."

"Thanks," I say. "And, yeah, any help you could get me would be fantastic."

I practically collapse against the door after she leaves. Holee-Clusterfolee, that was close. Thank goodness she didn't think the black backpack was weird. Or notice any of the ceiling dust sprinkled on my desk. I wait a few minutes, listening for her office door to close, for the sound of her footsteps trailing down the hallway. Then I pack a manila folder with every bit of information we have on the case study. And I decide that what I really need is the vending machines with the good chocolate.

Do you know how hard it is to simultaneously walk and eat a chocolate bar and hold a massive file of charts and notes and papers? Okay, honestly, not that hard. But it *looks* hard, and that's what counts. Because when you trip as you're passing Talia al Ghūl's cell, and the papers scatter in every direction like feral children, no one could possibly blame you for taking a long time to pick them up.

"I've destroyed everything," I tell Talia in a low voice as I bend over to pick up a scan of her brain. "Data. Schematics. Notebooks. All that's left is the chips themselves."

I keep my eyes trained on the papers. Don't want to look suspicious.

"Excellent work. Who knows how many lives you've saved."

I focus on not reacting when Talia answers. It's surprisingly hard not to turn your head when someone talks to you.

"You know the rest of the plan," she continues. "Wait until it's time. And then bring me the chips."

"I could just destroy them," I say, picking up another sheet of paper with excruciating slowness. "If I—"

"No!" Talia says it like a command.

I feel myself flinch, despite how careful I'm trying to be. "I thought destroying the chips was the plan."

"We could destroy them. But think about how much we could change this city if we *used* them. Not on innocent girls but on Gotham City's elite. We could bring this entire city crashing in on itself."

Suddenly, it all makes sense. I'm embarrassed I didn't figure it out sooner. Keep it together. Just for a few more minutes, Harleen. I finish picking up the papers, faster now. I need to get out of here.

"Harleen?"

I stand up straight with my folder. Don't answer.

"Harleen!"

I don't even think about turning my head as I walk off down the hallway. Did she know what she wanted me to do even when I was crying in the hallway that time and she comforted me? Was that all part of her master plan to get the chips?

I shake my head. She's been using me this whole time.

It wasn't just a jailbreak. It was a heist.

5:25 p.m.

I barely manage to deposit the papers on my desk before I keel over and the panic sets in. I am reeling. Talia's betrayal feels like being torn in half. I looked up to her. Talia was a mentor. A mother figure. A future I thought I could have.

I call Ivy, frantic. Spill the whole horrible story to her in one breath.

"I don't know what to do," I say, tearful.

"I'll help you however you want." And I knew she was going to say it, but still, hearing it makes me feel like she's wrapped me in a warm blanket. "Do you want me to meet you early? At the place where we're supposed to meet. We could talk?"

"There's nothing I want more."

Ten minutes later, I'm walking out the back door of Arkham Asylum and into the woods that surround the facility like a fairy-tale forest where terrible things befall bad little children. Ivy meets me at the fence that marks the end of the property. She was going to use her powers to rip holes in it with plants as part of the escape plan. Maybe still is. I don't know. I have no idea what to do about anything.

"Are you okay?" asks Ivy, her windblown red hair wilder than usual.

I rush toward her, even though there's a chain-link fence rising fifteen feet tall between us.

"I don't know if I can go through with it."

She waits. Quietly. Thinking. Knowing I'm not done.

"Talia says she has a way of destroying the chips so that they can't be replicated. But letting Talia go means giving her a weapon to unleash chaos on the city. And to control all the rich people." People like you. If I hadn't met Ivy, would

I still be so horrified by the idea? I try not to think about it. There are bigger issues at hand. "But if I don't help Talia escape, I'm basically handing the keys to The Scarecrow to do whatever horrific thing he's concocted. Because even if I destroy the chips myself, and even if there aren't backup files somewhere (which there totally could be!), Talia has the best chance of anyone of stopping the trafficking gang. If I don't let her go . . ."

Stella. Remy. Kylie. All those other girls. Bianca broke her back trying to find them. Helping them, avenging them—siding with Talia would be worth it, wouldn't it? I look into Ivy's warm green eyes, and I whisper the thing I'm most afraid of.

"I've been trying so hard to be like Dr. Morales. But I worry deep down I'm Talia."

Ivy grasps the fence with her hands. "Hey. Don't worry about choosing between them. Choose yourself. You're the bravest, most brilliant person I know. And you're fearless. When the moment comes, you'll know what to do. I believe in you."

It feels like a declaration of love. It's so different from what happened with Win. Always sweet, but always second-guessing me. I love the way I look through Ivy's eyes. I love Ivy.

HOLY CRAP, I'M IN LOVE WITH IVY.

And Ivy loves me too. At least, I think she does. Hope she does.

I clasp her hands through the fence. I swear, I would rip it apart with my bare hands just to be with her. She laces her fingers through mine. Leans so close that her forehead rests against the fence. She feels it too.

I lean in to kiss her.

And I wait. (No. Not then. I mean now. Where is the rest of this memory? Where is me kissing Ivy? Melting into her sweet lips until I feel positively dizzy. Feeling fireworks so big they could rip the sky in half. ARE YOU FREAKING KIDDING ME RIGHT NOW, AMNESIA???)

Amnesia is not kidding.

Apparently, she's kind of a cruel mistress. With a penchant for sadism. And making people imagine life-changing kisses a thousand different ways as some sort of divine torture.

I bet it was good, though.

6:45 p.m.

An alarm blares, piercing the sky like lightning.

"I have to go!" I call to Ivy.

Three minutes. There are three entire minutes I can't account for. DO YOU KNOW HOW MUCH KISSING YOU CAN DO IN THREE MINUTES?

I rush back inside Arkham. Up the stairs and down the corridors to the intern office. I repeat what Ivy told me like a mantra. *Choose me. Choose me.* Don't worry about Talia or—

Him.

The Scarecrow waits for me at the end of the hallway, turning the corner at just the right moment, so no matter how much I'd like to pivot and run in the other direction, it's too late. I skid to a stop in front of him, my body bending, fingers trailing the floor. He towers over me in that burlap mask. Tall and lithe and monstrous and diabolical. The stuff of ghost stories and nightmares and footsteps creaking in empty rooms.

His eyes barely show through the crudely carved holes, but I don't miss the flicker of recognition there. Don't miss the fact that the hallway he came from leads to the secret lab.

He knows the data has been destroyed. Knows someone stole his briefcase.

And now he knows that someone is me.

I try not to let my eyes flick in the direction of the intern office suite. If he so much as suspects that's where I've hidden the briefcase, it doesn't matter that it's still in the ceiling. He will tear the room apart until he finds it.

I can't let him get to those chips. If he takes them back, he wins. I shift my weight from foot to foot. A bandolier of unmarked black cans ripples down the front of his faded leather shirt. My chest tightens at the sight. It's the same spray that killed Kylie. Could kill me in minutes, maybe even seconds. If he sprayed me with enough of it.

Focus, Harleen. Make a plan. Do I try to juke around him? Slip through his legs?

I try to pump-fake and tear off in the other direction, but I never had a chance.

He sprays me directly in the face with fear spray.

6:55 p.m.

I'm running and I'm running, but it's already too late. The most dangerous predators of all don't chase you. Did you know that? Because they know you're already dead.

"There are different kinds of screams—have you ever noticed?" he calls in a hollow voice. I can hear his footsteps in the hallway, pursuing me, walking briskly but not bothering to go any faster. "The glee when you hit that first drop on a roller coaster. A scream of pain when a bone snaps in half. And then there are screams of abject terror. The ones that happen just before you go mad."

I can feel the terror setting in. The toxin coursing through my veins like a scalding-hot darkness. I'm too far away from my office and the fear chips. I'm not going to make it.

Talia's cell is closer.

7:10 p.m.

The Scarecrow hovers over me, sometimes with the face of a monster and sometimes my dad and sometimes Dr. Nelson and sometimes Kylie—dead and hollow and rotting and beautiful.

"Where did you put them?" he growls, mealworms crawling from his eyes and nose and mouth, darkness radiating off him in waves.

I open my mouth. I think I open my mouth. I want to tell him, *I don't know.* All that comes out is a scream.

He sighs, body sagging against the wall for a moment, almost like he's savoring it.

"I like to think of myself as a connoisseur of screams. Tasting each one on my tongue for notes of panic and revulsion. Horror and trauma and pleasure." He leans closer to me, and I think I stop breathing. "Yours are lovely."

His hand turns into my dad's, and he grabs me by my overalls and throws me down the hallway, only it's not like any of the other corridors in the asylum.

Because now I'm in the Attic.

This is how you get there—didn't you know?

The spray takes you there. All this time, and that was all I had to do. Take the spray. Be his prey.

HahahahahaHAHAHAHAHHAHA.

It's in your mind. Don't you get it? THE ATTIC IS IN YOUR MIND.

Under and never. Spring to and right. Open and closed. Wandering and lost.

The Scarecrow steps closer.

"I want those chips. It doesn't have to be this way, my dear."

His skinny foot stomps down next to me. The walls close in, and he picks me up by the front of my shirt.

"Scream for me, my dear."

And I do.

7:13 p.m.

It's so small in here, and it's getting smaller, the walls and the floor and the ceiling and the fear, pressing in on all sides. Breaking my bones and my teeth and my skull. Crushing until there's nothing left.

There's nothing left! Stop it, there's nothing left!

I can't tell where the shrieks are coming from.

I'm not a person, just a collection of nerve endings. My heart is a shorted-out battery. My mind is one long scream.

But my hand is still a hand. And I watch it swipe Win's card through the reader on Talia's cell.

7:20 p.m.

My dad is dragging me down the hallway, ready to throw me in the bathtub with Pop-Tarts and a blanket and leave me there until I'm dead. I blink, wishing the nightmare would go away. Wishing I could wake up.

I blink again, and it's Talia. Only now she's got the head of a demon, and she's dragging me down this hallway. The Scarecrow isn't chasing me anymore. I think she did something to him. I think I'm next.

I try to fight her off, but she hisses at me with a snake's tongue and tightens her arm around me like a vise.

We're still at Arkham. No, my apartment growing up. No, the Attic. No, trapped inside Kylie's coffin. And the walls change and the monsters change and Talia changes. I scream until my throat is ragged, and she puts a knife to my throat and tells me to be quiet.

She drags me across the yard toward a nightmare forest. And suddenly Ivy is there, and I feel a split second of relief, but then she turns into a witch and tears apart a fence with her magic plants. I'm fading in and out. I remember being strapped to a motorcycle. Hell and Gotham City whipping by in flashes. And there are blue lights and monsters, but I can't tell if they're after us or if it's my imagination.

Everything turns to darkness after that.

7:55 p.m.

The next thing I know Talia is stabbing a giant needle into my neck. I try to scream, but I don't have any voice left. We're in a place that smells like fire and brimstone, and there are ghouls around us with rusty nails for teeth and a shark-monster and a leprechaun and a killer clown from outer space and and and—

I'm fairly certain they all want to kill me. Even when I see that the leprechaun is The Riddler and the shark-monster is King Shark and the ghouls are just Talia's henchmen (henchpeople?). Is it just me, or did the effects of this fear spray get a heck of a lot lighter? Things are still pretty trippy, though. There are pink and blue dots floating around the warehouse (I think I'm in a warehouse?), and The Joker is acting like a cat. I blink and shake my head. The dots go away, but The Joker is still licking the back of his hand and wiping his hair with it, so I'm not out of the woods yet.

Wait. Nope. Pretty sure that's actually happening.

Talia holds a hand in front of my face. "How many fingers?"

"Um, two?"

Her mouth spreads into a relieved smile. "Hey, you answered this time. And you're not screaming anymore."

"Yeah, but I still think The Joker's a cat."

"Oh, no, that part's real. Apparently, he called The Scarecrow a 'one-note,' and Crane decided to inject him with a mind-control chip and tell him that he's a cat. Which reminds me." She gestures to some of her crew. "Hey, let's get them de-chipped." The Joker slinks over to her and starts rubbing his head against her calf and mewling. "Sooner rather than later."

I realize I'm lying on my back on a metal gangplank in a huge factory-type building, and there are vats of chemicals all around me, bubbling like a witch's brew. The fear continues to wash over me in waves that ebb and flow. Tense-tense-tense. Stop. Tense-tense-tense. Relief. But I'm able to make out a sign on the wall: ACE CHEMICALS. And watch as Talia deftly removes a chip from The Joker using a pair of forceps.

He comes to right in the middle of attempting to cough up a hairball and appears perplexed as to why he is on all fours with his back arched.

Police sirens blare outside. For us? For someone else. He doesn't wait around.

"That's my cue!" He hops onto a chain connected to a pulley and slides down, laughing all the way.

Talia throws his chip into some bubbling green chemical waste, and it disappears with a hiss-fizz.

"I don't want Crane to be able to use them to replicate new chips," she tells me. "And I truly do think using the chips is wrong unless you're using them the way I intend to—the end justifies the means there."

I don't answer. Still don't feel myself enough to stand up.

Talia removes chips from The Riddler and Two-Face. Apparently, a couple of her henchpeople were rushing in as we were escaping and managed to free multiple people. Sometime after I swiped Win's card through Talia's door. And she knocked The Scarecrow unconscious. And I showed her the location of the briefcase. Not that I actually remember any of that from my fear-induced stupor. Talia bends over King Shark next. But before she can remove the last chip from the last Super-Villain, The Scarecrow appears at the other end of the gangplank.

He mutters some words into his remote.

And King Shark turns on her.

8:05 p.m.

You would think that a petite woman with perfect hair would be no match for a colossal half shark. You would be wrong.

King Shark snaps his jaws at Talia's arm, and I expect to see a hand missing and blood spurting everywhere, like in a horror movie. But she must have whipped her arm back faster than I could see it, because she's using that same arm to punch him in the nose. Repeatedly. (Well, that *is* what they said to do in all my elementary school shark books.)

He plunges to the side with an angry gurgle, snapping at her again. She manages to escape this time too, only she drops the case. And without thinking, I rush to pick it up. I hurry toward the blinking exit signs, the ones on the opposite side of the warehouse from The Scarecrow.

"Stop her!" yells Talia.

I glance over my shoulder as I run. Watch her free herself from King Shark and leave him to her goons. Grab on to a thick metal chain and kick a lever and ride it all the way—

HOLY CRAP, HOW DID SCARECROW GET IN FRONT OF ME?!

"Hand me the case, my dear. This doesn't have to hurt."

My chest goes tight, heart pounding, some kind of residual effect of the fear spray or memories of what happened between us at Arkham clawing their way in. Is this what Stella and Remy feel like all the time?

I turn to run in the opposite direction, but Talia is already behind me.

"Harleen, there's no good way out of this. We need to work together."

The Scarecrow darts in and hits her with a burst of fear spray, but he darts back out just as quickly. He's smart. Knows he doesn't have a chance at beating her hand to hand. But this spray—I've seen what it does to people. With Talia incapacitated—

Talia is not incapacitated. In fact, she has just started laughing. At first I wonder if it's some weird effect of the fear spray, but then she's all, "I grew up on this stuff. There's nothing you can do to me that my father hasn't done already."

I don't know what in the frozen hell that means, but I don't have time to think about it, because Talia and The Scarecrow are circling me like sharks.

I freeze, stuck between them, clutching the case of mind-control chips to my chest. Should I give the case to Talia? Try to get past both of them so I can take it back to Arkham and turn it in to the police? Or to Dr. Morales? Because that's the real question. Dr. Morales versus Talia. Win versus Ivy. The striving, ravenous perfectionist in me versus my other side. Hot blood in my ears and desire in my belly and the singing feeling I get in my veins when I do something even I hadn't planned on. Vengeance and fire and power/rage/impulse.

Talia and The Scarecrow jolt closer at the same time, desperate for the chips. I react without thinking, leaping onto the railing behind me.

"Stop!" I yell.

They skid to a stop on either side of me. The sight of me

and the chips suspended over a giant vat of toxic waste is enough to make The Scarecrow swear and Talia suck in her breath with a hiss. The skinny black bar I'm standing on is thinner than a balance beam. More slippery too, with the condensation from the chemicals below. I use the strength in my core and every second of gymnastics training I've ever had to keep myself upright.

One misstep, one push—and I'm falling fast.

My body tenses, and for a brief moment I wonder if I'll survive this.

PART II

CHAPTER 23

People I Don't Recognize

I SIT UP IN THE HOSPITAL BED, FEELING LIKE MY BRAIN IS made of wet cement, tapping my pen against the journal. I wish I could remember more. I have all these vivid memories of childhood and high school and stuff. But when I try to think about what it was like starting at Gotham U last fall, everything just goes . . . blank. On the upside, it doesn't hurt my hands to write. (The gauze gloves had me kind of worried about what might be hiding underneath.) Footsteps echo up the hallway, slowing when they reach my door. I look up—a reflex. And, oh.

There is a girl in my doorway, green eyes searing into me, red hair falling to her waist. I don't remember her, but I wish like hell I did.

"You're awake!" Her voice sounds like hope made real.

She dashes to my bedside. I wonder if she's the person who's been sleeping in the blue blanket nest on the couch. And then she hesitates.

Is she going to ask me something? Explain how the heck I got here? Kiss me?

I wait, trying to be patient, but honestly just wanting whatever it is to happen already.

She opens her mouth. "Harleen—"

"Ohthankgoodness, you're awake." A boy—a sturdy, handsome Eagle Scout to end all Eagle Scouts, the friendly-eyed boy from my phone—runs across the hospital tiles and wraps me in a hug. "I'm so glad you're okay. I'm so sorry, Schmoopie. If anything had happened to you—"

He freezes like he's suddenly embarrassed by his public display of affection. Clears his throat and holds on to the bedrail like it'll keep him from tackle-hugging me again. Or like he's hanging on for dear life. He has a jaw you could cut stone with, and his eyes search mine like he's hoping to find forgiveness there. Apparently, he's my boyfriend. He's not what I would have pictured. Neither is . . . Schmoopie. My eyes flick to the red-haired girl. I wasn't sure if . . .

She makes this tightly pinched face like I smell bad and also she hates me.

Nope. Definitely not.

"I was so scared you weren't going to wake up," says Eagle Scout, this time more quietly. Evenly. He takes my gauze-wrapped hand and doesn't let go, and I stare at it, at his strong hand covering my small one.

It would be really great if I could remember his name. I keep looking—at his muscular arms and his kind eyes—waiting for something to happen. A spark of memory to burst into flame. Something. *Anything.* And the more seconds that pass, the more scared I get. What if I'm stuck like this?

My eyes dart back and forth between them.

His brows furrow in concern. "Harleen?"

"I'm sorry," I say, feeling small in my hospital bed. "I don't remember you."

He looks crushed. I can see it in the way his smile droops and his eyebrows scrunch upward. It reminds me of a puppy making a begging face even though your plate is already empty.

The red-haired girl turns her face to the wall real quick. Wiping her nose. Pretending to wipe her nose?

I can't help but cringe. "And I don't remember you either."

The ghost of a smile disappears from her face. "At all?"

I shake my head, feeling my heartbeat speed up but also HEARING my heartbeat speed up because there's a monitor to let everyone in the room know exactly how anxious I am right now, which is just super helpful.

I stare her right in the face and try, really try, like hamster-running-full-tilt-on-the-little-wheel-in-your-brain level of trying. I'm rewarded with a brief flash of me setting my lunch tray down in front of her in a dining hall. Also a headache.

"Ow." I rub my temple. "Thinking hurts."

Before I can torture my brain any further, a woman who has to be my doctor breezes in with a nurse trailing her. Not the same nurse as before. Hey! I remembered!! The new nurse has curly blond hair, and she flinches when she sees my face. That's funny. My hand automatically goes to my cheek on the side without the gauze, checks the outline of my nose. I don't *feel* like my face got mangled during whatever it was that sent me here.

The doctor is tall, with a sleek black bob. The kind of person who is always moving. She clears her throat, and the nurse stops gawking. I like her already.

She holds out a thin hand. "Ms. Quinzel. Hi. I'm Dr. Viswanathan. It's good to see you awake."

I have about a billion questions threatening to pour out of me, but it's hard to concentrate on where to start, so instead I just say, "Thank you."

She puts her stethoscope to my chest and asks me to take deep breaths. "Your vitals are looking much better," she says. "But you've been through a terrible ordeal. How are you feeling?"

Eagle Scout stays by my bedside, but he pulls out his phone, almost as if he senses my discomfort and he wants to give me a measure of privacy. Red perches on the couch next to the blanket—so it was her!

I shrug. "Okay?" There was so much pain before, the kind your brain tries to hide the memory of as a way of protecting you. (I think I remember learning about that in one of my classes.) It's mostly gone now, though. Now there are other things to worry about.

"Valentina said you were experiencing some gaps in your memory."

"Yeah." *Some gaps.* That's a nice way of saying I don't recognize my own boyfriend.

"Related to the accident?"

I shoot guilty glances at Eagle Scout and Red. "And other stuff."

"Oh." Her tone is compassionate, but it can't mask her interest. She pulls a wheely stool over to my bedside, making a problem-solving face. "Can you tell me your full name?"

I don't have to try. It just pops into my head. "Harleen Frances Quinzel."

Whew. At least I'm not totally hopeless. Though knowing your own name is maybe not an aspirational benchmark.

Dr. Viswanathan makes a mark on her clipboard. "Do you know what year it is?"

"Yes." I cross my arms as I tell her, and this makes her laugh.

"I'm just making sure. It seems like you have at least

some form of amnesia, likely brought on by your accident. A concussive injury or perhaps the trauma of the accident itself. We didn't find any brain damage in the preliminary scans we did while you were out, so it's more likely the latter. We typically see patients with trauma-induced amnesia recover much of their memories in days to weeks or sometimes months. I'd like to see where the boundaries are and help you get what we can of your memory back." She pauses. "What can you tell me about the accident?"

Eagle Scout's been playing with his phone, but now his hands freeze, and Red leans forward on her couch. I scrape the dark corners of my brain for some scrap of what happened. Something was coming. Something bad. That damn heart monitor starts beeping faster again. Falling-falling-falling. And then pain.

I shake my head like a dog trying to get water out of its ears. "Nothing. I mean, I remember falling, but that's it. Nothing besides that." Is it just me, or do they look relieved?

Dr. Viswanathan frowns. "I'll be honest—we don't know much about what happened. One of the night nurses said he found you leaning against the doors to the ER. There was a bag sitting next to you." She gestures to a small black camping backpack on the side table next to us and a plastic bag containing what I assume were the contents. "You were barely conscious, definitely not coherent."

I try to remember getting to the ER. All I've got is a glimmer of what happened once I was already there. Hands strapping me down. The flash of fluorescent lights passing overhead like buildings outside a train. And . . . nothing after that. I wish I could remember who left me.

"You were covered in some kind of chemical," she continues, eyes kind. The sort of pity that feels more like understanding than unwanted charity. "Something toxic. Chemical waste, most likely. An acid, perhaps?" She hesitates. "Most of your body was covered in burns."

My gauze-y Madonna gloves suddenly feel a lot more sinister. My mind spins horror stories about what my hands look like underneath them, until I start to feel dizzy. *It's fine,* I tell myself. *Whatever it is, I'm going to be fine.*

But when she moves to touch the gauze covering my face, I want to shrink away. I force myself to hold strong. Still as a statue. I close my eyes as she peels away the gauze. It stings, but that's to be expected, right? I can't smell anything, at least. And I don't feel like I'm oozing or anything. I'm sure those are all very good signs.

"You're healing remarkably quickly," Dr. V tells me.

See?

But then Dr. V grabs a mirror, and I can't help but gulp. How do you prepare yourself for something when you have absolutely no idea? Should I expect massive facial scarring? Gaping wounds? A third eye growing out of my cheek?

She holds the mirror in front of my face, and what I see makes me gasp. My skin is the palest white. Like sugar and starlight. Or a drowning victim. There's only one other person in the world I know of with skin like this.

"Looks like I'll be wearing SPF one million from now on, huh?" I joke because I don't like the way everyone is staring at me in horror.

They can all shut their mouths, quite frankly. I expected it to be a lot worse. Skin puckered and warped from burns, or maybe even missing entirely. A mangled eyebrow at the very least.

But even so, seeing my reflection—it shakes me. Someone did this to me. Someone doused me in chemicals and dropped me on the front steps of the hospital. And I can't even go after them because I can't remember who did it or why. I keep myself from smashing the mirror against the roll bars on my bed, but only just.

My hands are the same underneath the gauze gloves. Dr. Viswanathan says I've healed enough that I don't have to wear them anymore. I wonder if my whole body is like this. Is *his* whole body like this?

"I'm being called to surgery, but I'll check in again after that. Until then"—she hands me the plastic bag full of handbag detritus—"why don't you look through your things, maybe some photos on your phone, and see if they spark anything. And don't worry: it may take time, and that's okay. But I want you to start trying to piece together what you can, because the police will be by to ask you questions at some point."

My eyes widen. Did I do something? What the heck happened that night? It doesn't escape my notice that Red and Eagle Scout are getting all squirrelly again. Doesn't escape my doctor's notice either.

"Do either of you know anything about how she ended up like this?" she asks more than a bit sharply.

"No!" blurts the boy in the most obvious knee-jerk panic response of all time.

"Yeah, nope. Me neither." Red says it coolly, but I know she's lying too.

But that's the thing about lying. There are little white lies and catastrophic lies. Lies to save a friend and lies to bury them. But how do you know which kind of lie it is if you don't have enough memories of a person to trust your own judgment?

"Maybe that's for the best." Dr. Viswanathan continues

to stare them down with a gaze that I'm sure glad isn't directed at me. "It might be helpful for Harleen to recover her memories on her own. Without any intrusion of bias from other people."

Before she can say anything else, someone calls her name from the hallway.

"Be right there," she calls back. She places her hand over mine and squeezes (gently). "Take care, Harleen."

She disappears with a snap of her white coat.

And I'm left in a room with two people I don't know and no idea what to expect from the police.

CHAPTER 24

Alone with Her

"SORRY, BUT I HAVE TO LEAVE SOON TOO," MY BOYFRIEND (Winfield, I've learned his name is) tells me, squeezing my hand. "I have a class at ten o'clock."

"That's okay." I try to seem like a kind and easygoing girlfriend, when, honestly, I still don't remember the guy, so he might as well be a very ripped mannequin taking up space in my hospital room. "And, um, I'm sorry I can't remember you're my boyfriend. I'm sure it'll come back soon."

"Oh!" He drops my hand with a thump, and then his eyes bulge like he's worried he hurt me. "I'm not—I mean, it's okay if—" He stutters along until he catches Red narrowing her eyes at him. And then something in his face hardens. "I just mean to say that I'm not trying to rush you. We dated for four months, so I'm sure it'll come back. And I'm happy to help however you need." His eyes flick to Red again. "Don't you need to go too?"

She smiles like she's won something. "I don't have class on Fridays."

He hesitates, almost like he doesn't want to leave me

alone with her. Because she knows things about him? Because she's dangerous? She feels dangerous.

"If you need anything at all, call me, and I can come back, okay?" He directs these words at me like I'm the only person in the room.

"Okay." I smile at him, and wow, he must really like smiles, because his whole face lights up.

I watch him leave, and can I just say? I'm not mad at his butt.

Red clears her throat.

I turn. She's scary-gorgeous, in a nineties-grunge kind of way. Bitten red lips and lilac eye shadow and a tiny green T-shirt under overalls. I try not to stare.

The silence expands between us like a canyon, but I'm not having it because (A) I feel compelled to know her (or, well, to know how I know her) and (B) I am getting sick and tired of knowing nothing about anything. So I hold out my hand like we're meeting for the first time, and I say, "Hi! I'm Harleen! How do we know each other?"

She startles, surprised at my bluntness, which, hello, DOES SHE EVEN KNOW ME?

No, really. I'd like her to answer that. In detail, preferably.

"We're friends," she says. Only there was the tiniest pause between the words *we're* and *friends.* Just a fraction of a second, but there are entire universes' worth of subtext living in that pause—I'm sure of it.

Before I can think on it any further, she says, "I'm Pamela. Pamela Isley."

"Pamela," I say, testing the name out on my tongue. Something about it doesn't fit, but I don't know why.

She moves from the couch to the seat beside my bed. "You really don't remember anything about what happened?"

"No." But let me tell you how great it is having people ask me that. Repeatedly.

She nods and takes a deep breath like her lungs weren't working before and they only just now remembered how.

I fix her with my eyes. "Do *you* know anything?"

Again with the startle reflex. Pamela opens her mouth. And closes it. And opens it again. "I'm not sure I should tell you." I must be making a terrible face because she rushes to explain. "Well, you heard what Dr. Viswanathan said. And, you know what, I think she's right. It's just . . . a lot went down that day. That whole month, really. I don't think you should listen to anyone's version of the story but your own. There are people who wouldn't be honest with you."

Her eyes go to the door, tracing the path where Winfield left minutes earlier. *Him?!* Interesting. I thought he was a total golden retriever, but maybe he's hiding some darkness under that shaggy brown hair.

Though maybe that's not what he's actually like. How do I tell the difference between what's real and what are just stories I'm telling myself to fill in the gaps?

I scoot closer to Pamela and give her my best pleading eyes. "But that's why I need your help. *Please.*"

Please, please, please. I really need to remember something beyond moving into my dorm room last fall. And I don't know if there's something inside me making me trust her or if it's just that she's ridiculously stunning and her hair smells like wintergreen berries and fresh snow, but I want her to tell me everything she knows.

Her mouth purses sympathetically. She's thinking about it.

I grab her hand. "C'mon."

WRONG. Wrong thing to do. Pamela snatches her hand back like I've burned her. Runs her thumb over the skin on her knuckles like she's trying to wipe me off or something. Cool, cool. I've always wanted hot girls to regard me as something on the level of flesh-eating bacteria.

"Pamela—" I start to say, but she's standing now, probably to get farther away from me.

But, no. Her face is calmer. Less startled. Less pinched. She picks up the plastic bag full of my belongings.

"Here," she says, practically shoving it at me, careful not to touch me, barely even looking at me. "Why don't you look through this and see if it sparks something, like the doctor said?"

I take the bag, hurt but trying not to show it. Has she always flinched away from me like that? Something tells me it's new. Because of my appearance? Because of something else? I have a better chance of figuring out what's in this bag, so I focus on that. Inside are two tubes of lip gloss, a wallet, some keys, twenty million receipts, and a lanyard with a badge on the end (normal). Also, a headlamp, three glitter-filled balloons, a lockpick kit, and two glow sticks (less normal). It seems that I went to a rave or a six-year-old's birthday party or on an extended deep-sea diving trip. THOSE ARE ALMOST THE SAME THING, RIGHT?

I turn over the tube of red lip gloss. Electric Watermelon. Sounds about right. I tug on the badge. ARKHAM ASYLUM is written across the top in blocky letters. And underneath that, HARLEEN QUINZEL. INTERN. There's a photo of me posing with a very serious, tight-lipped face. I don't even remember having it ta—

Click!

You smiled again.

Well, duh. I'm getting my picture taken. It's impossible not to smile.

Holy crap. I drop the badge. Flinch away from it.

"Are you okay?" Pamela leans forward again.

Oh, *nowww* she's concerned. I glance back and forth between her and the badge. I'm not sure I want to do this when she's here.

"Um, yeah. Actually, I can't remember the last time I ate real food, and I'm feeling kind of weak. Do you mind getting me something?"

Keep your face calm. Keep the past locked up for just a moment longer.

"Of course," she says.

She stands up too quickly and looks too relieved. I watch her pick up her bag and walk to the door.

"Breakfast sandwich?" she asks, a small smile on her lips.

"Yes!" MAYBE SHE *IS* MY FRIEND!

But I can't think about that right now. I have to focus. As soon as she leaves, I pick up the badge again and I will the memories to flow through me.

CHAPTER 25

Gotham Memorial Hospital

I'M JUST WRITING DOWN WHAT I REMEMBER ABOUT MY first day at Arkham, people talking crap about me, King Shark being an inspiration to behold, rumors about The Joker and Talia and a masked terror, when I hear a gaggle of excited voices outside my door. I look up to see a whole slew of girls in lavender-and-yellow T-shirts pouring into my room.

"Ohmygosh, Harleen, are you okay?"

"We were so scared."

"Do you think you'll still feel good enough to go to Formal next week?"

"Can we get you anything?"

A girl with long brunette waves practically crawls into my bed so she can hug me close. "I love you so much. You can't die," she says.

When she pulls back, her face surprises me because I actually recognize it.

"Hey! I remember you!" I say, sitting up higher in bed. "You're Kylie's Little Sis."

Sophie. Her name is Sophie, and whenever Kylie brought me around her sorority last year (which was often), Sophie was one of my favorites. I remember we got even closer after Kylie died. Sophie seemed like she had missing pieces in all the same places as me.

Today, though, she stares at me, confused. "I'm also your Big."

I look around the room. Lavender and yellow. Alpha Kappa Nu. Kylie's sorority. These other girls must also be Kylie's sorority sisters. And apparently . . .

"I'm in Alpha Kappa Nu?" I really feel like I'd remember something like that.

The girls look at me sympathetically, unsure of how to answer, except for Sophie, who nods.

A voice pipes up from behind them.

"She's been having some gaps in her memory."

We turn, none of us having noticed when Pamela slipped into the room. She holds up a breakfast sandwich wrapped in yellow paper.

"The doctor thinks it's temporary," she says.

"What about her face? Is that temporary?" blurts out a girl who reintroduced herself as Gia earlier.

Ouch. But before I can process how I feel about it, Pamela comes back with: "I don't know. Is yours?"

She moves closer with the breakfast sandwich. It smells like cheese and melted butter and every good thing in the world. She sets it on this tabletop thing that rolls back and forth over my bed. I devour it. (The sandwich, not the tabletop.)

While I eat, the girls spill random campus gossip about people I can't remember, which sounds like it could be insensitive, but it's honestly the very best thing. It feels good to get a break from people staring at me like I'm a martian. It's almost relaxing to gasp and feign (appreciative) shock over Gia making out with some Sigma Delt on the fifty-yard line of the football field. To get excited over us crushing Tri Phi at intramural basketball. There's a part of me that wonders how in the world I was able to afford being in a sorority, but I'm not about to ask that right now.

Pamela sits tucked on the couch, sipping a coffee and flipping through a book called *Pitcher Plants of Borneo.* It's not awkward, though. More like she's content to be alone but glad to have us nearby. The girls don't seem to mind either. They're happy to make me laugh and squeal with story after story. Sophie's the only one who seems to notice when my reaction times are a little too slow, when the flicker of recognition doesn't spark in my eyes the way it should.

"How much *can* you remember?" she eventually asks.

The other girls go quiet. Pamela's hand grips the page of her book a little too tightly, and I get the sense that she's no longer reading, just pretending to.

I plunge ahead with an answer anyway. "As far as I can tell, I remember pretty much everything about growing up and my mom and dad and high school and everything. And . . ." I pause, searching. "I know I did a gap year last year."

I remember working in the Nelson lab, falling in love with Bernice. I remember the Reckoning—me, Bernice, Jasmin, Bianca, and Kylie. We started a vigilante girl gang dedicated to taking down the most misogynistic men on campus. And we succeeded. Until . . .

But I'd rather not think about that. I know I somehow got through the summer after my dad died. I moved into my dorm all on my own. I try to picture something after that and wince.

"I think I remember everything about the gap year. And the summer too. But the beginning of my first year at Gotham U—that's where things start to get hazy."

The girls are appropriately sympathetic. Sophie squeezes my hand. I should be trying to figure out what happened to me and find all the pieces that seem to be missing from my brain, but for a second I'm stuck on Jasmin and Bianca. Do they know what happened to me? They would have come by, right?

Out of the corner of my eye, I see Dr. Viswanathan breeze by the door, probably rushing from patient to patient. Crap. That reminds me.

"I need to remember what happened the day I got hurt. Dr. Viswanathan said the police would be coming to talk to me. I guess they're trying to figure out who did this to me."

The girls nod. Pamela is pretend-reading again. But Sophie—Sophie looks down at her lap.

"They might also be coming to ask you about the escape." She says it like an apology.

Alarm bells blare inside my head, but I don't know why. "What escape?"

Sophie side-eyes Pamela, but Pamela only doubles down on her pretend-reading. She seems to be trying to bite her way through the inside of her mouth, though.

Sophie turns back to me like she doesn't want to do this, but okay, sure, somebody's got to. I get an uncomfortable sense of foreboding, like the universe has a giant foot hovering over me, just waiting to stomp.

"The night you got dropped at the hospital after . . . whatever happened to you happened," Sophie begins. "That same night was the biggest jailbreak in the history of Arkham Asylum."

It feels significant. Life-changing. I can't even breathe because I can tell there's more.

Sophie squeezes my hand again.

"You were working that night."

CHAPTER 26

How Do You Know If You Did It?

I TRY TO PUT THE PIECES TOGETHER IN SOME KIND OF WAY that makes sense. I don't understand how this happened. I remember I started off the year trying so hard to be so good. Grades, class schedules, internships, color-coded day planners. And yet I can't help thinking that my accident had something to do with the Arkham jailbreak. Was I involved? I can't fathom how things went so bad.

I think about it, trying to evaluate myself the way I would a patient. Impulsivity and inattention and hyperactivity and all the other hallmark behaviors associated with ADHD; a fear of being trapped in small spaces that's on the border of PTSD and claustrophobia; a mother who died when I was young; a super messed-up childhood courtesy of my father. But all of that was on board prior to my fall semester at Gotham U. I don't understand what could have turned me into the kind of person who could have been involved in a jailbreak. I don't have enough information. About this past year at school. About that night. What the hell happened? Do Win and Pamela know something? Why didn't they tell me about the jailbreak? And since they didn't, can I really trust them?

I ask Sophie if she knows any details, and she pulls something up on her phone. It's a newspaper article about the jailbreak.

THE GOTHAM ENQUIRER

ARKALAMITY: GOTHAM CITY'S MOST DANGEROUS CRIMINALS ESCAPE IN BIGGEST JAILBREAK OF ALL TIME

Five Escapees—The Joker and Two-Face Among Them

All Are Still at Large

Circumstances Surrounding Escape a Mystery

GOTHAM CITY, Jan. 7 – Chaos broke out at Arkham Asylum Saturday night, and so did several notorious inmates. Likely led by The Joker, the five appear to have escaped without the usual explosions, helicopters, and tunnel digging, leading to speculation that The Joker had an accomplice on the inside. A police chase across the city culminated in a standoff with The Joker and Two-Face in the industrial district, near Ace Chemicals. A Gotham University student and Arkham intern is rumored to have been kidnapped and seriously injured, but no other hostages appear to have been taken. Sources say . . .

I scroll through the article, whispering parts of it aloud as I go.

"The largest of its kind . . . Several high-profile inmates escaped, including Talia al Ghūl, King Shark, Two-Face,

The Riddler, and the Clown Prince of Crime himself, The Joker. . . . The media is calling it Arkalamity."

The article doesn't mention me, though. Hope flares in my chest. Maybe I wasn't involved. Maybe I just *coincidentally* ended up covered in chemical waste on the same night as the largest jailbreak in the history of Arkham Asylum. I glance up from Sophie's phone to see every face in the room staring at me in judgment. Okay, so probably not. But I don't remember being there. Not yet, at least. *Why can't I remember?* The heart monitor starts beeping all erratically again, and Pamela gently puts her hand over the screen of Sophie's phone, wresting it away from me.

"All right, enough. You're scaring her. She's not ready for all that yet."

She glares at me, or maybe Sophie, or maybe both of us—it's kind of hard to tell. I don't know if she's mad that I'm getting closer to the truth or if she thinks she's trying to protect me somehow. I watch the way she deposits the phone into Sophie's hands like a venomous snake. Doesn't flinch when she touches Sophie's hands, though. Apparently, she saves that just for me. Something about all of it is suspicious. Dishonest, at the very least. I'm good at knowing when people are hiding something. I've had a lot of practice. And Pamela Isley is *definitely* hiding things.

I think back to the news article, sifting through the pieces to see whether there's any gold in this mess of sensationalized reporting. I'm totally and completely floored by what I just read. A gong upside the head, a punch to the gut, a lightning bolt to the senses. Just thinking about that night makes my pulse race and my chest tighten and my armpits start sweating. What I don't understand is why.

I was definitely at Arkham Asylum, according to Sophie,

even though I don't remember it. But was it more than that? Was I involved somehow? Did I help them escape? It sure would explain the huge visceral reaction I'm having. Because when I think about the article, a lot of feelings come bubbling to the top. And one of the biggest is guilt.

I look up to see the police standing in the doorway.

CHAPTER 27

Interrogation

NUMBER OF TIMES THE POLICE HAVE QUESTIONED ME IN MY whole life: 37. Maybe. I think. After the first ten, they all kind of run together.

Number of times the questioning was about my dad: 24. (Again, approximately.)

Number of times related to me being in a vigilante girl gang: 4.

Number of times that resulted in me getting a restraining order: 2. I DON'T WANT TO TALK ABOUT IT.

Number of times more unnerving than this one: 0.

At least last year whenever Montoya was questioning me, I knew what to lie about (Kylie, the Reckoning, my relationship with Bernice, my penchant for smashing things). Right now, I feel like the floor is covered in bear traps, and I'm the one who put them there, only now I'm supposed to walk through them blindfolded. It's about as fun as you would expect.

"And you were working at Arkham Asylum that night, is that correct?" asks the lead cop, who unfortunately is no

Officer Montoya. Buzz cut. No neck. Control freak. The kind of powerless person who is drawn to positions of power but wields that power like a club.

"I've been *told* I was working there."

He crosses his arms. They poke out of his uniform like two hams. "What's that supposed to mean?"

"I was in some sort of an accident. I don't actually remember anything about that night."

When I say the word *accident,* his partner's eyes practically fall out of his head. (For the past six minutes, he's been looking at my ghost-white face while trying to pretend that's not exactly what he's doing. The result? His eyes look like they're having an existential crisis.)

Buzz Cut doesn't notice. He barrels on with the investigation. "That's awfully convenient."

What. A. Jerkwaffle.

I've heard one of the best things to do when people are being jerks (especially jerks of the sexist/racist/homophobic variety) is to ask them questions that force them to restate their jerkiness.

"You think me having amnesia . . . is convenient?" I say it so innocently, like, no, I'm not pouring a bag of marbles all over the floor and waiting for you to slip on them.

"I . . . No. Well, I—"

Let me tell you how satisfying it is to watch him flounder. (VERY.)

"Do you remember how the accident happened?" asks his partner. He has a gentle voice. Glasses. Kind eyes. The type of guy who probably joined the force because he thought it meant he could help people. Until he got saddled with Neanderthal Man over here.

"I'm sorry, but I don't." I keep waiting for it to hit me, but it just . . . doesn't. "I really wish I knew how this happened to me."

"Is there anything at all you do remember about that night?" asks Buzz Cut.

"No." Luckily, I can say it honestly.

"And you're an intern at Arkham."

"Yes." Which I already told you. I try to keep the edge out of my voice, though.

"Which inmates did you interact with while you were an intern?"

I shake my head. "I don't remember that either." I know I wanted to be paired with The Joker, at least at the beginning of my internship. Though, hell, so did everyone else.

Buzz Cut huffs and crosses his arms, and I will bet you dollars to doughnuts the words *awfully convenient* are running through his head right now. And then he gets this look in his eyes—like his gears are turning. (It's honestly kind of scary.)

He pulls up a photo on his tablet. "Do you recognize this woman?"

It's a mug shot. A raven-haired woman with smirking lips and eyes filled to the brim with secrets.

A flicker of a memory plays in my head. Me talking to her in a room with a giant scanner. The lights going out.

"That's Talia al Ghūl," I say.

And then I wish I could suck the words back in, like pressing a button on a measuring tape. Am I *supposed* to know her? Did I just incriminate myself somehow? I wish one of my friends was here to help, even that mean-looking redheaded girl. If I could just glance at someone and they could tell me through frowns and eye telepathy whether I'm about to reveal something that's going to get me carted off to jail . . . That's probably why Officer Buzz Cut made them leave in the first place.

"Do you remember interacting with Ms. al Ghūl?" he asks.

I shake my head.

He pulls up a video clip on his tablet next. "This is from one of Arkham's security cameras."

Oh crap. Oh crap. Oh crap. My heart starts racing like it's trying to break the sound barrier. Is this the part where I find out I blasted a hole through Arkham's stone walls with a bazooka? Freed all the prisoners so we could go get midnight pancakes? Stole Mr. Freeze's suit and used it to put an ice sculpture of me riding a unicorn on every street corner? (Actually, that last one sounds pretty sweet.)

Officer Buzz Cut hits Play. "This is the night of the escape."

It's a hallway at Arkham. Gray-green floors and painted cement-block walls and feeble light bulbs enclosed in metal cages. I remember them and I don't at the same time. At first the dimly lit hallway is empty. But then someone appears. Two someones. Talia al Ghūl is moving down the hallway, practically dragging a body along with her.

My body. She has a knife pressed against my throat.

I gasp.

"It *is* pretty shocking," says the nice cop.

But I'm sighing with relief. I was being held hostage. I can see the fear in my eyes in the video as we get closer to the camera. You can't fake something like that.

"We know you've been through a lot, Ms. Quinzel, but please let us know if you remember anything," Nice Cop says with a kind pat on the shoulder and one last fleeting glance at my dove-white face.

Even Officer Buzz Cut takes a break from his incessant grilling.

They think I'm innocent, I realize. Maybe I *am* innocent.

I stare out the window for a moment, remembering a talk with a tall, curly-haired woman—Dr. Morales, I think—who I'm starting to realize was my mentor.

She's also one of the smartest people I've ever met. While we're in that room with Talia al Ghūl, you are not to speak to her.

This is for your own safety.

"I think I was assigned to Talia al Ghūl. As an intern," I say. "I remember getting some kind of debriefing before the first time I met her, but that's it."

The nice cop nods, but Officer Buzz Cut is relentless.

"Are you sure there's nothing else you can tell us about Talia? What about—"

He's cut off by the clearing of a throat. Not all that loud or emphatic, an unassuming sound, really, but you can tell the throat-clearer means business. A doctor in scrubs and a white coat enters. He's tall. Rail-thin. Not frail, though. On the contrary, his slenderness makes him seem composed entirely of sharp edges.

"Who gave you permission to speak to her?"

I rake my eyes over him, searching for context clues. Do I know him? The writing embroidered over his pocket reads JONATHAN CRANE, MD. And underneath that, ARKHAM ASYLUM. So, then, I probably *do* know him. Don't recognize him, though. (Story of my day.)

Officer Buzz Cut, who seemed frozen for a moment, recovers the ability to speak. "She's not a minor."

Dr. Crane narrows his eyes. "No, but she's been through a tragic accident, and she's in a vulnerable state. Here's my card. In the future, please don't question one of my interns without me present."

Oh-ho-ho! Take that, Buzz Cut! Seriously, he looks like

he just swallowed an entire liter of cherry-flavored cough medicine. For a second I think he's going to argue, but despite his frame, Dr. Crane cuts an imposing figure, towering over the officers like a tree in winter, casting his shadows at them until they vacate the premises.

As soon as they're gone, he folds himself into pieces so he can fit in the chair next to me. "Are you all right? Did they stress you out too much?"

"I'm fine. Thank you." I smile at him. A genuine smile, not the fake ones I've been serving up for the past half hour.

"Good. And I meant what I said. If they come bothering you again, you can call me at any time."

I thank him again, and there's an awkward silence, and then:

"What sort of questions did they ask you?"

"Oh. Um, just like, did I know anything about the escape and what happened to me that night."

"Right, right," he says, gnawing on his bottom lip. (Still furious at them but trying to contain it, I guess.) "And you said?"

I wince. I wish I could help him. He's probably in all kinds of trouble because of an escape at a place where he's the director. (Side note: How do I know that? Did I remember it?!)

"Oh yeah, that's the thing: I don't actually remember anything. I mean, I know who I am, and I remember my life and starting school this fall, but the jailbreak? Nothing." My eyes can't quite meet his. "I'm sorry, but I don't actually know who you are."

He is the very definition of taken aback. "Oh. *Ohhh*. I'm so sorry to hear that. I'm happy to help you work on recovering your memories, if that's something you're interested in. Memory was something of a subspecialty of mine in graduate school." He pauses. Checks to make sure no one is listening. "And just between you and me," he continues in a low voice, "if it turns out you were, ah, involved in anything—anything at all—we could consider that privileged information. I don't think there's any need to tell them, especially not that surly one."

I sigh with my entire body. It would be such a relief to know what happened that night, the last few months, to be able to go searching for it without having to be afraid of what I'd find.

"You'd really do that? For me?" And then my cynical side kicks in. "Why?"

"I want to help you. I feel bad that you got hurt on my watch." He rushes to say it and realizes it isn't endearing him to me the way it would to your average person. "Also, Arkham Asylum gets a lot of bad press. I'm concerned that this is somewhat my fault, and even if it isn't, the media will make it my fault. I'd like to figure out what happened, so we can release our own version of the story in a way that doesn't hurt the asylum and the good work we're trying to do there."

Sounds reasonable to me. I'm just about to tell him so when Dr. Viswanathan rushes in, followed by Pamela and Winfield and the woman from my memory, Dr. Morales.

"I'm so sorry they barged in here without me or another doctor present. Pamela came and got me. Are you doing all right?" Dr. V checks my vitals in case they're hiding any secrets.

"Harleen." The woman with the dark curly hair approaches my bedside. "How are you feeling?"

"Good," I say. "Better than I have been."

I search her face, trying to remember more of our time together.

"I'm Dr. Morales," she hurries to say, probably thinking

I don't recognize her. "You're an intern with my research group at Arkham."

"Oh, I remember." Is it just me, or did half the people in this room do a spit take? "Not everything, but I remember you were my mentor."

She smiles and gives my hand a slight squeeze. "Still am. You let me know if you need anything at all."

Dr. V clears her throat. She's finished looking me over. "So. You're looking a lot better, and we'll likely be letting you go home tomorrow."

"Well, that's wonderful news," says Dr. Morales.

"But I think it would be a good idea to continue seeing someone about your amnesia. Someone in outpatient," continues Dr. Viswanathan.

I think about Dr. Crane's offer to help me uncover what I've lost.

"That sounds great."

"I'm happy to provide you with a list . . ." Dr. V rummages in her pocket.

"I can recommend some excellent specialists as well," says Dr. Morales.

I appreciate the help, but sometimes you just have to go with your gut.

"I've already decided on Dr. Crane."

CHAPTER 28

Gotham Memorial Hospital

DR. VISWANATHAN REGARDS DR. CRANE LIKE SHE'S ONLY just realized he's in the room. (He does have a way of blending in and disappearing.) He offers a handshake.

"Dr. Jonathan Crane. I do have some expertise in this area."

She takes his hand skeptically, probably because they're just meeting and all. "Right. Well. As long as that's what Ms. Quinzel is comfortable with."

"It is," I jump in.

"Are you sure?" Dr. Morales's eyebrows practically disappear into her hairline.

Pamela looks mutinous, but then, doesn't she always?

"Definitely. I have a really good feeling about it."

Weird that Dr. Morales doesn't, though. Maybe I was supposed to pick her instead? I'm not even sure if she does that kind of work, though, and Dr. Crane says he's an expert.

"I guess that's settled, then," says Dr. V. "And on that note, Ms. Quinzel needs her rest. It's time for you to go."

Pamela frowns. "But—"

So does Win. "I thought—"

"It's time for *everyone* to go."

I actually wouldn't mind a moment alone to try to piece together some of this stuff. Drs. Morales and Crane leave, but Win and Pamela protest.

Win offers his best rich-people handshake to Dr. Viswanathan. "Winfield McCall Callaway. Harleen's boyfriend. I really don't want to leave her alone at the moment."

Pamela jumps in. "Me neither. I'd really like to spend the night."

"One person only. I've got to go, but when I pass by here again, I'd better not see the two of you arguing. She needs rest." Dr. V is making her I-am-not-to-be-trifled-with face.

She dashes off, but honestly, I kind of wish she had stayed, because Win and Pamela look like they're about to fight a duel over me, possibly to the death. In this corner, with fire-engine hair and more inexplicable tension than you can shake a stick at, we have . . . Pamela Isley! And in this corner, with preppy good looks and terrible taste in pet names, we have the triple-last-name triple threat, Winfield McCall Callaway!!!

Pamela comes out swinging. "I need to stay. I need to talk to her about some things."

Win counters with the jab. "You can talk to her tomorrow. She's supposed to rest, anyway."

IDK, I'm pretty exhausted, so I'm tempted to tell them to wake me up if someone cracks a chair over someone else's head. I get up to go to the bathroom because (A) I need to escape the awkwardness, and (B) I just saw an incredibly creepy teddy bear sitting on the windowsill, and I want to see who it's from. I pick up the card attached. *Hope you feel better soon! Sending love and gentle hugs, Stella and Bernice.* I thought the bear looked like something Bernice would make.

I wonder if there's anything here from the other Reckoning girls. I search all the flowers and stuffed animals for a note from Jasmin or Bianca, but they're mostly from my sorority sisters and my intern friends. I think about texting Jasmin. Or Bianca. I wonder if they know I'm in here. There's a part of me that's scared to find out the answer.

When I get back from the bathroom and back into bed, Winfield and Pamela are still going at it. Luckily, this battle is fought primarily through intense glances and quietly but emphatically exchanged words (they *are* both pretty rich and WASPy). Win says something into her ear, and she stalks off, but not before narrowing her eyes at me one last time. JUST IN CASE I HAD ANY DOUBTS ABOUT WHETHER SHE HATES ME.

Win posts up in the chair next to my bed, chest puffed up. Apparently, he wins this round. I look at his profile, at his nose that looks like it's been broken before, but in a good way.

"That was intense." I tip my head in the direction Pamela left.

"Oh." He makes this *aw, shucks* smile. "Sorry about that. I just think she's a bad influence."

And . . . Pamela just got 20 percent hotter. I think about saying something sarcastic like, *Thanks, Dad,* but there are things I need to ask him. I have to play this carefully.

"It's okay." I put my hand over his. "I'm glad we have a chance to be alone together."

He smiles in a way that feels bittersweet, and then he scoots his chair closer. "Me too. Also"—he eyes the door—"I think it was really smart of you to pick Dr. Crane to help you with your memory. I've been his intern for the last three years. He really is a genius."

"Good to know." (It actually is. A Boy Scout like Win

wouldn't steer me wrong. Right?) I should probably butter him up more. Start with some easy questions. But I've never been the most patient person. "I was hoping to ask you about the jailbreak. Were you there?"

For some reason, I feel like if I can solve the jailbreak, I can solve what happened to me.

His eyes go big. "No. I mean, yes. I mean, I was there that day, but not during the jailbreak. I left before it happened."

OMG, could he be any more suspicious right now?

"So you don't know anything?"

"I mean, I have some ideas, but I wasn't there, so they're really more like guesses. I left around two-thirty that afternoon, way before anything started, and honestly, you should probably be listening to, like, facts and your own memories and stuff rather than guesses from somebody else, right?"

Dude. Calm down. The way this guy is sweating, you'd think I just unrolled a case of torture devices. Also, if he wasn't there, then how does he know when anything started?

I put my hand against his cheek and gaze into his ocean-blue eyes. He really does have pretty eyes. I wonder why he's lying to me.

"It's okay," I tell him. *You can stop with all the vague answers and half-truths.* "Whatever happened, I'm not going to hold it against you. You're my boyfriend."

I don't miss how his lips twitch at the word *boyfriend*.

"Do you really still not remember me at all? Our relationship was kind of a big deal. To me, anyway."

He squeezes my hand while he waits for my answer. I wish I had a better one to give him.

"I'm sorry. I remember meeting you? I'm sure the rest'll come back soon."

"It's okay. I'll wait as long as it takes." He pauses and

closes his eyes, like his next words are costing him something. "I love you."

He looks like he means it. And I don't know if I can trust him, but I want him to believe I do, so I pull him by the hand into bed with me and snuggle up against him and let him think I've fallen asleep in his arms.

As soon as I hear him snoring, I pull out my phone.

There's a text from Pamela, all caps.

Pamela: DON'T TELL HIM ANYTHING.

Pamela: AND DON'T TRUST DR. CRANE.

CHAPTER 29

Past Lives

HUH. I STARE AT THE TEXT, WONDERING WHAT TO THINK. Interesting that Win didn't even try to get me to tell him anything. And Dr. Crane, he protected me from the police. Pamela asked me questions about what happened, though. Wanted to know what I remembered. And she seemed kind of nervous/angry/weirdly intense about it. But then, Win acted weird at times too.

I decide it's time to get serious. I'm going to piece the past together the best I can using photos and the stuff from my bag. I have to. It's exhausting trying to figure out who's lying to me and about what.

I unlock my phone, the wallpaper with me kissing Win on the cheek popping up again like blunt force trauma to my senses. I check to make sure he's still asleep. Then I flip through pictures of us, irrefutable photo documentation of a happy, if somewhat cringe-worthy, relationship. A grinning dance-floor selfie at a sorority party. Kissing in the woods on a hike. Dinner at a fancy-looking restaurant, me wearing a black dress that feels entirely too sensible. They're posted on his social media too, every last one. With hashtags. #TeamHarleWin #hangingwithmybae. I wince. Am I dating a thirty-five-year-old woman?

There's a photo of us eating lunch in a place I recognize as a courtyard at Arkham Asylum, though I can't remember how I know that or anything else about the day. I know he was the lead intern there. I remember meeting him that first day. Getting the VIP tour. Flirting. Was he involved in the jailbreak somehow? I know he said he had already left, but people don't act that nervous unless they're hiding something.

I make notes in my journal, chronicling the history of our relationship. Cobbling together what I can of the school year. There are photos of what feels like another me—waltzing/skipping/twirling through another life. I see this straitlaced, brilliant girl, starting school, doing sorority recruitment, going to parties and concerts and date dashes and football games, getting every gold star that's offered.

I linger on a photo of Pamela Isley.

We're at a football game, temporary tattoos on our cheeks, smiling carefree grins at the camera as we take a selfie. Gosh, she's beautiful. There are so many of us together. And it's weird because when I go back to the first ones, she's so withdrawn, shoulders slumped, hair hanging over her face, a hesitant smile—one that feels like she forced it just for the picture. And as the pictures go on, she changes. Her red hair is swept away from her face, and her smile goes from shaky to strong, and even her posture changes. I wonder what did that.

And it's not just her. *We* change. I mean, I'm still shooting for that pretty-paralegal look (which, *ugh,* Past Harleen, can we talk about that?), but you can see the shift in our relationship to each other. The first photo looks like it's from one of those elementary school class pictures where you have to stand shoulder to shoulder with someone, but you're trying not to touch them. But then in the later ones, we have our arms thrown around each other's shoulders, cheeks pressed together. Hell, in the last one, I'm sitting in her lap, and she's laughing in a way that would frankly seem unbelievable to anyone who has ever met her.

So, she's my friend. I think she's maybe even my best friend. Why does it feel so tense between us, then?

I think about this memory I have, of these girls talking crap about her in the dining hall. It was the same day I met her. They were talking about a lab. And an accident. And a professor. I search for *Pamela Isley accident*. The articles that pop up are shocking. I click on the top article.

RECENTLY LEAKED PHOTOS REVEAL WHAT REALLY HAPPENED TO WOODRUE LAB

Student allowed to remain at school—are we safe?

There was an incident. An explosion. Greener Earth Society was supposed to be a school club devoted to saving the planet, but apparently there's a dark underbelly to Gotham U's extracurricular activities—the group blew up a building. And a girl died.

Another article:

WOODRUE ACCUSED OF EXPERIMENTING ON STUDENTS

Lab Destroyed by Vengeful Undergrad

Woodrue fled before they could prosecute and/or fire him. It's the pictures that are unbelievable. I feel like I remember Pamela saying something about getting revenge, but I thought she just destroyed all his samples or something. (That's what she told me, right? I try to remember.) This is more than just unplugging a few minus 80s or dumping someone's research into biohazard waste. She rained down vengeance on an apocalyptic scale.

It's amazing she didn't get in more trouble for reducing a campus laboratory to rubble. The article says her parents are wealthy donors, though. I look at the photo again. How in the world did Pamela *do* something like that? Even if she had dynamite or a sledgehammer or something, it seems . . . almost impossible.

Hoping for answers, I read until my eyes grow heavy, but when I feel myself getting sleepy, I tuck my journal behind my hospital bed because I don't want my boyfriend to read it.

I don't know that I trust him.

But I don't know that I trust Pamela either.

I decide to check one last thing on my phone before I drift off. First, I comb Pamela's social media for any posts leading up to Arkalamity. (Nothing, but then, being on a posting hiatus is not really unusual for her, I discover.) Then I scroll through Win's. There's a recent photo of him and some friends clustered around a wood-paneled booth at a bar near campus that everyone goes to. Their faces are ghostly from the camera flash in the dim light of the bar, and their glasses are raised like they're having the time of their lives. I check the date.

Wait, this was the same night as the jailbreak. Win was out partying the night of Arkalamity? I check the time stamp. Based on when I got checked into the ER, this photo was probably taken hours after my accident. Maybe less.

I zoom in closer. Win's eyes are red, bloodshot or crying.

And his hand around the glass, it's too tense. His friends' faces smile too hard at the camera, trying to convince it of how much fun they're having.

The photo is staged. Which leads me to my question: Why would a person need to stage a photo in a bar on the night of Arkalamity?

CHAPTER 30

Echoes

THE SCARECROW TOWERS OVER ME, BUT WHEN HE SPEAKS, it's with my dad's voice.

Where did you put them?

I don't know what he's talking about, and I don't know if I'd be able to tell him if I did. The fear is too strong. It's pulling me under.

I DON'T HAVE TO LET YOU GO.

He throws me against the wall, my head banging against the cement blocks, stars exploding in front of me.

Where did you put them?

Breathe-in-breathe-out-breathe-in-breathe-out. My lungs/heart/brain are all are made of hummingbirds, beating their wings to death because flying against a window is better than being trapped. In here. With him.

He stomps/starts/lurches at me, rotting face looming large in front of mine.

Where?

I DON'T KNOW.

I scream it, and suddenly I'm awake, and I'm in a hospital

bed, and there's a warm body beside me. A hand on the small of my back. I take a couple deep breaths, but Win doesn't look alarmed. I guess the scream was only in my mind, then.

Win searches my eyes with his. "Hey, Schmoopie. You sleep okay?"

Something about it gives me the weirdest sense of déjà vu.

Today's the day.

Are you sure you want to do this?

Now I'm certain he knows more than he's telling me. Knows what happened the day of the jailbreak for sure. Was he involved? Somehow behind it? Did he trick me into doing something and then dump me in a tank of chemicals when he was done with me?

He brushes my hair from my face, concerned, but also like it's a wonder, just seeing me there in front of him. "Are you okay?"

"Yeah," I lie. "Just a bad dream."

He wraps his muscular arms around me. "I'm sorry."

Are you?

I press closer to him, curl my head under his chin. "I think it was about that night." I shiver like the weak, scared thing I'm not. "Is there anything at all you can tell me that would help me?"

His body tenses.

Crap. I pushed too hard too soon.

But I wait. Leaning away from him so I can look directly into his eyes. Channeling the most innocent, damsel-like version of myself. If I let the pause stretch long enough, he'll have to answer. He'll have to—

"I wasn't there during the jailbreak," he says, even though he's already told me that. "But the police keep asking me about it too. My ID badge went missing the night of the escape. Apparently, it was used to open a bunch of doors."

Wait, seriously?!

His eyes flick to the plastic bag of items that were found with me. Oh! Ohh . . .

"It wasn't in there. I promise." I hold the bag out to him. "You can look if you want."

Does he really think I stole it?

Before I can get too upset about it, he drops another bomb.

"Pamela was there that night." I can't help but notice the way he says her name. "And I think she was leading you down a bad path all of last fall."

His whole face changes, like saying that took a lot out of him, and now he's relieved or unburdened or something. (It seemed like a pretty painful process.)

I try not to laugh. "Why are you making that face?"

"I was worried about how you'd take it. I know she's your friend."

Oh. Yeah, I guess I should be worried because Pamela's been acting all weird and tense and she won't tell me anything and I don't know if I can trust her and also she apparently destroys labs.

But I don't know if I can trust him either.

I put one hand on each of his cheeks and kiss him to see if he kisses like a liar.

He pulls back, surprised, after only a second. But the kiss, it was sweet.

"What?" I ask.

His eyes dart around the room like he's searching for an escape route. "Things were complicated. Before. I wasn't sure if—I was scared I was losing you. But my feelings for you have never changed."

He presses his lips against mine like he's starving. Like a drowning man gulping down breaths of air. I probably shouldn't be kissing a person who staged a photo the night of Arkham's largest ever jailbreak, but something about the danger makes it even hotter.

I still don't know if he's the enemy.

But I know I don't want to stop.

CHAPTER 31

Discharged

DR. VISWANATHAN JUST TOLD ME THE GOOD NEWS. I'M well enough to go home now!

"We're not permitted to let you leave the hospital by yourself, but since you don't have a parent or guardian, I thought it might be best to call Dr. Morales."

"That makes sense," I find myself saying. And then it hits me. "Do I have medical bills?"

My brain starts to spiral. I can't even begin to imagine the cost for multiple nights in the hospital, intubation, meds, everything else they did to keep me alive. I feel like there are metal bands around my chest. This will ruin me. I don't have the money to pay this off. And even if they put me on some kind of payment plan, by the time I'm able to—

Dr. Viswanathan puts her hand on top of mine. "It's going to be okay. Payment of all your medical bills has been arranged."

"Wait, what?" This does not happen. I am literally an orphan. This is the kind of thing that leaves people like me destitute and homeless and in pits that just keep getting deeper.

"An anonymous donor has taken care of it."

I narrow my eyes.

Dr. V spreads her hands. "That's all I know."

It seems like she's telling the truth.

And of course I have no reason to distrust Dr. Viswanathan, but this is such a huge thing, it's impossible to make my brain believe it. I'm still recovering, but she has switched to business, making an appointment for a follow-up and giving me instructions on how to care for my injuries.

"If you have any problems at all, don't hesitate to contact me. And of course, if you have any issues with your outpatient care, please let me know."

"Sounds good, Doc. Thank you so much."

I give her a huge hug, and she startles but hugs me back.

She doesn't get up, though.

"There's something else. We removed a . . . well, I'm not even really sure. A chunk of plastic, I guess. We found it in your neck." She holds it up. And she's right. It does look like a melted chunk of plastic smaller than a pencil eraser. Weird. "We're going to send it off to have it analyzed, but I wanted to give you a chance to see it first."

I take it from her, turning it this way and that in the light. I have no idea what it could possibly be. And it was in my *neck*? I shudder.

"Dr. Morales should be here any minute to drive you back to campus. It was a pleasure taking care of you, Harleen." She clips out of the room like she's afraid of getting mushy if she stays.

I'm just thinking that I'll miss seeing her, when Pamela appears in the doorway. "You ready?"

I sit up straight in my hospital bed. "I thought Dr. Morales was coming."

"I am." Dr. Morales strolls into the room behind Pamela. "But I wasn't sure what dorm you were in, and I didn't know if you'd know, so I called your friend. Are you ready?"

I nod. "All clear." I look down and realize I am still wearing a hospital gown. "Ummm."

"I brought you clothes!" Pamela holds out a stack to me (jeans, old-school white sneakers, Alpha Nu T-shirt).

I go to the bathroom to change, holding my gown shut in the back so I don't flash them. My hair is an oily mess, so I put it in pigtail buns on top of my head.

"Ready!" I say brightly. (Not gonna lie, I am super excited to get out of this hospital.)

On the way to Dr. Morales's car, she chatters with me about how I'm doing and what progress has been made on capturing the escapees. (Not a lot.) Pamela is silent.

On the ride back to Gotham U, we discuss the project I was working on this semester—a case study on Talia al Ghūl's brain scans. Pamela is silent.

And it's almost tense, if I'm interpreting things correctly, and I'm pretty sure I am. I wonder what happened to make us like this. When we get to the turnaround in front of my dorm (Elliot Hall—I remembered!!), I thank Dr. Morales and tell her goodbye. Pamela says she'll walk me to my room. And as soon as Dr. Morales drives away and we're alone, Pamela actually speaks!

"I'm just two floors up. Call me or come by if you need anything. And I'll come check on you."

So, she hates me . . . but she wants to take care of me . . . ? Maybe she just wants to keep an eye on me. I cannot figure this girl out to save my life.

We take the elevator down to the Pit, even though I tell her I feel fine and could totally take the stairs. When we get to my room, she sets my stuff on my bed (I don't want to brag, but I got the top bunk), and then I kind of expect her to leave, but she just . . . doesn't.

"So, yeah, this is Elliot Hall. This is your roommate, Samantha. Do you remember her?"

Samantha glances up from her laptop and offers me a forced smile that does, in fact, feel familiar. I'm pretty sure she gave it to me when I suggested we have a Taylor Swift dance party as a study break. (It is possible I crooned "Lover" into her ear. Loudly. Turns out some people don't like that.) And after she caught me drinking her milk straight from the carton. And after I opened the window because it was hot, and it rained all over her desk.

"If you need any help finding your way to classes or anything, just let me know."

Pamela's saying nice things, but she won't even look at me, and it is SO weird.

Meanwhile, my roommate is alternating between machine-gun typing on her laptop and giving Pamela the stink eye. At least, I think she's mad that Pamela's here. She could also be mad because I'm home from the hospital and she was hoping to have a super single. Or perhaps her face just looks like that. On the plus side, she doesn't seem weirded out by my super-white skin?

Pamela makes that flustered face she gets when she doesn't know how to people, and she starts rearranging the stuff on my desk so she'll have something to do with her hands. (Note: Is it weird that I know that's a thing she does, but I don't know anything about her past our first meeting?) She eyes the parched remains of a plant in a flowerpot and doesn't even try to contain her disgust.

"You could have at least watered her plant while she was in the hospital."

Samantha closes her laptop with a snap. "I have an article due for the *Clocktower* tomorrow. I'm going to the study room."

Pamela watches her go. "Weird that she hates you so much."

I shrug, thinking about the time I borrowed her black tights without asking and gave them back full of holes. "Different personalities."

"Yeah." Pamela fiddles with her bracelet. "Look, I wasn't going to tell you any of this because of what Dr. Viswanathan said about coloring your memories, but Crane is a bad guy, and I don't want you to get hurt. Again."

Again. Is she saying what I think she's saying? I catch sight of my white skin in the mirror, and my breath hitches momentarily. It's like seeing a ghost, only the ghost turns out to be you. "So, Dr. Crane did this to me?"

Pamela purses her lips like she's profoundly annoyed. "I don't actually know. I wasn't there."

UGH. WAS ANYONE THERE?! Does nobody know anything useful or helpful or meaningful? How am I supposed to kick ass and take names if there aren't any names to take?!

I search Pamela's face for signs that she's lying, and for some reason, I'm reminded of this morning with Win. When I kissed him to see if he kissed like a liar.

"Okay, so we don't know who did this to me, but Crane is still bad and you want to protect me?" I'm not sure if I believe it, but it's important to know if she does.

"Yes."

Her voice is so firm. My stomach and my lips and my heart are telling me that there's an easy way to know for sure, but my brain just holds me back. There's no way I could have been involved with Pamela without cheating on

Win, and I feel very strongly that I'm not a cheater. But does it count as cheating if I'm just retracing my steps?

"Because you care about me?"

"Yes." She says it again, only this time her face goes so very soft, and everything else she's saying may be a lie, but this part, this is the truth. I want it to be the truth. I want—

Before I even know what I'm doing, I lean forward, hands reaching for her like they're aching to know if they've touched her before, lips parted ever so slightly.

"Hey, whoa, what are you doing?!"

Pamela breaks the spell just before my mouth completes its collision course, and the look on her face—she's horrified or repulsed or something else that makes me feel like I'm being stabbed.

I have misjudged this so, so badly. "I'm sorry. I thought maybe we were—"

"Well, we're not." Her cheeks flash red. "And that was a really terrible idea."

She flies out of my room before I can say anything else.

CHAPTER 32

Elliot Hall

AFTER SHE LEAVES, I CLIMB UP TO THE TOP BUNK AND FLOP onto my bed. (A limitation of the top bunk: it's less ideal for dramatic flopping.) I pull out my phone and start to text Pamela.

> Harleen: I'm so sorry.

Delete.

> Harleen: I absolutely should have asked first.

Delete.

I think about that awful, repulsed face she made, like she could only just barely tolerate me, and I shove my phone under my pillow. Maybe it's better if I give her some time to hate me less before I go apology-texting.

Today was the most physical activity I've had since the accident, and I guess I'm exhausted, because I fall asleep with my clothes on and I don't wake up until there's light streaming through the window. I'm parched. My tongue is stuck to the roof of my mouth, and it feels like there's sandpaper under my eyelids. The first thing I do is stretch down and grab my water bottle from my desk and chug the entire thing. The second thing I do is check my phone to see what time it is. I'm supposed to meet Dr. Crane before my classes for my first memory appointment. Nine o'clock at Arkham Asylum, bright and early.

My screen blinks to life. Oh, good, it's only 7:45. And . . . I've got, like, two hundred new texts from Pamela.

> Pamela: I'm sorry I freaked out before, but I really need to talk to you about Crane.
>
> Pamela: Harleen?
>
> Pamela: You can't just ignore me. This is serious.
>
> Pamela: He's bad. He's really, really bad. You can't listen to anything he says. And I don't want you to go see him. It's not a good idea to do your amnesia therapy with him.
>
> Pamela: Harleen???
>
> Pamela: Please don't go tomorrow, or at least please talk to me before you do.

And on.

And on.

And on.

Geez, I wonder what Dr. Crane ever did to her. Seriously, though, what could she possibly have on him? He seemed so nice. Well, maybe not in the traditional sense, but he seemed to want to protect me. To help me. That's, like, the definition of nice.

I text Pamela back.

> Harleen: Hey, I'm the one who should be sorry. Consent is really important. I screwed up.

I feel a pit open in my stomach as I wait for her to answer. It doesn't happen immediately, so I decide to take a shower. Did you know when you walk down the hallway to the girls' bathroom in a towel and skin the color of bleached paper, it's physically impossible for people not to stare at you? But, like, none of them ask about it. A couple offer some feeble "welcome back, glad you're okays," but most of them don't say anything. Almost makes me appreciate Gia's bluntness at the hospital. (At least I know who to trust when shopping for formal dresses and swimsuits.)

At first I just try to get through the gauntlet. But when I reach the bathroom door, I pause. "Wow, I knew I slept funny, but my hair must be really wild today, huh?"

I press on to the showers without waiting for a response because I can't bear it if no one laughs.

Luckily, the halls are emptier when I squish back to my room in my wet shower shoes. And there's a text from Pamela!

> Pamela: You're forgiven as long as you promise me you won't go see Crane.

I frown. I didn't realize her forgiveness was transactional.

> Harleen: Could we at least meet and talk about why first?

The three little dots appear. And disappear. And reappear.

> Pamela: Maybe it might be best if we keep some distance right now. But you could call me?

Wow. That's just great. I mean, she has every right to feel that way after what I did yesterday, but I don't know. It feels like there's some other reason. Something personal. And hurtful. I get dressed while I think about how to reply. Blow dry my hair. It's a silvery-white color now, but that doesn't bother me so much. It's actually kind of pretty. Plus, it seems like an invitation to do something exciting. Some bright colors. Maybe some ombré. My face, though? That's going to take some getting used to.

I dab some foundation onto my forearm as a test, the way Dr. Viswanathan suggested. A patch of peach floating in a sea of ghost white. I eat a yogurt and brush my teeth, but my skin doesn't seem to be itching or flaking or turning red or breaking out into painful boils (which may be reversible!), so I decide, what the hell, and smear it all over my face. But I get this weird feeling. Like I can't decide if I'm painting over the real me or uncovering her.

Another flurry of texts from Pamela come through.

> Pamela: Look, if meeting with me is what'll keep you from seeing Crane, I'll do it.
>
> Pamela: Just not now because I'm in class. Will you please please please wait for me to get out before you do anything?

She doesn't say *anything stupid,* but I feel like it's implied. And I don't know if I like being talked to this way. Like my amnesia means I can't think for myself or my impulsivity equals stupidity. Who died and made Pamela my keeper?

I fire off a reply.

> Harleen: Fine. I'll wait here, okay?

But then I slip my phone into my bag and go to meet Dr. Crane.

CHAPTER 33

Dr. Crane's Office

THE LEATHER CHAIRS ARE BUTTERY SOFT. AND THE LIGHTing is a pretty golden color, courtesy of one of those stained glass lamps; his has a pattern that looks like tree branches or maybe a spiderweb—it's hard to say. Dr. Crane has steered me through the pleasantries, made me feel safe and calm and comfortable. He's almost as good as Dr. Morales. But he has a tell. He steeples his fingers, leans over them in a way that is almost hungry, when he asks it:

"What can you tell me about the day of the jailbreak?"

My heart races, but I can't say why. "I—"

DON'T TRUST DR. CRANE.

He's bad. He's really, really bad.

"Well, um—"

I don't remember. I really don't. But if I did, should I tell him?

"Is there something wrong?" he asks. Kind. Careful. That hungry look is gone.

"My friend Pamela says not to trust you." And . . . there I go. Hope that was the right decision.

I wait for him to get angry, react somehow, but he just nods. "Well, let's unpack that. Why do you think a friend would say that to you? Is it possible she meant to discourage you from seeking amnesia treatment? Do you think there are things she'd like to keep you from remembering?"

You know, now that he mentions it . . .

"She did try to keep me from seeing the news articles about the escape. And she won't tell me anything, even though I'm sure she knows things. And then the way it feels when she's around. Ugh. Everything's always so tense. *She*'s always so tense." I realize how much I've been talking and blush. "Sorry. My friendship drama probably isn't going to help us figure out anything."

But Dr. Crane just spreads his arms wide. "You never know. Anything that feels important to you probably is that way for good reason."

I smile. "Thanks." It's such a 180 from talking to Win or Pamela or anyone else. Oh! And now that I'm thinking of it . . . "Do *you* know anything?"

He looks genuinely pained. "Unfortunately, I wasn't scheduled to work that day. I only wish I was. Maybe I could have somehow stopped all of this from ending the way it did."

He stares off at the wall, almost like his mind is running through all the alternative scenarios for that night. Then he recovers. "I'm sorry. I can get a little maudlin with the brooding. Are you certain you don't remember anything about that night?"

I shake my head. "I'm sorry."

There's a flash of something in his eyes, but it disappears just as quickly. "Not to worry, my dear. We'll figure it out."

My dear.

I'm in a darkened hallway.

It doesn't have to be this way, my dear.

I shake it off. I don't know what it means. The voice in my memory doesn't even sound human.

"Is everything all right? Did you remember something?"

I can't tell him the truth. It'll sound crazy. So I tell him part of it. "I remember being in a hallway, here at the asylum. I think it was that night."

He nods. "Were you alone?"

Except for the monster with the inhuman voice. "Yes."

"Interesting. Well, we'll keep at it." He flips a page in his notebook. "I'd like to shift topics a bit. What can you tell me about Talia al Ghūl?"

"I know I was her intern? Well, Dr. Morales's intern, but I think I worked with Talia."

"I think she's the key. She's an expert at manipulation. She pushes people. I think everything that happened that night leads back to her." His teeth grind together for a moment. I'm sure it must feel awful to have let her slip through his fingers. "Of course, I can't know for certain, but based on what I saw on the security footage . . ."

I remember the footage of Talia dragging me down that hallway, a knife to my neck. That petrified look in my eyes. "I think you're right. The police showed me . . ." I trail off, partly because I can't hold back a shudder and partly because he must have seen the same footage.

"Do you have any idea how to find her?" He leans over steepled fingers again. That same hungry expression.

"No. Why would I know that?" Holy crap, how guilty am I? What did I do?

"I think it's likely you may have been helping Talia that night. Don't be worried. It's clear she was using you," he rushes to add. "Do you have any ideas about what she may have asked you to do?"

I shake my head apologetically.

"That's okay. That's where I can help you. I want you to lean back in your chair. Close your eyes. Just relax. Feel the leather against your palms. The light on the outside of your eyelids."

I do as he says, taking deep, slow breaths in and out.

He continues in a soothing voice. "Now, I want you to go back to that night. Think about where you are. Notice the details."

It's the day of Arkalamity, I feel it. I'm standing in the intern office area with one of those small hiking backpacks. The same one that was next to me when I woke up in the hospital. And I don't know how I know it or why I'm going to do it, but I'm about to climb up into the ceiling.

I tell Dr. Crane what I see. (Well, the part about being in the office area, not the part about the ceiling.)

"Good. Keep going. What do you see?"

I climb up onto my desk. I move the ceiling tile, and the dust makes me sneeze. I'm on a mission, but I still don't know why.

"I'm supposed to be doing something for Talia."

"Can you remember what?"

"Um—"

I crawl into the ceiling, and I pull the powdery white square of tile back into place, all except for the smallest crack. And I wait.

Except, no, that isn't right. It's the wrong day. A different ceiling looking down on a different room, some kind of laboratory.

I try to pull my mind back to Talia and the jailbreak, but

the memory keeps going. My hands tense on the arms of the chair. My brain doesn't want to let me remember this right now.

Dr. Crane's voice tethers me to reality. "Just relax. You're safe here."

I'm going to strap you into the operating chair now.

Just relax.

My pulse pounds in my ears. I remember.

King Shark waits in an operating chair.

And Dr. Crane pulls on a mask and becomes The Scarecrow.

CHAPTER 34

Fear

"TELL ME WHAT YOU SEE," SAYS DR. CRANE, HIS SOOTHING voice more insistent now.

I don't know how I make it out of this alive. I am in a therapy session with The Scarecrow—quite possibly the person who did this to me—and I have to pretend I don't know what I know because if he realizes that I remember . . . If he suspects . . .

I force myself straight up in my chair, eyes wide open, gasping in shock or terror or both.

"Talia," I stammer out. "I see Talia."

"What happened? Are you all right?" He seems so sincere. It's unbelievable, really.

"I'm okay." I pant a little and hope I'm not overselling it. "But I think Talia did something to me. I think she's the reason I ended up in the hospital."

"I think you're right. And we have to stop her. Find her. Do you remember where she is?"

"I remember . . ." I screw my eyes shut, pretending to focus. "I remember falling-falling. And Talia. I know she was there," I say emphatically. "I'm sorry. That's all I've got."

"What about—?"

But I've already got my hand to my head, feigning a headache. "I don't feel so good. I think I need to go lie down."

His teeth clench again, just a little, just for a second. "I get the feeling you have unfinished business with Talia. That you won't be able to fully understand and reconcile what happened to you until you confront her."

The weird thing? I feel the same way. I guess he's a good psychiatrist despite being made of pure evil.

"I'd like to see you later this week so we can keep working on this."

I would rather give myself eighteen thousand paper cuts and then jump in a swimming pool with King Shark.

I paste on a bright smile. "I'd love that."

I rush straight to Pamela's after my session with Crane. *Knock-knock-knock.* C'mon, I need you to be home. IT IS LITERALLY LIFE AND DEATH.

She isn't there. Of course she's not. I'm only burning from the inside out with important questions that she and she alone might be able to answer. Things like: What was the mission I was doing for Talia? And who sprayed me with chemicals and left me for dead? And what was The Scarecrow doing to King Shark? And was I a hero the night of Arkalamity or a villain? But, no. It's cool. DON'T BE HOME OR ANYTHING.

I put my head in my hands and slide to the floor in front of Pamela's door. So, she's not here. I'll wait. She's got to come back sometime.

I jot down some notes on what I remembered during that session while I wait for her. Crane is The Scarecrow. I helped

Talia escape. But why? That's the part that doesn't make sense. I was trying so hard to be good. Why would I have helped her? Was she blackmailing me or something, or did I actually choose to help of my own free will?

Ten minutes later I realize that (A) Pamela is not here and doesn't seem to be coming anytime soon and (B) if I stay any longer, I'll be late for class. So I leave a note on her marker board: *I stopped by after my session (sorry!!). Come find me! —HQ*

Then I hurry across campus so I'm not late. They said I didn't have to attend classes this week if I wasn't feeling up to it. (My professors have actually been extremely cool about the whole hospitalization-and-amnesia thing—perhaps because they've deduced that I'm the Gotham U student mentioned in all the news articles?) But anyway, I *am* feeling up to it. And besides, today's lecture is on memory and the brain, which could not be more perfect for a person trying to regain her memory and unbreak her brain. I'm so close to figuring things out; I can feel it. A part of me knows I barely made it out of my session with Dr. Crane alive, but the other part of me feels like he really helped me tap into something. Multiple pieces of the past came back, and if I can just keep this snowball rolling, it'll be an avalanche in no time.

A professor I haven't seen before starts lecturing about learning and memory. We learn about how memories are encoded and how they decay. How they're stored in a part of the brain called the hippocampus, which looks like a seahorse. I take extremely helpful notes like, *Why is my seahorse broken?*

The next few slides are on declarative memory, the kind you explicitly remember. So, like, facts about the world or events that have happened to you. And some people have amnesia where they can't remember stuff in the past (yes, hi, me) and other people have a type of amnesia where they can't form new memories. But here's the wild thing—you could have a person like that practice a song on the piano every day or you could tape a tack to your hand every time you shake hands with them. And eventually they'd learn the song and they'd pull back their hand before it touched yours. But they wouldn't be able to say why. They'd just know that it felt like the right thing to do. Apparently, it's called implicit learning. I am fascinated. I wonder if I picked up any cool skills in the months I can't remember. Oh! I hope I know how to play guitar now! Or fly airplanes! I mean, I doubt it, but it would be cool.

I look up and realize I've missed the last couple of slides. Oops. I just missed everything he said on sensory memory. But now we're getting to the good stuff. False memories. Confabulation.

"Memories aren't perfect. Our brains aren't books or computers. Things change."

Apparently, if you ask people with a certain type of brain injury about an event they can't remember, instead of saying "I don't know," they'll make up a story on the spot, and they actually think it's the truth (confabulation).

The professor pauses. "Are there any questions?"

I raise my hand. Oh! Me! Pick me!

"Yes?"

(Success!)

"I was wondering, what are some methods for the recovery of lost memories or amnesia?" Just 'cause I'm curious. Not 'cause I have it.

"Good question. Emotion and personal significance are two of the things that help our brains classify a memory as special. A person could try cueing a memory with a song or a smell. Something connected to that memory when it was recorded."

Huh. Not sure they make a "Sounds of Arkham Asylum" ASMR. Or an eau-de-chemical-waste-scented candle.

"Things like photographs and letters can help too," the professor continues. "There's also a school of thought regarding state-dependent learning. If a person was in a particular state, emotionally or physically, when a memory was encoded—delighted, sad, alert, drunk, hypnotized, in pain, on ADHD medication—they would need to be in the same state to best retrieve the memory. Not that I'm suggesting any of you get drunk and study for this exam." He gives us a wry smile and progresses to the next slide.

I take notes, rapid-fire, until the class ends.

When I get back to my dorm room, I can't wait to try some of these memory techniques. After I snuggle up in about seventy-five blankets. And drink an entire gallon of hot chocolate. Good grief, what is wrong with me? I can't stop shivering. Part of me wonders if I'm actually cold or if looking at my white palms just makes me feel like I am. Either way, putting on a sweatshirt seems like the very best idea. I grab one out of my dresser and shove it over my head without bothering to close the drawer.

My roommate side-eyes the open drawer on her way out. It's practically vomiting jeans and tank tops. Absolutely nothing like her dresser, which has been Marie Kondo-ed within an inch of its life. As the door snaps shut, I am struck with the idea that the real reason she hates me has something to do with French class, but that doesn't make any sense.

I scowl and shove the drawer shut. Only it doesn't close all the way. It catches. Because of course I can't even do that right. I pull it open and smoosh all the clothes down and try again. It's still a couple of inches open. Ughhhhhhhh.

I wonder if a T-shirt fell behind— Wait a minute. Wait a minute, I remember this. Something about a box and some duct tape and making sure Samantha wasn't home. Something with this dresser.

I check Samantha's schedule, which she has neatly tacked to her bulletin board. She'll be gone for the next hour. I pull the drawer out one more time, wiggling it so that it comes off its runners. I balance the drawer on my desk chair and peek into the empty space where it used to be.

There's a box duct taped to the bottom.

CHAPTER 35

Elliot Hall

THE BOX IS WHITE AND ONLY AN INCH OR SO THICK, LIKE the kind a new tablet might come in, which I guess is how it fit between the drawer and the bottom of my dresser. I can see the gap between the dresser bottom and the runners now if I peer inside. Thick enough for a book, but not a dictionary. The top third of the box is mangled from getting smashed by the drawer. Repeatedly. Oops. Sometimes I should really do the problem-solving *before* the smashing.

I pull off the top, my hands leaving foundation-colored smudges, my mind already spinning about what could be inside. Weapons? Devices? Stacks of money? I really hope it's stacks of money. Or, like, the deed to a unicorn farm.

Files. Lots of them. And a notebook. I was kind of hoping for something more exci— Oh! At least this one's about King Shark. It's got his all his information (380 pounds, can you believe?), notes about sessions (every bit as intriguing as you'd hope), and photo (sharktastic). I feel like I can remember reviewing files like these with Dr. Morales. I wonder why I took this one home. I note the handwriting scrawled at the top.

> Majestic. Dangerous. Kind. King Shark could basically murder someone in cold blood at this point, and I'd still be smitten.

My handwriting.

Maybe I didn't want anyone knowing my private thoughts. After what happened last year with Dr. Nelson and the Joker paper, it makes sense.

There are other psychological profiles after King Shark's. Talia. The Riddler. The Joker. And then a list of names. At the top it says *Arkham Acres.* I realize it's more than just a list, really; it's a schedule of blood draws. I remember this. They were taking blood samples from all the girls at Arkham Acres with selective catatonia.

I was trying to help them. Someone . . . someone wanted to hurt them. Or at the very least, use them.

These girls. They could be why I would have worked with Talia.

I gaze around my room with new eyes. I wonder if I've got anything else hidden away in here. I lift up my mattress. Poke around in the back of my closet. Nothing.

That's when I notice the eyes staring out at me from the bookshelf over my desk. They belong to a jaunty, if somewhat aloof, taxidermized beaver, and he is staring at—nay, judging—me from his silent perch.

"Hey, I remember you." I say it out loud almost like I'm expecting him to talk back. (He does not. Much disappointment is had.)

I pick him up, my hands running over his lifelike fur. "Bernie, right? Bernice had all kinds of papers and stuff hidden in you."

That was last year. Easy to remember. I can't say whether

I have or haven't used him the same way, but I do remember where the secret hatch is. I feel for the little latch between his shoulder blades.

"Aha!"

The latch pops open. There aren't any journals or papers this time.

But there is a key.

It hangs on a plastic key chain with a glittery red cherry logo and the words *Cherry Bombz*. It's not particularly fancy—the key or the key chain. Like, when you find a secret key hidden in a taxidermized animal, you kind of hope it will be heavy and metal and covered with engravings of flowers and dragons and ancient languages and stuff. The kind of key that looks like it's meant to unlock pirate treasure or a book of incantations or a castle in France because, guess what, you've been a princess THIS WHOLE TIME. Not that I daydream about that; I'm just spitballing here. Anyway, this key looks like it unlocks all the secrets of a dirty gym locker or maybe a middle school diary—one of the high-end ones. But since I clearly went to the trouble of giving it an elaborate hiding place, I figure it has to mean something.

"Do you know what it goes to?" I ask Bernie.

He stares at me with those shiny black eyes.

"Yeah, me neither."

I try internet-searching *Cherry Bombz*. Apparently, it's a skating rink half an hour from campus. Weird.

I slip the key into my jeans pocket because I don't know what else to do with it. Then I sit at my desk and open the box of papers again.

I look at the list. I remember stealing it now. I remember that I made Win go get the car first. Because I thought he'd judge me for taking it? Because I didn't trust him with this information? And if I didn't trust him then, does that mean I shouldn't trust him now?

I pull Bernie closer on the desk. "I don't know. What do you think, Bern? Pamela said don't trust Crane. And she was right. And she also said don't trust Win, so he's got to be bad too, right?"

Bernie sits there with his square white teeth, so wise for someone so condescending. He really is a good listener, despite the resting beaver face.

"Yeah, that's a really good point."

I think back to how hard Graham had to fight to work with Dr. Crane. Win must have done the same thing as a first-year. You don't randomly get assigned to work with the director of Arkham Asylum.

Dr. Crane is a genius.

He can take the most hardened criminal, and they'll be sobbing and vulnerable when he leaves the room.

I think it was really smart of you to pick Dr. Crane to help you with your memory.

Win doesn't just work with Crane; he idolizes him. And he may seem like a golden retriever, but he's smart too. And dedicated. Always coming in evenings and weekends to work on some project he's never really told me any details about. I try to imagine some universe where Win works for Crane without knowing what he does.

And I just can't.

If Crane is injecting chips into people, experimenting with fear as a means of mind control, Win must be a part of it.

Two quick raps on the door, and I nearly jump out of my skin. Samantha wasn't supposed to be back from class yet. The handle turns, and I stuff the papers back into the box, quick, and shut the lid.

"Hey," says a deep voice that makes me wish I had locked my door.

I turn, and Win is standing in my doorway, grinning in that way he has. Except before I never thought it was hiding something.

"Hey, your face is different."

"Hey, yeah, I put on makeup." I position myself in front of the box and cross my fingers he doesn't see it.

He frowns. "What are you doing?"

"Trying to remember things." I shrug and smile and stare into his eyes while thinking about kissing him because I heard that can be very distracting.

He nods and seems to forget why he's here, so maybe it worked?

"So," I say, grabbing a coat and scarf from my closet. "We were learning about memory and stuff in class today, and I was thinking about trying to retrace my steps the day of the jailbreak."

I toss the scarf on top of the box instead of putting it on, and I hope he doesn't notice. (He doesn't. In fact, now that I think about it, he's glancing around the room like he's expecting the League of Assassins to pop out of the ventilation system.)

"Well, that's perfect," he says. Arms crossing over his chest. That nervous, searching look again. "I was just coming over to ask you to go for a drive with me."

CHAPTER 36

Win's Car

WIN TEARS THROUGH THE CITY IN A SPORTS CAR THAT probably costs more than two years' tuition at Gotham U, only instead of being candy-apple red or electric blue or some other douchebag color, it's slate gray. Old money and class and all that. It's still kind of weird to me that I'm dating him.

I never got the idea he was with me for the wrong reasons, though. To slum it with an East End girl or to shake up his parents or something like that. His suntanned hands grip the steering wheel as he hums along to a Top 100 song. I study his face. Freaking adorable dimples. Blue eyes that manage to be searing and kind at the same time. He must hide the darkness real deep.

Win takes the exit for Arkham Asylum—we figured it makes the most sense to start there. Or, well, I did, and he agreed. But now I can't help wondering why. Does he have an ulterior motive? Is he helping me pick up the pieces of that night or delivering me to The Scarecrow?

I narrow my eyes like that'll somehow help me see

through the Boy Scout veneer. Has he always had that scar over his right knuckle? It's purple, not a fading pink or a nearly invisible white. Maybe he got it in the last few weeks. Maybe the night of the jailbreak.

I realize I've inched away from him at some point, body practically pressed against the door, betraying my feelings. I make myself scoot closer. The Cherry Bombz key shifts in my jeans pocket so that it's poking me in the leg. I thought about mentioning the roller rink to Win. Going there and seeing if I could figure out what the key was for. But if it was important enough to hide the key, it's probably not something I want Win knowing about. No matter how much I'm dying to see what it is. I ignore where the key is digging into my leg and also my mind, and I lean closer to Win. Run my fingers over his hand that rests on the median near the stick shift. I trace the scar with the tip of my index finger.

"How'd you get it?"

He startles. "What?" Darts his eyes at the scar and then back at the road. "Oh. Um. Yeah, I don't really remember."

His jaw tightens, and he swallows what looks like an awful lot of spit. (People who aren't used to lying really suck at it.)

"Oh." I don't even try to pretend I believe him. Scars like that come with memories. And stories.

I lace my fingers through his, but his hackles are up. He pulls his hand away and runs it through his hair. Chest rising and falling with shallow breaths. Anxious breaths.

"So, how are you feeling?" he blurts out, breaking the silence.

Like I wish I could remember who doused me in chemical waste.

I force a smile. "Good. Well, better." I lean closer. "I wish

I could figure out what happened that night, though. I'm really glad you're helping me." I pause long enough for it to feel like I'm finished talking. Long enough for him to relax. "So, you really weren't there for any of it?"

"No. Not after I left you that afternoon."

I actually believe him this time. That or he's getting better at covering his tells. And then he grips the steering wheel, skin turning white at the knuckles.

"Pamela was there." His voice is different when he says her name. Not the softer, honeyed version he uses with me. It's got bite in it. "If there's anyone who can tell you what happened that night, it's her."

He's right. He's right, and his words settle on me like bricks. I don't even attempt to argue.

His eyes slide over me. "She hasn't told you anything yet."

I hate that he could pull the thought from my brain like that. It makes me feel naked.

"She's told me things," I shoot back. "About . . . things."

Nice, Harleen. Why don't you just hand him your heart and a microscope while you're at it.

But he doesn't look self-satisfied the way most people would. More like frustrated, with a side of longing. "Why do you think she's keeping things from you?"

I don't answer. I don't want to think about it. Here. With him. What if the answer hurts, or what if it's not the one I want, or what if there's a reason my brain won't let me remember it?

Win shakes his head. My non-answer is enough. He mutters something I can't quite hear. *It's always her,* or something like that. And then: "She's not what you think, you know."

I would have been good to you.

She's not what you think.

Holy crap. We broke up. An image of us on the day of Arkalamity flashes in my mind. Us, standing in the hallway outside the restricted wing. Me, breaking up with him. I don't exactly have all the details—I can't remember *why*—but I know I was the dumper and he was the dumpee. What is he doing pretending he's my boyfriend? Talking in front of Dr. Viswanathan, snuggling in my hospital bed, kissing—we have kissed MULTIPLE times—any of those times would have been an excellent opportunity for him to tell me we were no longer seeing each other.

Unless he has a reason not to.

A reason like working for Dr. Crane. Being his most devoted intern. His protégé.

What if Crane suspects that I remember who he is and what he's done? What if he's asked Win to do something about it?

Win's supposed to be some kind of Boy Scout. But Boy Scouts don't fake-date amnesia patients. He's been watching me. He's been watching me and reporting back to The Scarecrow.

The scenery outside the window shifts from concrete to trees, and I realize we're not on the road to Arkham anymore. When did that happen? Is he driving me out to the country so he can do something terrible and no one will hear me scream?

The winding black road grows thinner, changes to a packed-dirt path. Oh crap. Oh crap. Oh crap. We're in the legit middle of nowhere, and I bet there are no people for miles, and I wish I had found an excuse to make him pop the trunk because I bet it contains sharp objects and latex gloves and maybe even a body bag.

I glance across the car at my beautiful, lying golden retriever of a boyfriend and realize how much I don't know about him.

"Um. Where are we?" I try to keep my voice calm, but my lungs are traitors.

Win smiles in a way that does not look altogether hinged.

"You'll see."

CHAPTER 37

The Middle of the Woods Where No One Can Hear You Scream

WE HIKE FARTHER DOWN THE PATH AND INTO THE FOREST. I can still see the car behind us, but only just. The restless, pinned-in feeling grows inside me, and I feel an overwhelming urge to run—*now*—but I force myself to keep walking.

He doesn't have any weapons, I tell myself. It doesn't comfort me as much as it should.

Win touches my shoulder, and I jump. I can't help it.

"We're almost there." He cocks his head. "You okay?"

I nod like a bobblehead. "For sure. I'm great. What is it we're looking for again?"

A hidden weapons cache? Bear trap? Shallow grave?

He points through the trees. "There."

"Holy . . ." My voice trails off. "What is that?"

I take in the fence. Well, what used to be a fence. There's a great gaping hole through it—you can see where it's been patched, but some kind of vine/tree/plant/thing clearly tore it to pieces. A beast of a plant dives into the ground and back up again with humps like a sea dragon's (at least, I think it's the same plant?). On either side of the patched hole, vines curl to the sky, thick as a person, fairy-tale beanstalks with thorns like teeth. The fence looks like a plaything next to them. If you look carefully, you can see twisted pieces of it clinging to the vines, lying on the forest floor like dead bodies or pieces of silver lace torn from a dress. You can imagine how the vines tore apart the chain links and razor wire with an apocalyptic zeal.

And behind the carnage and metal husks and prehistoric botanical monster, Arkham Asylum rises in the background. Strangely, the plants only add to its Gothic glory.

"What could have done this?" I honestly feel like I might be hallucinating. That's how otherworldly this looks.

"That's what we're trying to figure out. Prison fences aren't the same as backyard fences, did you know? These are made of stainless steel. Extremely hard to climb. And to cut." Win cautiously runs a hand over one of the vines. "It happened the night of Arkalamity. This is how they escaped. We were hoping you might remember." His eyes flick over me, searching for a reaction or some sign of recognition. I wonder if *we* means him and Dr. Crane.

I stare at the colossal vines stupidly, my eyes still goggling. "I wish I knew."

He nods, but I can't tell if he believes me. Also, wait a minute, is this him slipping? Accidentally saying he knows I was involved in the breakout? What else does he know? And why isn't he being straight with me?

"Hey, why don't you look around or whatever. Try to jog your memory." He starts walking back the way we came. "I forgot something in the car."

A wrench to bludgeon me with?

He gets smaller and smaller, disappears into the trees. I check to make sure my phone still has reception in case I need to call 911. I should probably be alarmed by how much this all feels like a horror movie, but the vines winding through the fence are calling to me. Pulling me closer. Begging me to reach out my hand and— Hold up. I have read the fairy tales. I know what happens when the princess pricks her finger on the thorn of some magical/majestic/malevolent plant.

But I can't stop myself from touching it.

I am not sucked into the Phantom Zone. (Yet.) But there's something about these vines. The huge hole they left—the sheer level of destruction—it's weirdly similar to the photos of the Woodrue lab.

Plants shooting out of the ground.

Fence bursting at the seams.

And delicate vines spelling out *Harleen* on the roof of the library.

Ohmygosh, ~~Pamela~~ Ivy has powers. I remember now.

Ivy did this.

A branch snaps behind me, and I just about jump out of my skin.

"Win. You scared me."

My heart flutters in my chest as I turn to confirm that, yes, it is Win, not an ax murderer. Not that I've established the two are mutually exclusive.

He pulls out a knife.

"What are you doing?!" My eyes dart around, searching the woods for exits, legs tensing, ready to run. He's big, but I'm East End scrappy. Plus, I know martial arts.

He stalks closer, eleven feet tall and arms like tree trunks. Fleeing is no longer an option. Fighting it is.

I clench my fists at my sides. Ready myself to dodge the first blow.

And . . . he walks right past me.

"Dr. Crane asked me to get some samples of these weird plants." Win shaves off a few pieces of the vine and slips them into a plastic specimen bag. "You don't remember what could have done this, do you?"

I try to keep my eyes from falling out of my head. "NOPE. No clue. I got nothing."

He nods. Does he believe me? I think he believes me.

But then he sighs in a way that feels theatrical. "Bummer. I was hoping this would help you remember."

He heads back to his car, and I follow him, glancing over my shoulder at the vines and the torn fence one last time.

"Don't worry," he says, misinterpreting my expression. "I'm sure our next stop will help."

"Are we going inside Arkham?"

I stare at the dark spires of the asylum, and my palms start sweating and my pulse pounds in my ears. This is the part where he delivers me to The Scarecrow.

"No. We're going to Ace Chemicals."

CHAPTER 38

Ace Chemicals

OUR TOUR DOWN MEMORY LANE JUST TOOK A DARK TURN.

"Does anything about these roads feel familiar?" Win asks as he navigates through the heart of Gotham's industrial district.

I try not to let him see how scared I am. Partly because there's something about the grungy buildings and belching smokestacks that makes my heart race like it's trying to break the sound barrier and partly because Win has made a mistake. If Ace Chemicals really is the place that changed me (and my heartbeat is saying it is), Win shouldn't know that. Not if he really did leave when he said he did.

Of course, it's always possible he came back.

"You were on a motorcycle right around here." He catches me staring at him, and he must be able to read the suspicion in my eyes, because he quickly covers with: "I mean, that's what I've been able to piece together from news reports and social media and stuff."

Uh-huh. Or you were there that night. Maybe not with Talia and me during the escape, but following us. Lurking in the shadows. I slip my pocketknife out of my bag and into my coat pocket so it'll be easier to get to.

Win parks in the alley behind Ace Chemicals, a giant industrial eyesore in a string of giant industrial eyesores. Huge neon letters spell out ACE in a sickly-green color, the word CHEMICALS in red underneath. Smokestacks rise in four corners like turrets, giving the entire building the feel of a castle. A dark one forged of spray-painted bricks and corrugated metal. And inside there's a witch or a foreman or the person who made me this way. This is where it happened. I can feel it.

Falling.

Falling.

Falling.

Burnt-hair smell. Swimming pool filled with napalm.

But who pushed me?

The paint on the metal stairs is blistered and peeling, but Win doesn't notice as he grabs the railing, taking them two at a time. He seems almost excited. Or relieved, maybe. No, that's not right either. The keys jangle as he takes them from his pocket, his hands shaking with anticipation. That's what it is. The knowing that something is finally going to happen, and for better or worse, you'll be free of the weight of it.

I pretend to shiver so I can put my hands in my coat pockets. I wrap my fingers around my pocketknife.

"How do you have the keys?" I ask.

"Oh." He freezes, but just for a second. "Dr. Crane got me a set of keys. He thought it would be a good idea to take you here."

I bet he did.

Win takes me inside, and I didn't think it was possible to feel any more panicked than I did in the woods. Until now. I can't remember the metal catwalks or the vats of chemicals, but the terror they make me feel—that has to mean something.

He leads me up the stairs and onto one of the catwalks. Closer and closer still to a vat of chemicals that is different from the others. This one is surrounded by caution tape. And the chemicals inside are the most luminous shade of green.

"They've been doing a police investigation," explains Win.

I drift to the edge of the catwalk, drawn to the otherworldly green of the chemicals below, churning in their swimming pool–sized crucible. So, this is where it happened. The feeling washing over me is stronger than certainty. More like . . . destiny. Like some secret part of me knows I was always meant for the place, one single thread of razor wire drawing me here. Win leans against the metal railings next to me.

"We need to talk. I had an ulterior motive for driving you around today."

I get ready to throw him over the edge. Stake him through the heart. I'm pretty sure he tried to kill me to make his boss happy, and now he wants to finish the job.

"I've been lying to you. Ever since the accident. I've been pretending to be your boyfriend."

He searches my face, waiting to see how I'll take the news. I try to remain calm, but inside my jacket, I flip open my knife.

"When you woke up, you thought we were still together, so I pretended. Partly because I didn't want to hurt you, but also because it felt so nice. To be together again." He puts his head in his hands. "What kind of person does that?"

The kind of person embroiled in a sinister plot with The

Scarecrow? I expect this is all some kind of trick, a ruse, but then he actually starts sobbing.

I love you.

Do you?

I'd do anything to show you.

Anything?

Oh crap, Win wasn't manipulating me. It was the other way around. Extracting promises in the dark. Pushing him to do things. Stealing his badge. *I*'m the bad guy in the relationship. (Side note: Why is this such a shock?)

I slide my knife blade shut. This poor guy. I almost broke him. Maybe did break him. I pat him on the back while he hiccups. Eventually, he gets the whole thing out of his system. His sobs taper off to a sniffle.

"I have something else to confess," he says.

"Okay." You cheated on your third-grade spelling test one time? I know, man, you're hard-core.

He stares down at the noxious chemicals, blue eyes still shining with tears. "After I left, the day of the jailbreak, I know you told me not to, but I told Dr. Crane what was going on."

I tense next to him. Was the whole sobbing thing an act to lull me into a false sense of security? I don't think it was, but—

"I'm really sorry," he says.

Because he knows Dr. Crane is The Scarecrow? Because Dr. Crane is the one who pushed me?

"If I had gone to him sooner, this might never have happened to you."

Ohhh. Win still thinks Dr. Crane is one of the good guys. Wow, he's even more of a golden retriever than I thought.

"I was really upset with you. About the breakup."

Okay, now I'm even more confused. "You were fine with it," I blurt out. "It was like I was setting you free."

He recoils, looking legit horrified. "Uh, no. I was devastated."

"What?!" All of this makes less than zero sense. There's no way I could misremember/misinterpret/mis-whatever a situation so badly. "No. No way. I maintain we had a really nice breakup."

Like, maybe even the nicest of all time. No screaming. No restraining orders. Not even a drink in someone's face.

Win is still staring at me like I'm from outer space. "Nobody has nice breakups. That's like an oxymoron. At least one person ends up getting crushed. Usually both." He winces like he's in pain. "But sometimes it doesn't matter as much to the other person."

Oh gosh. This poor guy. I don't even know what to say, so I try to put my hand on his shoulder, but he shrugs me off, his face suddenly hard.

"Tell me the truth. Did you run to her the second you broke up with me?"

"What?"

He rolls his eyes. "Pamela."

Well, now that he mentions it, I guess I did, kind of. . . . "Yeah, well, you were in a bar partying right after. I saw the picture."

He shakes his head, his neck turning red in patches. "That's just what my friends made it look like on social media. They took me drinking because I was so messed up over you, and I ended up having way too many beers and punching a wall and crying in my room while listening to Olivia Rodrigo's 'Traitor' on repeat. Is that what you want to hear? Because that's how I spent the night of the accident."

Wow. Well, that's . . . unexpected. "Olivia Rodrigo, huh?"

I work really, really, really hard not to smile, but Win doesn't even notice; he's so full of tragic sincerity. "When she said, *Loved you at your worst, but that didn't matter,* she spoke directly to my soul."

The irony? I was trying my absolute hardest to be good this year.

"Also, I know you stole my ID badge. And the funny thing is, I would have given it to you if you'd just asked. Even after you dumped me."

Gah, this guy.

"Win, I'm really sorry. For all of it."

"S'okay." He simultaneously wipes his eyes and puffs up his chest, like you can see toxic masculinity having a battle for his very soul. "I've been thinking a lot about us and life and what I want since we broke up, and I think you were right."

"Yeah?" I go to pat his arm again, and this time he lets me.

"Yeah, like there are all these things I want out of life. I want to have a normal life and a normal job. I want three kids. I want to go to their Little League games and ballet recitals and let them eat cake for breakfast on their birthdays. Have a house with a yard, get a cocker spaniel or maybe a corgi, some chickens or something." He turns and looks directly into my eyes. Takes my hands in his. "And that's not you, Harleen."

I feel like I have been punched in the chest, but he keeps going.

"I mean, kids and dogs and fences? Can you picture it? You'd be miserable. If you didn't break me, I'd break you a different way."

I understand what he's saying, I do, and I know he's not

purposely trying to hurt me. But knowing that he thinks I'm incapable of any of those things makes a fissure open up inside me, a wound I have no idea how to close. There's a part of me that worries he's right.

He wraps his arms around me in a hug, probably our last.

I expected that Win was taking me here to hurt me. I didn't think it would be like this.

Win and I are quiet during the car ride home. Thinking. When he drops me off, I go inside like I'm going to my room, but instead I walk right past it and out the side door of the dorm in the direction of the subway.

A flurry of texts from Ivy pop up when I'm a block away.

Pamela: Harleen!

Pamela: I can be home in 30 minutes, and I promise to tell you EVERYTHING.

Pamela: Just please stay where you are and stop going to the cars and offices of people who I am certain are trying to kill you!

I snicker at the idea that I made Ivy break out the all caps. I also can't help but wonder if she really means it about telling me everything, or if it's going to be another skewed, sanitized version. Either way, I'm not staying put. I text her back.

Harleen: Meet me at Cherry Bombz

CHAPTER 39

Cherry Bombz

I GET TO CHERRY BOMBZ FIRST. IT'S . . . NICER THAN I EXpected. Middle-class nice. Not a dive, anyway. There's this kind of anteroom with a front desk where everyone-and-they-mean-everyone has to pay before entering. Just in case you were thinking of coming in with some sweet skates of your own and not paying—THINK AGAIN. I pay the entry fee and the skate rental too. Just in case I need to do any skating. Purely for research purposes.

I shuffle inside after a herd of middle schoolers. There's a giant rink—a lake of smooth, beige wood—with a disco ball hanging over the exact center. Spotlights in red and purple and green and blue. Other than that, it's pretty dimly lit. To set the mood? So that you can't see how much gum has been ground into the art deco indoor-outdoor carpet in the last two decades? PROBABLY BOTH.

On one side of the rink are tables and a pizza-popcorn-slushies-cotton candy place. On the other, benches and a massive wall of lockers. My heart beats faster as I approach them. The metal on their locks matches the key burning a hole in my pocket. This is it. I'm going to find out what I've been hiding from myself.

And then it hits me. I have no idea which of the 237 lockers this key goes to.

Instead of trying them all in order or something equally suspicious, I decide to lace up my skates and skate around. I used to love skating when I was younger, but I haven't done it recently. At least, I think I haven't. I glide around the rink easy as walking. And then I pick up speed, turn around so that I'm skating backward for a bit, do a double spin as I return to skating forward. Turns out I'm good. Really good. Shockingly good.

"How. Are. You. Doing. That?" Pamela hobbles across the rink on newborn-colt legs. Like, she's gonna bust her butt any second. Like, it's almost hard to watch.

I crack up laughing at her expense because I am such a nice person. But also I skate over to help her. (I'm not a monster.)

Before I can reach her, though, there's a three-kid pileup, crash-crash-crash, right in front of her. Pamela's eyes go big. She knows she's way out of her depth, and she doesn't seem to have discovered how to use the brakes yet. I speed up, figure-eighting around two sets of couples holding hands, but then another kid slide-crashes right in front of me, and I have to leap into the air to avoid hitting him. Which sets me careening straight for Pamela and her Twister pile of children. I flip into the air—it's more muscle memory than anything—doing an aerial over the kids and stopping on a dime as I land.

Pamela gawks at me. "How did you know how to do that?"

"I have no idea." I'm panting. But I'm okay? I'm okay! So

are the kids, which, thank goodness. I did not need to take out any tiny humans today.

"Hey! HEY!" a voice yells from the side of the rink.

Oh crap. I'm in trouble.

But the person the voice is attached to doesn't look pissed. They jog over in their bare socks, short brown hair flapping as they approach.

I lean down to help Pamela up.

"Hey, that was sick! Any chance you'd be interested in joining derby? We really need—"

I look up at the person wearing suspenders dotted with custom buttons (I <3 SKATING, JAMMER, TALK DERBY TO ME, THEY/THEM, THEY SEE ME ROLLIN') over a T-shirt that says CHERRY BOMBZ.

"Oh. Ninety-Two. I didn't realize that was you."

"Huh?" I have never met this person in my life. (That I know of.) Wait. "Did I join a secret elite derby squad and not know it? Also, why, out of all the cool derby names out there, did I choose the number ninety-two?"

"Well, that was your number when you tried out, but you were worried you wouldn't have time with school and interning and everything." They hand me a card. "But, hey, if you ever change your mind about joining skate club, let me know." They smile and help me help the rest of the kids up before jogging back to their post. "See you around, Ninety-Two."

Pamela regards me curiously. "You tried out for derby?"

I shrug. "Apparently, I did. Apparently, I was even good at it."

I slip the card into my pocket, staring at the bank of lockers again.

See you around, Ninety-Two.

It's worth a shot.

"What?"

Oops, I guess that was out loud. "I said it's worth a shot. I found a key with a Cherry Bombz key chain, and it looks like it goes to one of the lockers here, but I couldn't figure out which one."

I do not explain where I found the key. I'm pretty sure it's safe to trust Pamela with whatever's inside that locker, but that doesn't mean I'm ready to tell her about my dead pet beaver that was a gift from my ex-girlfriend and that maybe probably talks to me.

"Ninety-two?" Pamela asks.

"Ninety-two."

Pamela holds my arm (read: clings for dear life), and I manage to get us both to the side of the rink, despite the fact that she is touching me WITH HER OWN BARE HANDS. It's one of the first times we've touched since my accident that hasn't resulted in her jerking away like my skin is made of fire. In fact, she grips my arm so tightly, it leaves white streaks on one of my forearms where the foundation was rubbed away.

Locker 92 looks just like all the others, but it *feels* different. Or rather, something in me feels different when I stand in front of it. Like all my cells are buzzing in a way that is tuned to this specific locker.

"Do you have any idea what's inside?" asks Pamela.

I shake my head.

Then I check to make sure no one is watching. And I insert the key. And I turn it.

It works! I mean, of course it works. This is not surprising. I open the metal door with the vents like shark gills. The locker is small, only about the size of two basketballs stacked on top of each other. There's a duffel bag inside! It's not mine; at least I don't think it is. It's plain black and kind of boring-looking. I set it on the bench behind us and start to unzip it. And then I hesitate.

"What if whatever is inside isn't something I want to open in public?" I ask Pamela.

"We could go back to the dorm?"

"Yeah, that's probably the best plan." Even though it kills me because I want to open this bag IMMEDIATELY. I think about how long it will take to get back to my dorm room so I can unzip this supersecret mysterious duffel bag that may or may not contain clues or weapons or stacks of money. I think about opening it in front of my roommate. Yikes. "Also, can we do this in your room? My roommate'll flip."

"Sure," says Pamela, smiling even.

I breathe a huge sigh of relief. "Thanks, Ivy. You're the best."

Pamela freezes.

"You called me Ivy."

The way she looks at me makes me stop breathing. I'm frozen just like she is, the entire moment existing in a snow globe as the world passes by around us. It's just a name—hers—but it feels so different from when I call her Pamela. *I* feel so different. The very air we're breathing has changed, and now it's made of electricity and fire and intangible things that pull me toward her.

"Well, yeah, I've been remembering things." I manage to string the words together, six of them, but I've just remembered something else.

Ivy, meeting me outside Arkham that day, clasping each other's hands through the fence.

Choose yourself. You're the bravest, most brilliant person I know.

I believe in you.

I think that was the day I realized I was in love with her.

Pamela/Ivy/the most beautiful and maddening girl I've ever met stares at my lips in a way that I'm convinced means she's thinking about our kiss through the fence. She looks nervous as all hell that I might be thinking about it too.

CHAPTER 40

The Floor of Ivy's Dorm Room

I PLACE THE DUFFEL BAG IN THE CENTER OF IVY'S ECO-friendly rug, and we huddle over it. Moment of truth. The bag unzips with a buzzing sound that only makes me more excited to see what's in it.

The first thing is fat manila file with a rubber band around it and a sticky note that says *If anything should happen to me, find Nyssa.*

"Do you know who Nyssa is?" asks Ivy.

I shake my head.

I carefully pull out the file and set it on the floor. Underneath it are night-vision goggles, a flare gun, colorful smoke grenades, comms units, and some other stuff.

"What's that?" asks Ivy, her eyes fixed on a pink remote control/phone thing.

We reach for it at the same time, hands brushing for a fraction of a second. And like every other time since I woke up after the accident, Ivy jerks her hand back with a sharp intake of breath. Except this time I do it too. Ivy notices. And she gulps.

I remember us kissing through the fence now. Well, the lead-up, anyway, but I'm pretty sure we kissed. And that it was awesome. *Of course* a passionate kiss with Ivy would be one of the things my brain would conveniently decide to keep cloudy. I accidentally look at Ivy's mouth. Ohmygosh, STOP thinking about kissing Ivy right now. I pick up the object and turn it over in my hand, noting the telltale pair of metal prongs at the end.

"It's a Taser," I say. "Apparently, they come in pink now."

Luckily, the pink Taser defuses the catastrophic awkwardness of the situation, and we can get back to the file Talia left me. I don't know how I know it, but that sticky note is in her handwriting.

"I know I thought I left myself this bag, but I think it's actually from Talia," I tell Ivy.

Ivy surveys the weird assortment of contents. "What do you think she wanted you to do with it? Other than get it to Nyssa if anything happened to her, like the note says."

I shrug. "Maybe all this stuff was in case it was hard to get the file to Nyssa?" I open the folder, and we read the first page.

To: jonathan.crane@gothamu.edu
From: anton@gothammail.com
Date: Thursday, April 7, 4:34 p.m.
Subject: collaboration

Dear Dr. Crane,

It was a pleasure chatting with you yesterday over scotch. (Remind me to send you a bottle from my private collection sometime!) My partner and I were intrigued by your idea that fear could be used to enhance our behavioral modification technology. As we discussed, the chip my partner developed has not proven as robust as we would like it to be in recent trials, and there have been . . . lapses.

Would you be available to discuss this further? We feel that there may be the opportunity for a collaboration here.

Best,
Anton

"This is it. The people Crane's collaborating with." I wrinkle my nose. "*Behavioral modification technology* is a hell of a way to say *mind control.*"

"Right?" Ivy leans closer to the paper, sending a wave of pine and vanilla toward me. I forget to turn the page, and also, do you think it would be weird to swear fealty to her right now?

"Harleen."

I shake my head. I have no idea how long I was out. Hopefully not too long and hopefully not with doe eyes? I flip the page to find another printed email.

To: anton@gothammail.com
From: jonathan.crane@gothamu.edu
Date: Thursday, April 7, 6:15 p.m.
Subject: Re: collaboration

Anton,

Thank you for your email. I was also quite excited by our conversation and the potential to pursue some truly innovative and special ideas. I believe fear is a natural motivator, and I've had great success with a spray I've developed in rodent models of fear, both as a pure fear toxin and a fear toxin/sedative combination drug. I'd be very interested to pair it with your chips, perhaps in a slow-release fashion.

Let's meet to discuss specifics. Perhaps next week?

Warmly,
Jonathan

Jonathan Crane
Professor, Department of Psychology, Gotham University
Director, Arkham Asylum

It's just like Ivy was telling me on the way over here. There was a bigger plot, and it involved girls being taken all over the city and experimented on at some other location. That's why Talia wanted my help. That's why I would have helped her. But April was ages ago. I don't understand.

I flip to the next email and the next. Ivy and I read through at least a dozen. It seems the modified chips took more fine-tuning than they expected. The first batch induced heart attacks in the experiments at the other location. The second was too mild. But this next one, the one Dr. Crane was testing himself at Arkham, this was supposed to be the Goldilocks batch.

There's an email dated September asking Crane how things were coming along with the modified chips. They were hoping for a February launch.

"Launch of what?" asks Ivy.

I wish I knew. I had already started at Arkham by September. Crane was already injecting chips into the patients there. There's a mention in one of the emails of Crane successfully using the test subjects to mass-manufacture fear spray in Arkham's basement—apparently that's what he was getting out of the deal. But what are Anton and his partner getting?

"I don't know," I say, flipping back through the emails. "They never really say. The Scarecrow just says that things are going better than expected and that they should arrange for a shipment. It was scheduled for the day after the jailbreak."

Ivy lets out a whistle. "Ohhh, I bet those guys are not happy that Talia stole their chips."

"Nope."

Ivy and I go through the rest of the folder. There are newspaper clippings reporting an increase in kidnappings: girls living on the streets, girls with no one to miss them. A few paper flyers—the HAVE YOU SEEN ME? kind with photos on the front. Clues jotted down about a location. Talia seemed so close. And then pictures of an empty warehouse. Makeshift rooms stacked with three sets of bunk beds apiece, the sheets still on the beds. She must have just missed them.

And then it's clear her plan took a different tack, because Arkham blueprints appear, along with detailed information about the mayor's schedule, his security team.

I never miss.

"Holy crap, Talia never meant to shoot the mayor." I cup my hand over my mouth in shock.

Ivy searches my eyes like she's trying to figure out what I'm on about.

"The mayor. Talia got put in Arkham for attempting to assassinate him. She took out every last person on his security detail with tranquilizer darts. Solo. But then she misses the mayor when she has the shot?" I shake my head. I'm not buying it. "She told me she never misses. I just didn't get it until now. She was never trying to kill him. She was trying to get sent to Arkham so she could figure out what was going on and steal the chips."

"That seems like an awful lot of work to get arrested." Ivy wraps a strand of red hair around her finger. "But it makes sense."

We go through all the papers again, and I go downstairs and grab my box of notes too. We have to figure this out. Now. Not only so I can figure out what happened with Talia and the chips, but also so I can think about the best way to pin something on Crane and get him locked away. We sit on the floor of Ivy's dorm room for ages, trying to solve the puzzle of what happened after Ivy last saw me and who did this to me and where Talia might be.

After a couple of hours, I get up and stretch my legs. Ivy's room is smaller than mine, since it's a single, so I'm really just walking back and forth between her closet and her desk. On my third trip, I notice a framed picture of a girl with light brown hair.

"Who's that?"

Ivy gets a sad, faraway look. "She was my girlfriend."

I'm pretty sure this was the girl who died in the Greener Earth Society accident, but I don't remember what the girl really looked like from my disturbed-perspective morgue memory, and I can't bring myself to ask.

We keep working, late into the night, ordering Chinese takeout and sitting closer than we should. Why is it like this? Why does being with Ivy feel so tense, like something terrible happened, but also like we might start making out at any given second?

I wonder how I misread the situation so badly. Now that

I know we've kissed, I can't help but wonder if that's why Ivy acts so weird. Because we kissed and I didn't remember it and I thought I was still with Win? It feels like more than that, though.

I sigh. Loudly.

"You okay?" Ivy raises her eyebrows at me over the psychological profiles she's reading.

"Yeah, just frustrated. I wish I could remember more."

She nods sympathetically.

And it's not just about Ivy. I hate that I don't know who did this to me. I'm terrified that I won't be able to stop Crane properly or keep Talia from using the fear chips herself unless I get my full memory back. I think about the things that have helped: reading through files, looking at photos, going to places, talking to people. Though, if I'm really being honest, there was one thing that helped more than all the others. My session with Dr. Crane.

"Hey, Ivy?"

She eyes me suspiciously. "Why do you look like a kid who's about to ask for seconds of dessert?"

"I have an idea for how to get the rest of my memory back. But you're not going to like it." There's a part of me that doesn't even want to tell her. That wants to just do it.

But then she leans closer and says, "What?"

And I blurt out, "I think I should go to my next session with Crane."

Ivy's jaw drops. (No, really, we may need someone to surgically reattach it.) "Are you kidding me?"

I don't answer.

"That's the worst idea ever."

I still don't answer.

"And so dangerous. You could die. *He could kill you.*"

Again with the not-answering.

Ivy scoots closer to me. "Please promise me you aren't going to do that."

"It would be really dangerous," I say. "And stupid."

But I don't promise. Because I'm not about to make a promise I can't keep.

CHAPTER 41

Elliot Hall

THE TERROR IN THE BURLAP MASK IS CHASING ME THROUGH the halls of Arkham Asylum, and I run—faster and faster—but I can't get away. It doesn't matter how many times I pinch myself. It doesn't matter how hard I scream. There is no waking from this nightmare.

I sprint around a corner and curl myself against a wall, hiding.

Please, I whisper, tears streaming down my cheeks. *Please, someone, help me.*

She finds me in the place between awake and dreaming. Her soft hands pluck me out of the jaws of my demons and carry me to the surface.

"Hey, hey, you just fell asleep for a second," Ivy says in a delicate voice. "You're okay. I've got you."

Her arms are wrapped around me, holding me together, and the screams recede up my veins. I look around. I am safe, I tell myself. I'm in Ivy's dorm room surrounded by papers and notebooks, not in some haunted, secret, mind-melting-fabrication level of Arkham, being chased by a madman.

"Maybe we should quit for the night." Ivy stares into my eyes like she's trying to find me amid all the fear. "It's almost midnight."

I don't think I can work anymore after this, anyway. But.

"I'm scared to go to sleep," I whisper. "The nightmares are getting worse."

Did you know you can see someone else's heart break on your behalf? I didn't until I saw it on Ivy's face. She smiles at me so softly and says, "C'mon," then takes me by the hand and helps me up.

I wonder where she's going to lead me, but she just sits me down in her desk chair while she builds a fort out of bedsheets. Green-and-white cotton banners that stretch from the lofted bed to the dresser. She holds them down with books. And then she builds walls and doors and a pallet of blankets for us to sleep on, a single flashlight shining between the two pillows.

When she's finished, she appraises her work, first proud and then sheepish, trying to look at the blanket fort through my eyes and hoping I'll see it the way she does.

I'm mostly just trying not to cry. "I love it."

Her chest twitches at the word *love.* At least, I think it does. The next second she looks like she usually does, and she's saying, "This is what I used to do when I was home alone and scared, and my parents were out of town, and the nanny was across the house."

We go inside and lie on the blankets. Facing each other. So close but not touching.

We gaze into each other's eyes until I feel like I have to say something to break the spell. "So, this is what it was like?"

Ivy smiles. "This is better."

I smile back. "Yeah?"

She nods. "Because now I'm not alone."

For the first time since the accident, I sleep like a baby.

◆

The next morning, my phone wakes me up while Ivy sleeps next to me. It's amazing what a good night of sleep can do for you. I wonder how many nights a week Stella and Remy get through without a nightmare. I feel like my symptoms are much less extreme than theirs. Maybe I got dosed with a different formula? Or maybe it was because I was given the antidote? I think I was, at least. The effects of the spray seemed to leach out of me, like the poison being sucked out of a snakebite, sometime after we got to Ace Chemicals.

I check my phone and find a forwarded email from Dr. Morales explaining that she's not sure if I'll remember this, and of course she's happy to discuss further, but the Arkham Acres inquiry we initiated last semester has failed to uncover any wrongdoing. She says she's so sorry for this hard news, don't worry, we'll try again.

I know better.

There is only one way for me to stop this, and it involves me staring fear directly in the face and winning.

Why can I fight everyone's monsters except mine?

Not today. If I can face my dad, if I can survive whatever chemicals did this to me, I can handle The Scarecrow. Talia has some way of beating his fear toxin, conquering the adrenaline. If she can, then I can too.

I think about that lecture on memory, the part about state-dependent learning. What if that state is fear? What if meeting with Crane, giving in to the fear, is the only way to recover the last of my lost memories and find out where Talia is hiding?

I will go to our session today. I will vanquish my monsters. I will do whatever it takes.

I slip out the door while Ivy is still asleep.

CHAPTER 42

Dr. Crane's Office

WHILE I SIT IN A LEATHER CHAIR AND WAIT FOR DR. CRANE, I have several minutes to review just how bad an idea this is and to consider sneaking away. Instead, I try to keep my mind busy by texting a huge, long update to Jasmin about everything that has happened (might as well check off everything I'm scared of today). I think about texting Bianca too, but I remember a conversation I had with Jasmin from before the jailbreak. I don't want to bother Bianca if she's still recovering from her back surgery. I hope Jasmin isn't still mad at me, though I understand if she is. I try not to think about what it means that she doesn't reply right away.

There's a quick two knocks on the door, and then he enters. It reminds me of being at the doctor's office, like for a physical or something. And I feel just as naked as if I was covered with one of those flimsy paper sheets.

"Sorry to keep you waiting." He crosses his slender legs as he sits in his mahogany desk chair. "Have you had any progress since the last time we met?"

"I have, yeah."

He leans forward ever so slightly, steepling his fingers.

"I've got most of fall semester now," I continue. "But I'm still having trouble with the more recent stuff. I know Talia stole something that night. A *case* of something."

He stops breathing.

"I can't remember what was in it." (Lie.) "But it feels very important to find it. And I feel like I know—or, well, *knew*—where Talia would have gone, but I just can't remember. I was hoping you could help me."

His mouth spreads into a slow smile. "Nothing would make me happier."

I feign a sigh of relief. "Oh, good."

"You know, Talia stole some very valuable technology from me that night. I wonder if that's what was in the case."

"It might have been." I try to make my eyes as wide and innocent as possible. "I'd be happy to help you find it. If I can." And then I knit my eyebrows together, scared, hesitant. "There's something else."

"What is it?"

I don't have to pretend to be anxious when I answer, because this next bit is legitimately terrifying. Will he believe me? And if he doesn't, what will he do to me?

"I remember a creature in a burlap mask." Don't freak out. Don't freak out. You can do this. "He sprayed me in the face with some kind of chemical. It was terrifying." I shiver for real, and I see that he notices. "I'm worried that it's some kind of state-dependent learning. That I'll only remember where Talia is under the effects of the chemical. But I have no idea how to go about re-creating something like that."

I try to ignore how greedy his eyes look. Otherwise I'll sprint out of the room and never come back.

"I've got an idea," he says slowly, gears turning. "When

we were searching Arkham after the escape, I found a vial of this fear spray, and I was able to develop an antidote. I do study fear, as you know. It would be a huge risk, but I could try to put you under and ask you about Talia and then bring you back. Of course, it might be incredibly dangerous. We probably shouldn't—"

"I'll do it." I rush to say it, then wish I hadn't. Do I seem too desperate? Does he know?

But in the next instant, he's pulling the vial from his desk, and he looks as desperate as I am. He screws the vial into an atomizer, a hungry gleam in his eye.

"Ready?"

My breathing and heartbeat are already speeding up, even though we haven't started yet. I almost choke on the word: "Yes."

He brings the nozzle to my face and presses a button to spray it. I have time for only one thought before the chemicals hit:

What if he doesn't bring me back?

The first thing I remember afterward is gasping the way people do after they've been brought back from drowning. I breathe in and in and in, my eyes roving around the room, taking in the glossy wooden bookshelves, the boat-sized desk, and Dr. Crane, peering over me, doing his best to appear concerned.

"Are you all right? Did it work?"

Yeah, like you don't know. I try to slow my breathing as much as possible. Calm my heart rate. I read an article about biofeedback once. You're supposed to focus on information about your bodily functions (heart rate, breathing, muscle contraction), and you try to change your thoughts or emotions and use that bodily information to tell you how well you're doing. I swear it works. (It could also be the antidote.)

"So? Did you remember where Talia is hiding?" asks Crane eagerly.

I am genuinely puzzled by his question. "Didn't I tell you while I was under?"

Because that's the thing. The whole experience was so intense, it really was like being anesthetized with fear. I can't recall *everything* that happened after a certain point, but I do remember about Talia.

Crane shakes his head. "You told me some things, but not that. But there was a moment. When I thought . . ."

He waits for me to finish his sentence. Jump in with some revelation about Talia.

I stay silent.

My lack of an answer nearly undoes him, but he forces himself to stay calm. "You really can't tell me anything about where she might be? Or the—technology?"

Chips. He almost said *chips.* If he's slipping, then he's letting his emotions get the best of him, and if that's true, then I need to get out of here. Fast. It isn't safe, if it ever was to begin with.

"I'm really sorry," I lie. "I thought this was going to work too. I really needed this." The tears well up in my eyes, and I don't try to hold them back.

He rolls his eyes when he thinks I can't see. "Well. It's all right. We can try again next week."

"Okay." I sniffle and walk to the door, and it's like my legs only just realized how lucky I am to be alive, because they turn to Jell-O on me. I have to place a hand on the door handle to steady myself. Count to two before I open it.

"Goodbye, Harleen," he says as he sits back down at his desk.

"Bye."

I close the door behind me, and I take a deep breath. I don't allow myself to smile until I'm out of the asylum.

I know where Talia is. I remember freeing her now, and I know where she's going.

I should feel better than I have in days—victorious—but there's something nagging at me, gnawing. Like a hangnail in your mind or a scab you can't stop picking. It's not until I'm on the shuttle calling Ivy that I realize what's bothering me.

He let me go too easily, and I can't figure out why.

CHAPTER 43

Gotham Subway

GOTHAM CITY WHIZZES PAST THE WINDOWS OF THE SUBway car. Sometimes the train lurches and sends Ivy bumping against me. Sometimes I pull away as soon as I should.

"I'm still pretty furious with you. You could have died, you know." She has said this approximately two dozen times since I got back from my session with Crane. I brace myself for another lecture, but instead she leans toward me and lowers her voice. "But also, what's going on? Did you remember where Talia's hiding?"

"I remember everything! Where Talia's lair is. The showdown at Ace Chemicals." It's the very best feeling, not having to stumble around your own life with a dimly lit flashlight.

Ivy's tenses next to me. "Everything?"

"Well, not everything. I have no idea how I ended up covered in chemicals—that's still a black hole. But Crane was right. Talia didn't just want to destroy the chips and then escape. She wanted to steal them. She was running away with them. And Crane was there too, I remember. Also, I think she kidnapped me?"

She nods, less worried now. Weird.

"Anyway, I think she has the chips, and I know where she would have taken them. Although if she does have them, why hasn't Gotham City been plunged into chaos?"

"Right. That makes sense. And that would definitely be, like, terrible. The chaos and stuff. So"—she bites her lip—"do you remember anything about . . . me?"

Do I?! "Yeah! The fence!"

Ivy's eyes bulge. Oops. I got excited and accidentally said it a little too loud.

"You opened the fence, didn't you? 'Cause I was pretty sure you did, but now I actually have a memory of you doing that." (Quieter this time.)

Still don't remember our kiss, though, which is just SUPER annoying.

Ivy grips the pole next to her, clenching her fingers around it tightly, like she's trying so hard to keep herself from spilling some terrible secret. Or maybe she's just really concerned about sudden stops.

She nods, still tense.

"It's okay," I whisper. "I know you have powers. Also, I think you're a badass."

Her eyes go wide. "Right. Yes. Powers. Glad that's out in the open." The relief is clear on her face, but she still doesn't relax her grip on the pole.

I wish I knew what she was hiding.

CHAPTER 44

Talia al Ghūl's Lair

IVY AND I ARE HIDING BEHIND A COLLECTION OF STATUES (gargoyles?) that dot the roof. Next to the infinity pool. Which is next to the helipad. (Talia clearly likes to keep a low profile.)

Ivy skeptically eyes a fountain of a golden lady wrestling a lion. "Are you sure this is where we should be?"

"Yep!" I say brightly. "I just wish I could remember more about what happened to the chips. And to me. I really thought it was going to hit me when Win and I were at Ace Chemicals."

She looks like she's trying to eat her own lips. This happens frequently when I talk about Win.

"I broke up with him, you know. The day of the jailbreak. Did you know that?"

Ivy doesn't say anything, but she does gnaw on her lips a bit less.

I think back to that day at Ace Chemicals. About what he said.

"It's not like I care or anything. That we're broken up.

We're way too different. But that doesn't mean someone can't still hurt you, you know?"

I try to keep the sunshine in my voice, but Ivy can see right through me.

"What did he do?" she asks quietly. The deadly/scary/dangerous kind of quiet.

I don't know that I want to admit this to her. I can feel in my bones how much it will hurt. But she's Ivy, and so I tell her anyway. "He said I'd never be the kind of person who has kids and dogs and fences. Can you believe that? Like, I'd never be able to live a normal life or work a normal job or be the kind of person who gets married or whatever."

I wait, breath held, hoping she'll tell me he's wrong and he doesn't know anything and of course I can have all of that. Instead, she replies:

"Is that really what you want?"

I'm confused. "To get married?"

Ivy's cheeks turn pink. "No, I mean, to have a boring, drab, colorless cookie-cutter life."

I snort. "Well, when you say it like that . . ."

"But, seriously, when you picture your future, is that what it looks like? Leading the PTA and mixing a cocktail for some husband who gets pissy if you shine too bright?"

"No. Gosh, no. I wouldn't marry someone like *that*." I know she doesn't actually think that about me, that this is more of a thought exercise, but it's still irritating. "When I picture the future, I—" Well, now that she mentions it, it's kind of hard to picture past med school. Or even college. Should it be this hard? Aren't regular girls supposed to have their whole lives planned on mood boards filled with wedding dresses and houses and the secret names they dream of giving their children but don't want anyone else to steal?

"Well, I know I'll go to med school," I say firmly, defiantly, proving-a-point-ly. "And maybe I can't exactly picture the rest, but so what?" Ugh. Why is this so hard? And does it really matter that I don't have some super-solid fifteen-year plan as long as I have a five-year one? Ivy looks annoyingly smug, so I throw out, "What's your future look like?"

I mean it as a challenge, but she doesn't take it as one.

"Oh!" She gets that look people have before they give you a whole entire dissertation on some topic. "Well, I'm going to be a doctor too, but I'll probably get a PhD, not an MD. And I want to live in a big, old Gothic house with vines climbing the outside and a conservatory and a hedge maze and the most magical gardens you've ever seen. And I won't depend on my parents for money. And I'll never have to talk to them, or to anyone, if they aren't kind to me. And maybe that means I'll live alone, but I don't mind a bit. I want to grow old with my live oaks and my man-eating pitcher plants, and I'll be that crazy old lady at the end of the street who all the neighborhood kids whisper is a witch." She realizes she's been going on and suddenly looks embarrassed. "Or something like that."

"No. That's—that's amazing."

"You don't have to—"

"I mean it. I'm jealous. I want to live in your Baba Yaga house with you and rattle around in dressing gowns like in the old movies, the kind that tumble to the floor and are trimmed with lace and peacock feathers and stuff."

Ivy shrugs shyly, but it's so freaking obvious how pleased she is. "There could be a room for you. With a fainting couch."

I scoot closer to her behind the statue of a fire-breathing dragon. "I'd like that."

"You can't ruin my street cred with the kids, though."

"Oh, I wouldn't dream of it," I say, crossing my fingers behind my back because if I ever have any kind of money in the future, I am totally going to be THAT PERSON who gives the full-sized candy bars on Halloween.

Hey! That's a future plan! See? I can do this. Maybe all it takes is some thinking and brainstorming. And Ivy. Who am I kidding—this is Ivy bringing out the best in me.

I put my hand over hers. "Thank you. For always seeing me in ways no one else does."

I expect her to brush off the compliment. Say something modest. Maaaybe even return it if I'm lucky. I do not expect her to snatch her hand back, sitting up straight and peering over the statue, all business.

"Are you certain Talia would enter this way?"

Are. You. Freaking. Kidding. Me.

Every time. Every freaking time I get close to this girl. Every time we're together. With the tension and the meaningful looks and the mother-effing blanket forts. Every time I feel like we're having a moment, she gets weird and pulls away.

And every time before today, I brushed it off because I didn't want to make things even more awkward, but today I just can't.

"What did I do?" I'm practically shouting it. "Why does it feel like you like me one minute and hate me the next?"

Ivy looks like she's being ripped in half. She runs her fingers through her red hair, distraught, and I can see the moment when she changes her mind and decides *screw it.*

"Because we can't be together!"

CHAPTER 45

Behind a Statue of a Fire-Breathing Dragon

"DO YOU REMEMBER THE DAY OF THE JAILBREAK, WHEN WE were by the fence?" Ivy asks.

Her declaring that she believes in me. Lacing her fingers through mine.

Me leaning in to kiss her.

Honestly, it feels like grinding salt into a wound, but Ivy looks so sincere that I push down my sarcasm. "Yes. Well, kind of. I remember us starting to kiss, but it gets kind of hazy after that."

(Not the part where you acted weird to me for the next two weeks, though. That part's clear as a bell.)

"We didn't kiss," says Ivy.

Wait, what?

She looks positively sick. "I pushed you away."

Oh. Ohhh. How many times have I tried to kiss this girl when she didn't actually want me to? What in the actual hell is wrong with me?

"I'm so sorry. I didn't realize that you didn't—"

"I did." Her mouth is a firm line. "I really, really did."

"I don't understand."

She closes her eyes tightly, hands clasped together like she's begging the universe for a different fate. And then her eyelids flutter open. "I'm scared I'll kill you if we kiss each other."

"Why would you think—? Oh." My mouth falls open. Oh, that time in the morgue with Ivy's girlfriend and that memory where I was outside myself and couldn't see the girl's face.

I'm a monster. He turned me into a monster.

"Harleen, I killed my girlfriend. I didn't mean to, but I'm pretty sure I did." Ivy's eyes well up with tears.

My brain gets suddenly blindsided with the memory of that day in the morgue. The *whole* memory. I guess I always thought Woodrue killed that girl—because of what Ivy said about her getting the same lines when he injected her and because he's the kind of person who experiments on students and also because he had the motive. But now a vision of the girl with the light brown hair swims in front of me. She was lying in that metal drawer with bloodless skin and eyes serenely closed. Her mouth, though. Her mouth was clearly the route of entry because her lips were greenish-black and there were all these veiny blackish lines radiating from them. Ivy did that?

I sigh, trying to expel all the poison inside me the way Ivy's girlfriend never could.

Her lip quivers as she watches my reaction. "Do you think I'm a bad person?"

"No. Are you kidding me?" I throw my arms around her neck, squeezing her tight. "I think you're the best person I know."

This time she doesn't pull away. Even though the skin

of my forearm is touching the skin of her neck. A thought occurs to me.

"Is it a skin-to-skin thing? Because you always jerked away before, like I'd burned you, but now—"

Ivy shakes her head. "No," she says between hiccups. "Because I've touched other people, but she's the only person I k—" She winces like the word causes her physical pain. "Kissed."

I want to ask her more, but just sitting with her, being here with her, feels like the rightest thing to do.

After a minute, she stops crying. Her eyes lift toward mine. "I was scared if I touched you or got too close, I wouldn't be able to stop. The whole time since you woke up in the hospital, I've been like: I'm in love with her. I'm in love with her, and I can't be with her, and if she can't remember falling in love with me, maybe that's for the better. I tried to keep it from happening all over again."

"But you couldn't."

I wipe a rogue tear from her face. Damn, she's beautiful. Burnt-auburn eyebrows and eyes that see you—the real you—and cheekbones that make you want to hold your breath. People have no business looking that beautiful while crying.

She smiles sadly. "No. I couldn't."

She's crying again, and I start to cry too, but then you know what? No. We don't have to just roll over and take this. We can fight it somehow. We just have to figure it out. Let me think. Let me think. Let me think.

"Okay!" I say, splaying my fingers in front of me like a magician. "Okay, are we or are we not brilliant scientists?"

Ivy's eyebrows rise practically into her hairline. "I fail to see how that makes you immune to poison."

"Yet."

"Ummm . . ."

HOW IS SHE NOT GETTING THIS? I grab her hands and shake them.

"We science each other up. We figure out a way to *make* me immune. Or to make you not pass on the toxins. Something."

"But that could take years!"

"Then I'll wait."

"But it might not even work!"

I know it will by the way my pulse races in my ears. I just have to convince her what my heart already knows. "It WILL. If I have to alter my own DNA, if I have to inject myself with antivenin daily, if I have to break into Wayne Industries and steal classified technology, I will kiss you, Pamela Isley. And if you died, I would invent time travel so I could go back and keep it from happening. And if you got some rare disease, I'd search until I found the cure. And if I got sucked into an alternate universe, I would fight off every demon in that post-apocalyptic hellscape so I could build a portal and come back to you. I would break every law of nature and physics to be with you. Don't you understand that—"

I gasp mid-sentence. Ivy's lips are inches from mine. How did I get so close to her without realizing it? How did my arm end up around her waist? I pull her closer so I can feel more of her body warm against mine. (Apparently, that's how.)

Ivy's lips are parted, and it would be so easy to kiss them. To absolutely drown in her.

"Harleen."

I lean closer. I can't go another day—another second—without knowing what it would feel like.

"Harleen!"

I tear myself away from her and fall to my knees, chest heaving, gripping the edge of a decorative planter until my knuckles are white because I don't know how I'm supposed to hold myself back otherwise.

"Freaking A! This sucks! We need to invent the cure already!"

Ivy's lips are a half-moon smile, but at least she's not hopeless anymore. At least she thinks there's a shadow of a chance that we could do this.

Her smile disappears just as quickly as it came. "What's that on your shoe?"

"Huh?"

She leans closer, pointing, and I look where she's looking, and sure enough, there's a square of black plastic stuck to the bottom of my platform sneakers, right where the arch is. I peel it off. Whatever it is, it's electronic.

"Was there any time during your session with The Scarecrow that you lost conscious thought?" asks Ivy tightly.

"You don't think—"

"That he put a tracker on you to follow you here? That's absolutely what I think."

It totally makes sense now. Why he let me leave so easily. Why he seemed unperturbed. How did I not expect something like this? I set the tracker on the planter next to me and smash it with a nearby rock. Repeatedly. Vigorously. Excessively? Must be, because Ivy cracks a wry smile and says, "All right. I think you've killed it."

I stare out at the horizon and frown, like I'm expecting him to come floating over the side of the building on a broomstick. And as I'm watching, a sound builds in the distance. It starts out small—the buzzing of a single bee landing on a single flower. And then it grows—to the hum of a whole hive and the whir of a lawn mower and the angry grind of an industrial shredder.

Ivy and I have to duck down quick. Talia's helicopter has arrived.

CHAPTER 46

Talia al Ghūl's Helipad

THE BLADES SPUTTER TO A STOP, AND TALIA DISMOUNTS, wearing a cream linen suit that is basically a testament to her dark magic—it would be a mess of wrinkles on anyone else after a helicopter ride. She strides across the brick pavers, and I realize I don't have a plan other than just to show up here. So I do what I do best. I run out of the shadows, waving my arms and yelling, "Hey!"

And I block her path.

Her eyes widen. "Harleen."

In the time it took her to process who I am, she has whipped a dagger out of thin air or possibly her sleeve. (A fair response.) But then she relaxes.

"How are you doing?" She says it like she actually cares.

I'm not letting her fool me again.

"You betrayed me," I say, hot tears pricking my eyes. "You were lying to me the whole time."

I know that's not what I came here to say to her, but it's what comes out.

She looks regretful, but a lot of people can fake that. "For the greater good. And only about the chips. I really do see something special in you." She stretches out her hand, the one without the dagger. "Come with me, Harleen. I'll make you into the kind of revolutionary who blows the whole world away."

There's a part of me that is so, so tempted. I think about Stella and Remy and the nameless, faceless girls who are trapped somewhere in this city. I'll never be able to change the world the way I want to if I keep to the path I'm on. I'll never be able to stop The Scarecrow. I feel like I'm on the cusp of some huge realization, when the shouts distract me.

The scuffling sounds come from every corner of the rooftop courtyard, and Talia and I turn, both on high alert, both ready to fight any threat with fists and blades, sharp knives and sharper wit.

"Ummm . . ."

"What—?"

Every last one of Talia's henchpeople looks like they're taking part in a piece of weird ecoterrorist performance art. One sits in a fig tree, caged in by branches like the hired-goon version of a songbird. Another three are tangled in vines, unyielding plants coiled around their wrists and ankles. The last is stuck like a sausage in a trumpet flower that is the size of a full-grown man, and purple morning glories form a flower crown on his head. (You have to admire Ivy's style.)

She pops out from behind a planter and shrugs at us. "Just in case?"

For the first time, Talia's eyes flash with fear, just for a moment. We've got her caught. Cornered. I could deliver her to the police. Be the hero. Or I could go with her. Be a different kind of hero.

"I just need you to hand over the chips," I say.

She frowns. "You don't remember? I don't have them."

"Stop lying."

She slips a hand into her pocket, and I tense, assuming it's a weapon.

Talia's face falls. "I wouldn't hurt you."

I hesitate. And the memories of that night hit me in a completely different way. Talia didn't drag me down the hallway; she helped me. She didn't threaten me with a knife; she protected me by keeping up the facade that I wasn't involved in the prison break. She didn't stab me with a needle; she dosed me with an antidote.

"Here," calls Talia.

She tosses me a small black electronic device. I turn it over in my hand.

"It's a GoPro that I strapped to one of my people during the jailbreak. Watch it."

I click Play on the video Talia has cued up. And I plummet back in time.

CHAPTER 47

ARKALAMITY—8:15 P.M.

TALIA AND THE SCARECROW CREEP CLOSER AS THEY TALK. We're at Ace Chemicals, and I still don't know what to do with these chips, but I know I'm running out of time.

"Harleen, weigh the consequences. Is keeping them from me really worth the risk of him getting them back?"

And I'm thinking and I'm weighing, and I'm not paying nearly enough attention to the fact that The Scarecrow's arm radius is about 40 percent wider than you'd expect it to be. I only realize it once he's lashed out a lanky arm and snatched the case from me. There is no way in hell I'm letting him keep it.

I jump down from the railing and do a roundoff back handspring, front handspring, twisting aerial down the catwalk. There are skinny black pipes suspending it from the ceiling, and I leap through the air, grabbing one of the pipes and swinging around, my body a horizontal line suspended over a pit of bubbling green. My feet connect with his chest with the most satisfying *thwack*.

He tumbles to the ground, all six feet three inches of him,

wiry arms and legs splaying in every direction. The case of chips breaks free from his fingers and hits the metal-caging floor of the catwalk, bouncing once, twice. Teetering on its side near the edge of the catwalk, so very close to falling, falling. One more push is all it would take. I kick myself up onto my feet again, ready to lunge for the case. The Scarecrow lunges too, and his arms may be longer, but I'm faster. I'm just putting my hands on the case when Talia screams behind me.

I turn, realizing in horror that (A) King Shark has escaped the henchpeople he was fighting and (B) he's got Talia cornered. He towers over her, jaws open wide, snapping left, right, and center. She hits the floor, slipping through his legs and coming up behind him, jumping onto his back. He shakes his head back and forth, viciously, like a dog with a squirrel. If she could just hang on. If she could just reach a little higher to the telltale wound on his arm. When he finally stops shaking, she slips her hand into her pocket and pulls out a pair of forceps.

I don't get to see if she's successful, because The Scarecrow wraps a bony arm around my throat. He leans close, burlap mask rough against my cheek, and despite my thrashing, I can't break his hold. His arms may be skinny, but they're strong. He jabs me in the neck with a needle as he whispers into my ear,

"And now, my dear, you are mine."

The thought of being his puppet is perhaps the most terrifying thing that has happened all night, and that's saying something. And then another thought dawns on me.

"You forgot one thing," I say, wrenching myself away from him. "Slow release."

I see the meaning of it come together in his eyes, but he's too late. I roundhouse-kick the case into the vat of chemicals. I don't choose The Scarecrow or Talia or the future of Gotham City. I choose myself.

"NOOOOO!" Talia screams from across the catwalk, pressing herself against the railing like she's thinking of jumping in after the case.

King Shark sits on the floor next to her, his chip now removed, his arms wrapped around his knees in a very kid-like way.

"Did I hurt anyone?" he asks quietly.

I shake my head. I don't know what he can remember. I'm *not* telling him about the ladybug. He stares at the chip in his finlike hand for a couple moments before placing it between his teeth and chomping it to oblivion. I have this urge to rush to him, make sure he's okay—I promised him I'd take care of him—but there's still The Scarecrow to think about.

He crosses his arms, looking smugger than he should, honestly, given what just happened. Whatever he's thinking, whatever plan, whatever scheme, whatever attack, I will counter it. I will stop him. No matter what it takes or how much it costs. I am beating this man.

"I'll just reverse engineer them from the chip in your neck."

The chip. My hand flies to my neck. I can't let this happen. I can't be his pawn.

And I won't.

"Like hell you will," I say.

And then I double backflip into the acid.

Falling-falling-falling. Through the air into something that smells like bleach and burnt hair and batteries. It feels like fire. Like taking a napalm shower, swan diving into a swimming pool made of knives. I guess I should be worried I'm going to die, but I'm not.

If The Joker can survive it, why can't I?

CHAPTER 48

Talia al Ghūl's Lair

OHMYGOSH, TALIA WAS TELLING THE TRUTH. SHE REALLY doesn't have any chips. Every last one was destroyed.

And it wasn't Talia, or even The Scarecrow, who did this to me. I did this to myself. Because I'm brave. And a badass. And, okay, maybe a little too impulsive for my own good.

I touch my hand to my cheek. The way I look—it feels different now that I know I was the one in control. Like a badge of courage or an act of defiance.

Talia, who up until now has had her head cocked to the side in concern, speaks.

"I was the one who pulled you out of the chemicals and took you to the ER."

It's hard to have a whole lot of shock left after what I've just learned. And besides, what she's saying makes sense. It explains why someone saved me but didn't stay. The pieces finally fit. And if I strain every last neuron in my brain, I can picture Talia's face before it all went black.

The police sirens sound in the distance.

"We have to hurry," says Ivy. "Crane might have called the police."

I listen, and I think she's right. It feels like the sirens are coming closer, closing in. But there's so much I still need to ask Talia. So much I could learn from her.

She betrayed you. And she'd do it again.

But then I remember something more important than any of that.

"So, things are going to be okay? If there aren't any chips to use, did we do it? Did we stop him?"

Talia shakes her head, her face taut with conviction. "As long as he's still out there, he's a threat. Those kidnapped girls are still being held somewhere, and who knows what they're doing to them. If we're lucky, we pushed back whatever their launch date plans are, but we didn't stop it."

The sirens are right outside the building now. And then there are footsteps on the stairs. They're coming for Talia.

She looks at me, desperate. "We could stop them, though. Together. Come with me."

I could capture her. Or I could run. Hero or villain. Those are my choices. Those have always been my choices.

Banging on the door to the roof. Any second now, they'll burst through.

And suddenly I know exactly what to do. Just like with the fear chips, just like with the chemical waste, just like Ivy said.

I choose me.

And not just partial me, pretend me, the me that checks off every box and keeps every dark thought strapped down so tight. All of me. I let the darkness loose in my mind, and it bursts through like a comet or a champagne cork or a thousand ravens taking flight, spreading like ink spilled on a white tablecloth, shimmering like an oil slick. I always feared this moment because I was so sure the darkness lurking inside me would be terrifying. Obliterating. It's beautiful. Without the darkness you can't see the stars. You can't smell the type of jasmine that blooms only in the dead of night.

I watch as Talia jumps into her helicopter. (Ivy follows suit by releasing her henchpeople and shrinking all the plants back to their natural size because, let's be real, that was going to be a pain in the ass to explain to the police.)

Talia calls out to me one more time. Waits for just another second. And . . .

I let her go.

But I don't go with her.

The door is open now, and the police are everywhere. A couple of them fire warning shots at Talia's helicopter. A couple more check on Ivy and me.

"Where is she? Did she hurt you?"

I shake my head and try to look brave and traumatized and resilient and innocent.

"She got away," I tell them. "But I've got everything you need to put away The Scarecrow."

CHAPTER 49

Arkham Asylum Grand Rounds

I NEVER EXPECTED HIM TO SCREAM SO MUCH WHEN THEY took him away. Here I am, sitting next to Dr. Morales at grand rounds, gripping my pen so tightly that it really should have shattered by now. I'm dutifully taking notes while Dr. Crane presents a case study on Killer Croc, when what I really want to do is leap down the rows of burgundy seats and unmask him (mask him?). That's when the police start flooding in.

They stream down the stairs from the back entrance and pour in through the double doors closer to Crane. They don't listen when he protests. They read him his rights. And then there are the handcuffs. That's when the screaming really starts.

"What do you think you're doing? I haven't done anything wrong. I'm the director of Arkham Asylum! I'll have your jobs for this!"

I smirk at him happily.

I also glance at Dr. Morales to see how she's taking it. Calmly, and with great poise and professionalism TO THE

SURPRISE OF NO ONE. And, okay, to be fair, she *did* kind of know this was coming, because I *may* have gone to her in tears after the first time I tried to convince the police that Crane is actually a deranged fear addict with antisocial personality disorder. Turns out Dr. Crane is *such* an upstanding member of society that the police didn't originally believe me when I said he was The Scarecrow. (Apparently, they've never attended one of his fear lectures.)

When I came back a second time with Dr. M, and the police told her their hands were tied (translation: we actually do believe you that he's a bad guy now; we just don't care), she suggested we go to every major newspaper in Gotham City. I told her we should start with the *Clocktower.* Oh! That reminds me! I have to text Samantha.

> Harleen: Guess what! Guess what! They're arresting him RIGHT NOW

Samantha replies in seconds.

> Samantha: Please tell me you're filming it.
>
> Harleen: No, but my friend Ansley is.
>
> Samantha: YESSSS. This is giving me life.

So, Samantha and I are friends now. (I think it really helped that I started buying my own milk. Also, that I gave her the biggest scoop of her journalism career thus far.) She put all the footage from Talia's GoPro and some of the other proof we found onto the *Clocktower* website two days ago—I'm honestly surprised it took Gotham City's finest this long to act, but ah, well.

I watch as the police drag Dr. Crane out of the room with one last flap of his white coat.

"I'll make you pay for this! I HAVE WAYS OF MAKING YOU PAY!"

Dr. Morales stands and clears her throat, and despite the clusterfluff we are currently experiencing, everyone goes quiet. "I think it's pretty clear Dr. Crane isn't who we thought he was. I'm going to go speak with the police to make sure they have everything they need. If everyone else could wait a few minutes to make sure the hallways are clear, I think it would be safest to wait until Dr. Crane is out of the building. We'll reschedule grand rounds for another day this week, during which I'll do my best to answer all the questions you may have."

She exits our row, and I follow her. The auditorium erupts in gossip.

Crane is already out of sight by the time we get to the hallway, but there are still plenty of officers milling around and having coffee, including the beef neck–buzz cut guy who interrogated me in the hospital.

He body-blocks Dr. Morales. "Miss, you'll have to remain in the lobby here for your own safety."

"I'm not attempting to leave," she says, like she'd rather staple her lab coat to her arms than talk to this guy. (Can't say I disagree.)

"Is Montoya here?" I ask, all sassy-like. "We need to talk to Montoya."

The second time I say *Montoya,* a familiar head of dark brown hair pops up. Thank. Goodness.

"Montoya! Hey, Officer Montoya!" I call out.

She startles when she sees me. Not that I can blame her. After what happened on Talia's rooftop, I stopped covering my skin with makeup. I dip-dyed my hair again too—blue and red this time. This morning I put it in braids: a red braid with blue roses clipped at the top and a blue one with red roses. And I'm wearing cut-up red jeans and a black-and-red cropped leather jacket and the most ass-kicking combat boots you've ever seen. I'm done playing dress-up as the bland version of me.

"Harleen. Are you okay?"

"Oh, yeah, I'm great. I'm so glad you're back. The department really falls apart when you're on vacation. Last week, we tried to tell this bunch of—"

Dr. Morales clears her throat next to me.

"Right, so this is Dr. Morales, my mentor. We have a lot of stuff to tell you." I lower my voice. "But can we tell you away from the guy without a neck?"

Montoya rolls her eyes, but she's smiling. "Sure."

As we walk a short distance away from the others, I hear one of the officers complain that they've been working overtime for weeks, still trying to round up King Shark and The Joker and everyone else. I sigh. I'm really gonna miss those guys.

"What is it you need to tell me?" asks Officer Montoya.

Dr. Morales and I exchange glances.

"Let me take you to his secret lab."

CHAPTER 50

Soon

IT'S SUNNY WHEN I LEAVE ARKHAM ASYLUM, BUT THIS TIME I'm not disappointed by the lack of thunderclouds. I am the storm. And I'll rain down vengeance on anyone who comes for my friends. Or for me. Or for any of the other girls in this city.

The metal gates loom large before the shuttle, and I watch the letters pass me by as I head for a different Arkham. I just heard from Remy that Stella is allowed to have visitors again after her heart attack, and I'm on my way to see them.

This time we don't play games in the rec room. Remy and I perch on wooden stools that were painted with crescent moons and sunflowers during art time, while Stella stays in her bed, doctor's orders. The covers are tucked up all around her, and her skin is still pretty pale, but she's smiling. It gives me this weird sense of déjà vu because she looks so much like Bernice when I visited her in the hospital last year.

"How are you feeling?" I ask her.

"Tired. But better."

"Awesome." I wait till the nurse steps out of the room to

whisper the next part. "I don't want to stress you out, but I wanted you to know that we got the person who was supplying the stuff to the other person."

I watch her face. Did that make any kind of sense? I wanted to tell her that Dr. Crane, aka The Scarecrow, was arrested, but without saying *fear spray* or *Dr. Nelson* or anything else that might send her heart racing.

Stella heaves a huge sigh of relief. *Ohthankgoodness.*

So does Remy. "So, it's over?"

There's so much hope in her voice. I hate to be the one to shatter it.

"Not exactly."

I'm reminded of my debriefing with Officer Montoya in the secret lab.

It's always you. Are you certain you're keeping our agreement?

Yes, ma'am. The last time I did any Reckoning stuff was last year.

(Technically true. Everything with Ivy and Talia and The Scarecrow was non-Reckoning-related.)

Montoya looked less than convinced. *So I shouldn't expect to see you again? This ends with Dr. Crane's arrest?*

Not exactly.

I told Montoya, and I tell Remy and Stella now.

"This is part of something bigger. I don't know who Crane was supplying those chips to, but they've kidnapped girls all over the city. And there's some kind of launch coming up. Crane may be gone, but I think we have to proceed like they're still moving ahead with it."

We? Montoya had replied with a raised eyebrow.

You! The police. I just want you to catch them. I'll give you everything I've got.

And you won't get involved?

No, ma'am.

But I crossed my fingers behind my back when I said it.

"You're not really going to leave it to the police, are you?" asks Remy, tucking her pink hair behind her ear.

Now that she mentions it . . .

"No. No, I'm not." It feels good to say, even though I have no idea what I'm doing yet.

But as Remy and Stella and I talk about where the girls might be and how they're being taken and what Anton and his partner are doing with them, an idea starts to take shape inside my head.

I just need to figure out how to get the other people involved to agree to it.

Though, now that I'm thinking about it, one of those people is Jasmin, and I don't believe she ever messaged me back. I check my phone, just to be sure. Nope. Definitely not. And there's a part of me that feels pretty hurt by that, but honestly, I get it. I wasn't there for her and Bianca when it counted this year. But we're going to be okay. I'll earn back their trust. *Show them* I'm different. When they see how I go after these trafficker guys, they'll change their minds, I just know it.

I take the shuttle back to Gotham U and go back to my normal life. *Pretend* to go back to my normal life.

Samantha and I gleefully watch the video of Crane being taken away.

"I'm so excited about how much press my article is getting! The *Gotham Globe* actually *quoted* me." She squeals it, and let me tell you, she is not a squealer.

"That's amazing!" I tell her. "And, uh, I actually may have something else for you soon."

Her eyes light up greedily. “Really?”

But she only has so long to ponder her Pulitzer Prize acceptance speech, because she has class in fifteen minutes, so she grabs her shoes and jacket. Meanwhile, I go to my dresser and open the bottom drawer and pull out a costume I haven’t touched in months.

Black and red and fierce and glittery. It holds so many memories of last year—of rage and cleverness and laughter. It’s perfect.

“What’s that?” asks Samantha, peeking over my shoulder.

“Just this thing I used to be a part of.”

“Huh.” She slips her book bag over her shoulder. “I’m gonna go to Nighthawk’s for coffee after class. You wanna come?”

“Nah, you go. I’ve got some stuff to do here. But next time?”

“Next time.” She smiles at me as she leaves.

I hold the costume in my hands. I choose me. I’m not locking any part of me up ever again. And I want to solve the mystery of where these girls are being taken and what’s happening to them (and find them and save them too, obvs!), but I don’t want to do it Talia’s way or Dr. Morales’s way or Montoya’s way. I want to do it my way.

There’s a knock at the door, and I set my costume on my desk.

“IVY!!!” I practically tackle her in a hug. “You’re just the person I wanted to see!”

“Cool. Also, I would like to continue breathing, if you don’t mind. It’s one of my hobbies.”

“Sorry!” I release her. “What are you doing for spring break?”

She shrugs. “Nothing. Why?”

I feel my eyes glimmering in a way that I am certain is diabolical. "Want to go on a road trip where we steal all the things we need to cure our kiss problem and also save a bunch of girls?"

She smirks at me. Gosh, I love it when she smirks. "I do have a pink convertible we can take. But we still don't know how we're going to cure ourselves. It might just lead to heartache. Are you sure you want to do this?"

"OF COURSE I'M SURE!" I can't help jumping up and down when I say it.

"Me too. Let's do this, Harleen."

I twirl my red braid around my finger, and my eyes go to the costume on my desk, and the rightest idea in the history of right ideas pops into my head.

"Call me Harley."

HARLEY'S FILES

Arkham Acres							
Blood draw schedule for patients with selective catatonia							
December							
M/TH		**12/4**	**12/7**	**12/11**	**12/14**	**12/18**	**12/21**
Stella Watkins		KLP	KLP				
Remy Hughes		KLP	KLP				
Alana Myers-Ruiz		KLP	KLP				
T/F	**12/1**	**12/5**	**12/8**	**12/12**	**12/15**	**12/19**	**12/22**
Taylor Levinsky	KLP	KLP					
Flora Knight Mayer	KLP	KLP					
Serenity Lee	KLP	KLP					

Arkham Asylum Patient Information Form

THE JOKER

Name: Unknown (Aliases: Clown Prince of Crime, Harlequin of Hate, Ace of Knaves)

Sex: Male

Height: 6'2"

Weight: 192 lbs. (87 kg)

Eyes: Green (formerly brown)

Hair: Green (formerly brown)

Other distinguishing characteristics: Ghostly-white skin

Age: 22

Powers and Abilities

- Resistance to pain and Joker Venom as well as other toxins
- Heightened intelligence with probable genius IQ
- Moderate skill in hand-to-hand combat, particularly due to speed and chaotic fighting style
- Expertise in explosives
- Disguise and theatrics, including creative weaponry: lapel flowers that spew acid, joy buzzers that cause electrocution, bombs disguised as toys, Joker teeth, razor-sharp playing cards, unusual guns, Joker Venom (poison that causes victims to laugh themselves to death with permanent grin on their faces)
- Violence, intimidation, and sheer force of will

Psychological Profile

- Potential diagnoses include: Psychopathy, antisocial personality disorder, sadism, malignant narcissism, pseudobulbar affect
- Extremely violent, devoid of empathy and regard for human life

- Warped sense of humor
- Pathological liar
- Marked obsession with Batman
- Recently blew up Gotham Clock Tower

Not what I was hoping, but you can't deny he's dreamy

Arkham Asylum Patient Information Form

KING SHARK

Name: Nanaue

Sex: Male

Height: 7'2"

Weight: 380 lbs. (172 kg)

Eyes: Black

Hair: None

Other distinguishing characteristics: Is half shark

Age: 15 (housed at Arkham Asylum due to special requirements not available in a juvenile center)

Majestic. Dangerous. Kind. King Shark could basically murder someone in cold blood at this point, and I'd still be smitten.

Powers and Abilities

- Ability to survive on land and in water
- Superstrength and stamina
- Heightened sense of smell
- Teeth (Big ones. Razor-sharp. Lots of them.)
- Possible ability to communicate with other ocean life
- Excellent swimming ability
- Extreme skill in hand-to-hand combat due to size and strength

Psychological Profile

- Autism spectrum disorder, severity level 3, with accompanying severe aggression in response to change in routines and ritualized patterns
- Exhibits uncontrollable bloodlust or feeding frenzy in response to smell of blood
- Displays high levels of empathy for other creatures, including penchant for releasing any ladybugs found in Arkham Asylum

Arkham Asylum Patient Information Form

THE RIDDLER

Name: Edward Nygma

Sex: Male

Height: 5'10"

Weight: 145 lbs. (66 kg)

Eyes: Green

Hair: Red

Other distinguishing characteristics: Glasses

Age: 27

Powers and Abilities

- Criminal mastermind with genius IQ
- Expertise in riddles, puzzles, mind games, and deductive reasoning
- Tactical analysis and manipulation
- Escape artist with penchant for elaborate death traps
- Moderate skill in hand-to-hand combat with Riddler's staff

Psychological Profile

- Obsessive-compulsive disorder that renders patient unable to complete crimes or day-to-day functions without incorporating riddles
- Narcissism

Recently visited by the face in the burlap mask. Mentioned being taken to a place called "the Attic."

Arkham Asylum Patient Information Form

TALIA AL GHŪL

Name: Talia al Ghūl

Sex: Female

Height: 5'8"

Weight: 141 lbs. (64 kg)

Eyes: Brown

Hair: Black

Other distinguishing characteristics: None

Age: Unknown

Intriguing
Dangerous
Revolutionary
Genius
Mentor
I don't know what to do

Powers and Abilities

- Criminal mastermind with genius IQ
- Leadership, entrepreneurship, ability to evoke an almost cultlike following
- Tactical analysis and manipulation
- Expertise in explosives
- Escape artist
- Trained assassin and expert marksperson (blades, firearms)
- Extreme skill in hand-to-hand combat due to martial arts training
- Resistance to toxins and all forms of torture

Psychological Profile

- Machiavellian in her manipulation of people, possibly stemming from childhood trauma
- Justifies unspeakable acts using her warped worldview, likely the result of growing up in a cultlike environment
- Perfectionism
- Brain scans suggest an early-onset neurodegenerative disease
- Possible connection to League of Assassins

Arkham Asylum Patient Information Form

THE SCARECROW

Name: Jonathan Crane (Aliases: Straw Man, Scarebeast, Dr. Nightmare, King of Screams)

Sex: Male

Height: 6'3"

Weight: 140 lbs. (63.5 kg)

Eyes: Blue

Hair: Brown

Other distinguishing characteristics: None

Age: 46

Powers and Abilities

- Genius in the realm of psychology, particularly fear and phobias
- Expertise in biochemisty; developer of powerful experimental fear toxin
- Possible immunity to fear toxin due to repeated exposure
- Martial arts training

Psychological Profile

- Marked obsession bordering on addiction with fear and phobias, including desire to incite fear in others
- Inferiority complex due to childhood trauma, including vicious bullying
- Suffered from corvidophobia (fear of crows) in childhood
- Lack of empathy suggests antisocial personality disorder, while motivation by childhood fear suggests paranoid personality disorder

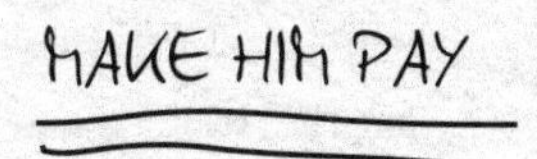

Arkham Asylum Patient Information Form

HARLEY QUINN

Name: Harleen Quinzel

Sex: Female

Height: 5'7"

Weight: 140 lbs. (63.5 kg)

Eyes: Blue

Hair: Blond

Other distinguishing characteristics: Ghostly-white skin

Age: 19

Powers and Abilities

- Genius intellect, particularly with regard to science, invention, and manipulation
- Expertise in gymnastics
- Lockpicking
- Advanced skill in hand-to-hand combat due to speed, agility, and grit (including with baseball bat and Dissent Cannon)
- Growing expertise in martial arts

Psychological Profile

- Childhood diagnosis of ADHD; patient takes medication and receives accommodations
- Grief counseling after death of mother
- Claustrophobia and PTSD stemming from childhood trauma
- Patient mentions persistent battle with "darkness"
- Potential diagnoses include: (1) borderline personality disorder due to patient's history of unstable personal relationships, abandonment issues, heightened emotional responses, and impulsivity; and (2) histrionic personality disorder due to

patient's pathological need for attention, dramatic displays of emotion, theatricality, shallow style of speech, and provocative behavior

Rude! IDK, these just sound like ways to say I'm a girl who's fed up with the patriarchy.

Arkham Asylum Patient Information Form

POISON IVY

Name: Pamela Isley

Sex: Female

Height: 5'8"

Weight: 120 lbs. (54 kg)

Eyes: Green

Hair: Red

Other distinguishing characteristics: Faintly green skin

Age: 18

Powers and Abilities

- Genius IQ with expertise in botany, biochemistry, and toxicology; uses this knowledge to create everything from love potions to truth serums
- Immunity to toxins, bacteria, and poisons
- Manipulation of all plant life
- Secretion of pheromones with the power to seduce and control
- Production of a lethal toxin by lips
- Moderate skill in hand-to-hand combat
- Is rumored to be part plant due to experiments performed by Dr. Woodrue

Psychological Profile

- Suspected childhood trauma/neglect
- Extreme misanthropy
- Potential diagnoses include: (1) Antisocial personality disorder due to patient's aggression, recklessness, exploitation of others, and prioritization of plant life over human life; and (2) borderline personality disorder due to patient's history of unstable personal relationships and emotional instability

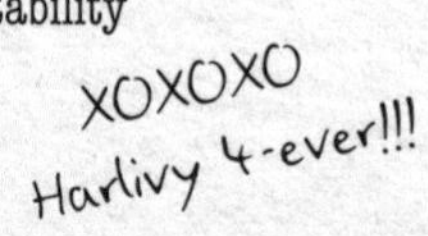

ACKNOWLEDGMENTS

This book wouldn't be a reality without the help of a whole bunch of people:

To my incomparable critique partners, Alina Klein, Dana Alison Levy, and Kate Boorman, thank you for brainstorming and reading drafts and helping me figure out plot holes and being the very best friends. I love y'all.

To Maryann and Jenn, thank you for all your help with the outline! And to Maryann and Gilly and Mayra, thank you for the very best supervillain/hero brainstorming sessions!

To Shinban Liu, thank you for helping me with Harley's medical chart!

I'm really lucky to be part of an amazing writing community. Huge thank-yous to the MoB, the Drafted Tavern, High School English but with Wine, the Korner, the LBs, the Not-So-YA Book Club, and my Atlanta buddies, especially Kelly, Becky, Aisha, Julian, Mayra, Marie, Kim, Kate, Vania, Jessi, Lee, Angela, Elizabeth, Addison, Becca, Katie, Lauren, Dana, and Terra.

To the most spectacular local bookstores in the entire world, Little Shop of Stories and Brave + Kind Bookshop, and to all the librarians, bloggers, teachers, and readers who make writing for kids such a cool place to be—thank you. Book people are the best people.

To my agent, Susan Hawk, thank you for making my dreams come true again and again and again. I am so very lucky to work with you!

To Sasha Henriques: *Ravenous* was a tricky one, and I'm glad I had you with me on this journey! Working on *Harley* with you is one of the highlights of my career. And to Sara Sargent, thank you for your passion for this project! It has been wonderful getting to work with you! To Lois Evans, Ben Harper, Janet Foley, Barbara Bakowski, Regina Flath, the Random House Books for Young Readers marketing and publicity teams (special shout-out to Kris Kam and Madison Furr!), and anyone else at PRH or DC who worked on this book in any way: Y'all are amazing, and I would leap tall buildings and fight Super-Villains for you. And to Kevin Wada, thank you for making the most butt-kicking version of Harley I have ever seen. I am obsessed.

To my family, especially Mom, Mica, Maxie, Dennis, Dad, Julie, Hannah, Matt, Little Zack, Bekah, and my new BIL, Jonathan: I love all of you so much!

To Zack, Ansley, and Xander, I love you all more than words can say. If I ever got sucked through a portal into an apocalyptic alternate universe, you'd better believe I would science my way back to you.

ABOUT THE AUTHOR

RACHAEL ALLEN is a scientist by day and kid lit author by night. She is the winner of the 2019 Georgia Young Adult Author of the Year Award, and her books include *Harley Quinn: Reckoning, 17 First Kisses, The Revenge Playbook, The Summer of Impossibilities,* and *A Taxonomy of Love,* which was a Junior Library Guild Selection and was among the 2018 Books All Young Georgians Should Read. Rachael lives in Decatur, Georgia, with her husband, two children, and two sled dogs.

rachaelallenwrites.blogspot.com

SELINA KYLE IS CATWOMAN.

TIME TO SEE HOW MANY LIVES

THIS CAT REALLY HAS.

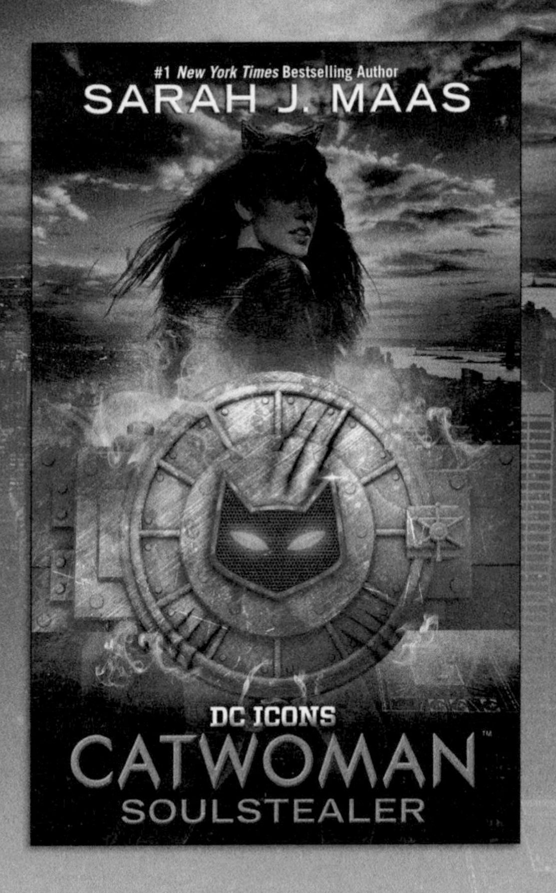

DON'T MISS THIS DC ICONS STORY FROM

#1 *NEW YORK TIMES* BESTSELLING AUTHOR

SARAH J. MAAS!

CHAPTER 1

The roaring crowd in the makeshift arena didn't set her blood on fire.

It did not shake her, or rile her, or set her hopping from foot to foot. No, Selina Kyle only rolled her shoulders—once, twice.

And waited.

The wild cheering that barreled down the grimy hallway to the prep room was little more than a distant rumble of thunder. A storm, just like the one that had rolled over the East End on her walk from the apartment complex. She'd been soaked before she reached the covert subway entrance that led into the underground gaming warren owned by Carmine Falcone, the latest of Gotham City's endless parade of mob bosses.

But like any other storm, this fight, too, would be weathered.

Rain still drying in her long, dark hair, Selina checked that it was indeed tucked into its tight bun atop her head. She'd made the mistake once of wearing a ponytail—in her second street fight. The other girl had managed to grab it, and those few seconds when Selina's neck had been exposed had lasted longer than any in her life.

But she'd won—barely. And she'd learned. Had learned at every fight since, whether on the streets above or in the arena carved into the sewers beneath Gotham City.

It didn't matter who her opponent was tonight. The challengers were all usually variations of the same: desperate men who owed more than they could repay to Falcone. Fools willing to risk their lives for a chance to lift their debts by taking on one of his Leopards in the ring. The prize: never having to look over their shoulders for a waiting shadow. The cost of failing: having their asses handed to them—and the debts remained. Usually with the promise of a one-way ticket to the bottom of the Sprang River. The odds of winning: slim to none.

Regardless of whatever sad sack she'd be battling tonight, Selina prayed Falcone would give her the nod faster than last time. That fight . . . He'd made her keep that particularly brutal match going. The crowd had been too excited, too ready to spend money on the cheap alcohol and everything else for sale in the subterranean warren. She'd taken home more bruises than usual, and the man she'd beaten to unconsciousness . . .

Not her problem, she told herself again and again. Even when she saw her adversaries' bloodied faces in her dreams, both asleep and waking. What Falcone did with them after the fight was not her problem. She left her opponents breathing. At least she had that.

And at least she wasn't dumb enough to push back outright, like some of the other Leopards. The ones who were too proud or too stupid or too young to get how the game was played. No, her small rebellions against Carmine Falcone were subtler. He wanted men dead—she left them unconscious, but did it so well that not one person in the crowd objected.

A fine line to walk, especially with her sister's life hanging in the balance. Push back too much, and Falcone might ask questions, start wondering who meant the most to her. Where to strike hardest. She'd never allow it to get to that point. Never risk Maggie's safety like that—even if these fights were all for her. Every one of them.

It had been three years since Selina had joined the Leopards, and nearly two and a half since she'd proved herself against the other girl gangs well enough that Mika, her Alpha, had introduced her to Falcone. Selina hadn't dared miss that meeting.

Order in the girl gangs was simple: The Alpha of each gang ruled and protected, laid down punishment and reward. The Alphas' commands were law. And the enforcers of those commands were their Seconds and Thirds. From there, the pecking order turned murkier. Fighting offered a way to rise in the ranks—or you could fall, depending on how badly a match went. Even an Alpha might be challenged if you were stupid or brave enough to do so.

But the thought of ascending the ranks had been far from Selina's mind when Mika had brought Falcone over to watch her take on the Second of the Wolf Pack and leave the girl leaking blood onto the concrete of the alley. Before that fight, only four leopard spots had been inked onto Selina's left arm, each a trophy of a fight won.

Selina adjusted the hem of her white tank. At seventeen, she now had twenty-seven spots inked across both arms.

Undefeated.

That's what the match emcee was declaring down the hall. Selina could just make out the croon of words: *The undefeated champion, the fiercest of Leopards . . .*

A thump on the metal door was her signal to go. Selina checked her shirt, her black spandex pants, the green sneakers that matched her eyes—though no one had ever commented on it. She flexed her fingers within their wrappings. All good.

Or as good as could be.

The rusty door groaned as she opened it. Mika was tending to the new girl in the hall beyond, the flickering fluorescent lights draining the Alpha's golden-brown skin of its usual glow.

Mika threw Selina an assessing look over her narrow shoulder, her tight braid shifting with the movement. The new girl sniffling in front of her gingerly wiped away the blood streaming from her swollen nose. One of the kitten's eyes was already puffy and red, the other swimming with unshed tears.

No wonder the crowd was riled. If a Leopard had taken that bad a beating, it must have been one hell of a fight. Brutal enough that Mika put a hand on the girl's pale arm to keep her from swaying.

Down the shadowy hall that led into the arena, one of Falcone's bouncers beckoned. Selina shut the door behind her. She'd left no valuables behind. She had nothing worth stealing, anyway.

"Be careful," Mika said as she passed, her voice low and soft. "He's got a worse batch than usual tonight." The kitten hissed, yanking her head away as Mika dabbed her split lip with a disinfectant wipe. Mika snarled a warning at her, and the kitten wisely fell still, trembling a bit as the Alpha cleaned out the cut. Mika added without glancing back, "He saved the best for you. Sorry."

"He always does," Selina said coolly, even as her stomach roiled. "I can handle it."

She didn't have any other choice. Losing would leave Maggie with no one to look after her. And refusing to fight? Not an option, either.

In the three years that Selina had known Mika, the Alpha had never suggested ending their arrangement with Carmine Falcone. Not when having Falcone back the Leopards made the other East End gangs think twice about pushing in on their territory. Even if it meant doing these fights and offering up Leopards for the crowd's enjoyment.

Falcone turned it into a weekly spectacle—a veritable Roman circus to make the underbelly of Gotham City love *and* fear him. It certainly helped that many of the other notorious lowlifes had been imprisoned thanks to a certain do-gooder running around the city in a cape.

Mika eased the kitten to the prep room, giving Selina a jerk of the chin—an order to go.

But Selina paused to scan the hall, the exits. Even down here, in the heart of Falcone's territory, it was a death wish to be defenseless in the open. Especially if you were an Alpha with as many enemies as Mika had.

Three figures slipped in from a door at the opposite end of the hall, and Selina's shoulders loosened a bit. Ani, Mika's Second, with two other Leopards flanking her.

Good. They'd guard the exit while their Alpha tended to their own.

The crowd's cheering rumbled through the concrete floor, rattling the loose ceramic tiles on the walls, echoing along Selina's bones and breath as she neared the dented metal door to the arena. The bouncer gestured for her to hurry the hell up, but she kept her strides even. Stalking.

The Leopards, these fights . . . they were her job. And it paid well. With her mother gone and her sister sick, no legit job could pay as much or as quickly.

The bouncer opened the door, the unfiltered roar of the crowd bursting down the hall like a pack of rabid wolves.

Selina Kyle blew out a long breath as she lifted her chin and stepped into the sound and the light and the wrath.

Let the bloodying begin.

Girls have been disappearing all over Gotham City, and no one seems to care about looking for them—except for Harley Quinn. With her darkest instincts unleashed and Ivy fighting next to her, will she find herself on the right—or the wrong—side of the story?

Read the thrilling conclusion to the Harley Quinn trilogy in

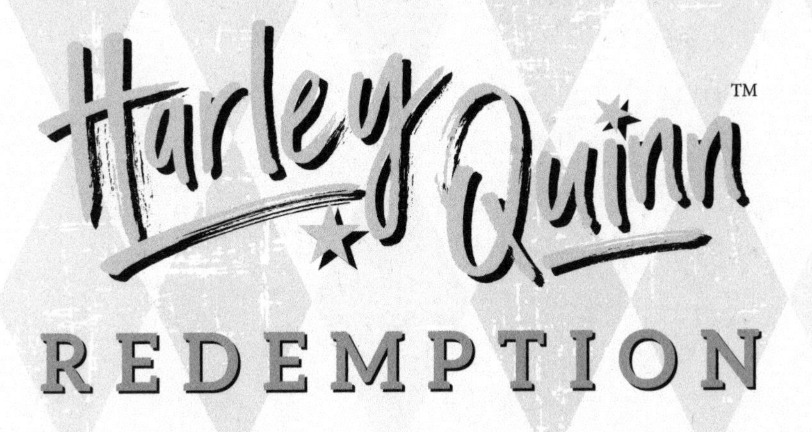

Available Spring 2024